SEPTSTAR

STAR TRIBES: BOOK THREE

BLAZE WARD

KNOTTED ROAD PRESS

SeptStar
Star Tribes, Book Three
Blaze Ward
Copyright © 2020 Blaze Ward
All rights reserved
Published by Knotted Road Press
www.KnottedRoadPress.com

ISBN: 978-1-64470-141-6

Cover art:

ID 125360035 © Freestyleimages | Dreamstime.com

Cover and interior design copyright © 2020 Knotted Road Press

Never miss a release!
If you'd like to be notified of new releases, sign up for my newsletter.

I will never spam you, or use your email for nefarious purposes. You can also unsubscribe at any time.

http://www.blazeward.com/newsletter/

Flight of the Star Dragon

Call of the Star Dragon

Shadow of the Star Dragon

Trial of the Star Dragon

K'BARI

ONE

Daniel still wasn't quite sure why he was alive, but the Commander had said that she wasn't going to allow him to die just yet, so he supposed that he still had a purpose. Whatever was that terrible thing that the gods had chosen for him had not been made clear yet, but after the last year or so, he knew at least that they had a cold, black sense of humor about them.

What that meant for mere mortals was left to the imagination.

And cooks like him to uncover.

Daniel had no idea what to expect, though. The gem at the base of his throat still contained the thousand or more victims of Urid-Varg's crimes against the entire galaxy, so he had those memories to deal with. That would not change as long as he was alive. At least that was his more pressing fear.

His great ship, the Star Turtle, was dead. Gone forever. Plunged into the heart of a star after having been mortally wounded by that Septagon's Axial Megacannon. Daniel had almost gone with it, but for the help of his friends.

It was good to have friends.

And the refusal of the Commander to let him die in peace.

He sat today in the wardroom where the comitatus would join him soon for their evening meal. *SeekerStar* was a starship, forever traveling the darkness of space, but the Commander still kept something like the hours of the planet-bound, even if the ship itself never slept and there was always someone on duty.

Three meals per day. Plus the odd snacks and treats as the women needed or Daniel wished to experiment.

Cooking was Daniel's job.

Originally, he had trained Ndidi to replace him as the Commander's personal chef, on the presumption that he would be far too busy with other tasks and adventures to reliably cook for all these women. And they were all women.

Commander Kathra Omezi. Twenty-two other warriors, with various retirements, who flew the Spectre fightercraft into combat when necessary. Plus Ndidi, who had been accepted into that inner circle in spite of being as short as Daniel and needing glasses to see anything more than two meters away.

The young woman approached him now, the apron on her front stained with use. The smells emanating from the kitchen told him that the big casserole dishes had gone into the oven and were undergoing their own brand of magic.

Soon enough, he would rise from his bench and go back there to help her prep vegetables, but there was time.

"What's today's task?" she asked as she sat directly across the long trestle table from him.

"More translation," he said, looking down at the book on his left and the small datapad on his right. "Ovanii this time."

The first book he had translated, Daniel had done by hand, writing everything out slowly in a reasonably clear hand, so that it could be typed into the system later by anyone else, but that had turned out to be him as well. This time, he was just skipping the middle step. It made the raw translation slower, but the overall task faster.

Efficiency, if not art. Not something he wanted in his kitchen, but good enough for the rest of the galaxy to deal with.

Daniel held up the book he had found in a junk shop at the most recent TradeStation stop for advanced supplies. It was written in Ovanii, which he supposed qualified as a lost language today, as nobody was even aware where the Ovanii homeworld was, or where any modern descendants might be found.

Ndidi took the book from him and turned it to her. She carefully held a finger to mark his page in the middle and then flipped randomly through the rest, not that it would do her any good.

Ovanii was a language that used letters to build words, like Spacer or French, but the letters were completely different, and there were thirty-seven of them. At least that made it easier, as Daniel didn't have to figure out complex sounds like *th* or Ӝ.

She handed it back a moment later.

"So what did you find?" she asked.

Ndidi had frequently accompanied him on his station jaunts, usually when Erin ferried them over, in that woman's job as Commander Omezi's second in command.

"It turns out to be a collection of poetry and drama," Daniel smiled and took it back from her. "Nobody in my head speaks Ovanii, but it was just close enough to written Anndaing that one of my ghosts could translate it for me."

"Anndaing?" Ndidi perked up. "The ones that uplifted A'Alhakoth's people?"

"The same," Daniel nodded. "The Anndaing have

apparently been traveling over several regions of space for a long time, trading whenever people get advanced enough, but leaving the more primitive societies alone. Protecting them from outsiders, as it were."

"And the Ovanii?" she asked.

"Raiders," Daniel felt his face turn a little sour. "Like all the bad vid show representations of Vikings from the ancient times on Earth, with none of their advanced culture discussed. Well, that's not true, and I wonder how much is filtered through my ghost's personal opinions. You have to be pretty sophisticated to build valence drives and starships. And they wrote lovely literature, at least as well as I'm able to translate it. This person might have been their equivalent of Shakespeare, or Rumi, or Gibran."

"What happened to them?" Ndidi cocked her head a little.

"I'm not sure," Daniel shrugged. "My ghost is not sure, either."

"Have you asked A'Alhakoth?" Ndidi perked up. "Her people might have legends, you know."

Daniel blinked. He had not thought that the Kaniea woman might know about the Ovanii, but it made sense. Her people had been raised to technology by the Anndaing just a few generations ago. Who knew what the Anndaing might have told them?

"Thank you," he said. "I shall ask her. Now, did you have a reason to emerge from our kitchen, or were you just lonely?"

She shared his grin. Technically, it was still his kitchen, but he was merely the Executive Chef now, and Ndidi was his *Chef de Cuisine*, rather than his *Sous Chef*. Perhaps he was her *Chef de Tournant* at the same time.

It was probably not inappropriate to sometimes think of

her as something like a daughter that would inherit the family business someday soon .

It didn't really matter. She was his peer in everything except for the actual business of running a bistro somewhere on a planet. He would still need to take her someplace rough, like Brest or Nice, back on Earth, so that she could learn to deal with farmers and fishers that had other options besides selling to her.

Still, that could wait. She ran the kitchen as well as he did.

"You need to prep carrots and sweet peppers," she said, rising now with mock-sternness in her voice. "I'm making a red rice, and we'll have two dozen or more hungry women to feed shortly."

Daniel rose as well, closing up the datapad and the book and carrying them with him, where they would be safe up on a shelf until later. He had no idea what terrible task the Commander would have for him next.

But as always, he would be prepared.

TWO

Kathra Omezi was Commander of the Mbaysey. Daughter of Yagazie. Inheritor of that woman's dream to free the Mbaysey tribe from their slavery, both economic and literal, back on Tazo, and get them away from the Sept Empire.

Yagazie had convinced the women of the tribe to buy a small starship that they could use for trade. And it had been almost all women by then, with most of the men off to seek work in the factories off-world or inducted into the military. Even today, eighty-five percent of the tribe was female, with just a few men kept around, where they handled the softer jobs. Child-rearing, or art.

Nothing to challenge their delicate sensibilities.

One starship had turned into a second, and then a third. And then they had built the first ClanStar, and learned how to permanently live in space without gravity field inducers, spinning their ships slowly like tops instead.

Today, there were twenty-two ClanStars in the Tribal Squadron. Two *WaterStars* to raise fish and kelp. *ForgeStar* to reduce iron and other metals mined from asteroids into bars and sheets. *IronStar* to turn all that metal and make it into useful parts that kept the squadron in motion.

And *SeekerStar*, her new flagship that had replaced the now-destroyed *WinterStar*, lost in the same battle as Daniel's Star Turtle. She was sorry that her mother had not lived to see what her dream was turning into, however slow.

Kathra still owed the Sept for the assassin they had hired.

But for the need to trade for advanced electronics and foodstuffs more easily produced on planets, Kathra might never visit another station or human world. Just sail off into the galactic interior and leave everything else behind. The tribe was large enough these days to be self-contained, with over seven thousand women and a large sperm bank to raise several generations more without risking inbreeding.

She was certainly never returning to sectors claimed by the Sept Empire and Earth. These days, Kathra wasn't even sure that the Free Worlds were safe for the Mbaysey, since Septagon *Vorgash* had chased her halfway across even those worlds to ambush her.

She paused to think about that again.

The Lords of the Sept were so displeased with her that they had sent a Septagon and all its attendants that far. Four hundred thousand men committed to killing one woman. And her chef.

They had almost succeeded.

SeekerStar and the Tribal Squadron were clear out on the far edge of the Free Worlds now, having fled as far as their maps would take them.

Kathra knew that there were many other sectors out there that were inhabited, even civilized, but humans on nearby worlds were a bare majority now, and out there farther they might be so few and far between that Kathra Omezi and her comitatus were the first humans that some of the aliens she would encounter had ever seen.

She had a decision to make. A hard one.

One that only the Commander of the Mbaysey could undertake, and then she would need to convince the others, because this was not something she could just order and expect it to be obeyed.

The tribe wasn't that far removed from their generations on Tazo. The Elders on the twenty-two ClanStars would need to agree with her. Anything else risked fracturing the tribe at the very moment when they needed their unity.

Kathra checked the clock and put down the book reader she had been largely ignoring. Right on time, a knock at her hatch, followed a moment later by it opening and one of her comitatus warriors poking a head in to check.

"Ready?" the warrior asked.

Kathra nodded and the woman entered.

A'Alhakoth ver'Shingi. Spectre Twenty-Three. A native of Kanus.

The first alien, true alien, in her comitatus, those warriors sworn to serve the Commander body and soul.

Hopefully not the last.

THREE

A'Alhakoth took a deep breath to settle the fluttery insects in her stomach and rapped her knuckles on the metal door. She opened it and looked in, confirming that the Commander was prepared for their meeting.

"Ready?" A'Alhakoth asked, just in case.

The Commander nodded and A'Alhakoth entered, sitting in the chair on the left.

It didn't matter which chair she chose, as her feet would dangle in the air either way. These chairs were made for humans. Tall humans, she had learned to understand, in spite of being female.

The Kaniea had a much stronger sexual dimorphism than humans did. A'Alhakoth was only one hundred and fifty centimeters tall, as the human measured things. Fifty kilograms. Petite and wiry, compared to the Commander's other warriors, who started at half a head taller than her and ranged all the way up to the Commander.

A'Alhakoth barely came up to Kathra Omezi's collarbone.

Daniel Lémieux was only half a head taller, and apparently short for a human male. Shorter than her brothers or father, but all of them would look up to the woman across the desk from her.

At least the Commander was smiling today.

It was always strange, looking at the Commander. Kaniea like her had periwinkle-colored skin, while the Commander's was such a dark brown that it appeared truly black in most light. A'Alhakoth's cobalt hair was straight and fine, where the Commanders was a thick, brown collection of tight rings when it got longer. Right now, the woman's was buzzed tight.

At least their eyes showed a similarity. Navy blue and darkest brown, surrounded on both by bright white eyeballs.

A'Alhakoth let seriousness be her distinguishing feature today, calmly waiting while the woman studied her. She was used to that, being the sixth child and second daughter, even if she had been her father's favorite, generally.

Sit quiet and wait, rather than fidgeting.

"What was it that brought you to human space originally?" Commander Omezi, Kathra, asked.

A'Alhakoth blinked in confusion, already not sure where the conversation might be headed.

But it had been a serious question, and Commander Omezi was not a woman given to frivolous things.

"The Anndaing are primarily traders in our sectors," she replied. "Once they were known as great warriors, and have it in them, and so they have also been the protectors of my kind."

She paused and traced her thoughts back to Kanus itself.

"Understand that all children of the Jarls, like myself, are always sent out on some sort of spiritual quest as part of their adult ceremonies, even before modern technology, as well as since," A'Alhakoth paused for Kathra to nod. "The old woman told me I would go farther than any other Kaniea. Out and away long before I would ever return."

"Out?" Kathra asked.

"As close a translation into your language as I can come, Commander," A'Alhakoth replied. "It had connotations of going beyond our world or our two small colonies on Anndaing worlds. Beyond mapped space might be a better way to phrase it. There was a Se'uh'pal ship that happened to be in system and I was able to buy transit and then work my way along for a while as a crew member. That got me eventually to Tavle Jocia, where I met Erin and the others."

The Commander stared at her for a long moment, but A'Alhakoth would not fidget.

"Any proven psychic abilities in the Kaniea?" she asked finally.

"Only dangerous old women who like to tell people they're witches," A'Alhakoth grinned. "Nothing verified."

"So we're not part of some Chosen One quest that you're on?" Kathra laughed.

"Well, if we are, then I've already somehow managed to slay a dragon," A'Alhakoth noted in a dry tone.

The Commander grew more serious. Dreadful. Implacable.

"Oh, no," she said in a voice that might frighten the most jaded veteran warriors in Father's Longhall. "We haven't slain him. Merely surprised that dragon and made our escape when he wasn't looking. I have no doubt that he's still seeking us, out there in the darkness."

"How can I help, Commander?" A'Alhakoth asked, reverting to a neutral voice.

She didn't feel like the Chosen One so much as the troublemaking youngest child who was never going to be content living a boring life on Kanus. She would never be satisfied in the family Longhall that mixed all the old touches of the primitive culture that had met the first Anndaing visitor when her great-grandsire was young, combined with the modern touches of a stellar civilization.

But A'Alhakoth ver'Shingi had been raised to be a warrior, on Father's correct assumption that Kanus would never hold her.

"We are standing on a ledge, Spectre Twenty-Three," Kathra said, invoking A'Alhakoth as part of the comitatus, rather than the only non-human on this deck.

One of *them*.

A'Alhakoth nodded her understanding. She had proven herself to them, both physically, nearly dying with *WinterStar*, and otherwise, when Daniel had brought the other women into her mind and shared his own with her.

Family of blood, rather than the waters of the womb.

"That dragon will never cease stalking us," Kathra said. "Before, we had the Star Turtle as a threat to keep them at bay, however little Daniel was interested in mass murder by attacking one. Now, we must either flee beyond the Free Worlds, or find a way to turn ourselves into pirates and fight back against the Sept."

A'Alhakoth waited. The Commander had not asked a question.

"What will we find out there?" Kathra finally asked.

A'Alhakoth considered her answer for a long moment. It had been the first thing on the tip of her tongue, but Father had taught her that such things were frequently wrong, if not well thought out.

The thought did not change it.

She felt her shoulders come back and her chin come up. Humans had the same body language, she had learned, so Kathra Omezi would understand what she meant.

Understand the implications of the answer.

"Friends."

FOUR

Tavle Jocia.

Imperial Naupati Amirin Pasdar had never been to this system before, nor traveled this far beyond the borders of Sept space. He would never have likely come here, even if the Sept had decided to finally conquer the Free Worlds, as it would have taken a generation to spall off all the chunks closer to home than this.

However, conquest wasn't his mission.

Today.

He had chased the Mbaysey Tribal Squadron this far. Nearly caught Kathra Omezi and her flagship by surprise in orbit of this very planet, not far from the station that Septagon *Vorgash* was currently trailing.

The image probably reminded many of the locals of a small child holding the reins of a warhorse, considering the relative sizes of the TradeStation and his monstrous Septagon.

Of course everyone was behaving themselves exceptionally well today. One Septagon could not destroy all the various squadrons that made up the Free Worlds naval forces if they came here, but with the four Patrols he currently had at hand, he could scrub orbital space of Tavle Jocia clean in a matter of hours.

But again, that wasn't his mission.

Amirin Pasdar, Naupati of Septagon *Vorgash*, Destroyer of Worlds, was a customer.

He allowed himself an ironic smile looking out the porthole as his transport finally docked with the main station, shutting down local gravity field inducers with just the slightest blip as the station's gravity came in range and caught everything again.

He waited patiently while his combat troops filed out onto the traveler's concourse and took up station. It wasn't that he was planning a physical assault, although Pasdar still had the scar from his left forehead that ran all the way back on his shaved head, caused by a rebel's blade that just missed penetrating his eyeball so many years ago.

A Naupati had no business leading troops into ground combat. These forces were to remind the locals that he could, if he had to. He wore a field uniform instead of his normal command uniform. This one included a pistol and a medium blade, just in case he needed to actually kill people.

Finally, Pasdar emerged, greeted by an amazingly-nervous local that represented the man Amirin Pasdar was here to see, rather than the station authorities. He wondered what the man would tell those folks after he was gone.

"Naupati," the man bowed deeply at the waist, Imperial style, which Pasdar found impressive, this far from home.

Doubly so because his records suggested that the man this majordomo represented specifically had no direct trade whatsoever with the Sept Empire, all of his hulls stopping at Free Worlds TradeStations and not crossing even imaginary borders.

The man rose again and waited with patient care, surrounded by Pasdar's troops.

Amirin nodded and the man immediately turned and began to walk at a pace somewhere between a sedate jaunt and a purposeful stride. Probably trying to not do anything to offend the Naupati following him, presumably.

It was not a long walk. Up an escalator, rather than cycling lifts, and they were onto what Amirin's operatives told him was the personal quarters level of the station.

Through a door, Amirin found himself in an impressive waiting chamber of a salon with an enormous fish tank taking up one whole wall, but they did not pause there, crossing into a deeper chamber, where a half-dozen of Pasdar's troops took up station around the walls.

Factor Mikhail Isaev was standing on the far side of a conference table, with only two other men with him, neither of whom was armed, nor looked like guards of any kind.

Mechanics, perhaps.

Isaev bowed as well. Not as deep, but he was possibly the wealthiest human in the sector, so perhaps he saw himself as only slightly below Pasdar on the local social scale.

But then, Amirin Pasdar was a Pasdar of the Founders. One of the seven clans that had conquered first Earth itself, and then expanded into the Sept Empire and included more than half of all human-colonized worlds.

And was slowly taking over that other half.

"Naupati, it is my great honor to be allowed to host you," Isaev said, speaking like a Court merchant rather than a barbarian from beyond the lines of civilized culture. "I am given to understand that tea would be appropriate, but that you would not trust Free Worlders with your health?"

Pasdar nodded. Too easy to poison him, even accidentally, and upset too many plans in motion. But Pasdar had also reviewed his reputation within and without the Sept, and decided to make changes to how he did things.

It was never a good thing for the most powerful politicians to consider one merely a warrior.

"Indeed," Pasdar sat, so that the others could as well. "However, I have brought my own tea master instead."

He turned his head enough to nod to the man, an ancient, wizened scholar of Chinese ethnicity, whom he did trust. Who had been with his family for more decades that Amirin Pasdar had been alive.

The look of shock on the merchants face was fleeting, but telling. This was a man who seemed almost an artificial construct, with a bald pate covered up with implanted hairs that were not graying at the same rate as the hair on the sides. The tan on his skin was an unnatural color, such as you got from taking pills, rather than the proper ultraviolet lighting in the shower every morning.

Possibly the only thing real about the man was his money, and the power that the Trade Factor did exercise locally as a result. Factor Mikhail Isaev owned the largest ships foundry in the sector.

That was why Pasdar was here.

Time passed. For Amirin, amiably, watching his tea master work and seeing the others fidget as things progressed. Then on to small talk about meaningless things while enjoying tea and biscuits baked this morning on *Vorgash*.

After all, if Amirin Pasdar was going to be taken seriously by serious people, it was not enough to be an exceptional Septagon commander. He must also be a Sept gentleman.

Isaev was not his peer, but Amirin could practice more important things on the man, secure that nothing this merchant did or said would matter later on.

"There is a particular reason I have called upon you, Factor Isaev," Amirin Pasdar eventually got around to turning serious. Thirty minutes was a good use of his time to just chat. He needed the practice being human, and not just an effective naval officer.

"Sir?" Isaev's face again lost all coherence for the briefest moment, almost gone before it happened.

But this man had never visited the Imperial capital at Rhages. That was where you learned what *cut-throat politics* really meant.

"Commander Kathra Omezi was a recent customer of yours, Factor," Amirin smiled, perhaps twisting the knife into the wound just a little bit. "I'm given to understand that she sold you a handful of interesting shuttle craft for your personal collection, acquired from parts unknown."

"That is correct, Naupati," the man said carefully, probably wondering if the Sept were going to demand he give them up.

A Septagon parked nearby at the optimal distance to use the Axial Megacannon on this station was a powerful inducement to behave however a Naupati demanded.

"I am less interested in those vessels, Isaev," Amirin smiled genially. "Rather, she commissioned a vessel from your factories. *SeekerStar*, I believe, was the name."

"She did indeed, Naupati," Isaev's fake tan lost even more of its luster as blood drained out of the man's face.

Wealth brought power, and this man was probably as powerful as they came in places like this.

Not that it meant anything when the Sept Empire arrived.

"That vessel was armed," Amirin noted in a neutral tone. "Including Ram Cannons, which I am given to understand are not legal on a private vessel in Free Worlds space."

He dangled that out there and watched the man swallow carefully.

"There is legal precedent," Isaev replied slowly, carefully.

"The Mbaysey are not members of the Free Worlds, but consider themselves an independent star nation engaged in legitimate international trade, sir."

"Do they now?" Amirin let his face grow just a little more serious.

"I am a merchant, lord, not a politician," Isaev deflected the blame, just a little.

If Amirin was willing to allow it. He decided to let the technicality slide. He still needed this man.

"Indeed," Amirin nodded with a warmer smile, prompting the man to continue.

"Additionally, it was her stated intention to remove that vessel from Free Worlds space as soon as she could, so that local authorities would not be threatened," Isaev offered.

"Ah," Amirin Pasdar, Naupati of Septagon *Vorgash* smiled now. "That is why I am here."

"Lord?" Isaev asked, completely pale now, aware that the Sept Empire itself had taken notice of him.

"Do you know where she is headed?" Pasdar asked. "I have already destroyed the other vessel, the older one known as *WinterStar*, as well as her strange, alien allies. But *SeekerStar* has eluded me, for the moment."

He watched the implications of his words play out in the eyes of the merchant.

Destroyed, just like that.

Rats that fled.

Mikhail Isaev seemed to be wracking his brain for clues and tidbits that might deflect his possibly-impending doom.

"I seem to remember my spies pointing out that Omezi had recruited one alien while she was here," he stammered after a moment. "The ClanStars, her other vessels, recruited perhaps a hundred people while in system, mostly human but with a smattering of aliens as well."

"Why is this one alien important, then, Isaev?" Pasdar asked.

"She was attached to *WinterStar*, Lord," the man said. "Presumably as crew for *SeekerStar* as well, if you destroyed the one, as they did not recruit sufficient crew while here to man both vessels simultaneously, unless they stripped the ClanStars first."

"Interesting," Pasdar noted, leaning back and nodding to the tea master to refill his mug.

It also allowed some of the tension to bleed out of the room. That would be important.

"I would like to see that report, Factor," Pasdar continued, granting the man some comfort by using his title, like a regional noble. "If they have fled from me now, perhaps that will give us some clues, when we again take up our pursuit later."

"Later, Lord?" Isaev asked carefully.

"Indeed, Factor Isaev," Pasdar smiled warmly now. "I want you to build me a warship of a class like *SeekerStar*."

The shock on the man's face was worth all of the rest of the discomfort Amirin had endured today, traveling off his Septagon and dealing with Free Worlders.

Indeed.

"Why would you need such a thing, Lord?" Isaev asked with a stammer. "You have a Septagon. Patrols of craft. Enormous firepower."

"A Septagon is a slow, implacable Leviathan, Factor," Pasdar said. "Omezi can continue to elude me, as long as she has something light and fast, like *SeekerStar*. My mission, from the Emperor himself, is to hunt this woman down and destroy her. If you build me the vessel I need, the Septagon and this squadron can return to Sept Space and the Free Worlds can return to normal. All will be well."

"Where will you go, Lord?"

"Into the darkness, Isaev," Amirin Pasdar said. "I will pursue her wherever she goes and kill her. You will be well rewarded for forging me the sword, the steed that I will need to do it."

FIVE

Daniel had taken to retreating occasionally to the little white ship, sitting off to one side down on the flight deck. It was the only shuttle they had left from the bizarre collection that he had inherited when he took command of the Star Turtle over Urid-Varg's dead body. All those individual ships belonging to the various people that the Conqueror had captured and ridden, all those centuries.

Kathra had sold four others to that Trade Factor back at Tavle Jocia, getting the funds to build *SeekerStar*, even if some of it had been the promise of future things to sell.

The rest were all gone now. Destroyed when the big ship fell into that nameless star, already mortally wounded by Septagon *Vorgash*. He wanted to feel rage, but most days, just getting out of bed was nearly too much effort.

He'd understood depression in a clinical sense before this. Witnessed it in others from time to time. Understood that the best solution, most of the time, was for outsiders to just keep in place and offer positive thoughts, while the person suffering worked it out on their own.

It had never been him at the bottom of the pool, slowly

drowning in the critical voices racing madly around inside his head.

Daniel was used to hearing strange people, but these new ones were him, rather than all the aliens that existed as ghosts inside the gem. The loudest one was *Doubt*, with his cousins *Fear* and *Irritation*. Daniel had to focus on not reacting to things, most of the time, lest he flee from everyone or lash out unprovoked in an unexpected rage.

When he was not cooking, he used to go over to the Turtle and try to inventory all the strange trophies he had collected. Or Urid-Varg had. Something.

The shuttles, for instance, many of which used technology he didn't understand but could repair from someone else's memories. The skulls of victim races as well as beings Urid-Varg had ridden. Ground vehicles of every technology Daniel could imagine. The strange orchards the man had accumulated over the centuries. Millennia.

All of that was gone now. It was probably a good thing, when Daniel thought about it, but it still left a hole in his soul and he hadn't figured out how to fill it. So he again found himself down on the flight deck of *SeekerStar*, just sitting and staring at the strange shuttle that he and Erin had been able to use to escape the Star Turtle at the end.

Everyone always wondered if this thing was made of glass, internally lit by bands of white light. It had that look, and the skin had that texture, but it wasn't transparent, and it absolutely flew in space. Plus, he knew it was tough enough to resist Daniel pounding on it with the biggest hammer he could lift.

It helped if you envisioned a series of hexagonal pieces of indestructible crystal, stacked upright on top of each other. Each of the rods was about a meter and a half wide, and the ship was nearly sixty long, but didn't have any sort of thruster nozzles or anything that marked even one end from the other.

Looking in a visual database, Daniel had seen a rock formation from Earth called the Giant's Causeway that was shaped in a similar manner, although he had no idea if the ship was the result of natural processes or a bizarre design aesthetic so alien that he could not understand it.

In the end, he didn't suppose it mattered. The vessel worked. Nobody could explain how, but it would fly through space and had something vaguely equivalent to a valence drive, if utterly different. It also required no fuel at all, and had no working parts that Daniel had been able to find.

Even his ghosts mostly just shrugged when he asked. That was how old the vessel was.

But it brought him solace.

Nothing of Daniel Lémieux had been lost with the Turtle, as all his personal gear had already been aboard *SeekerStar*.

But the memories of others haunted him.

As did the young woman walking towards him now with a purposeful stride.

Spectre Twenty-Three. A'Alhakoth.

Daniel twisted his torso, flexed his shoulders back, and popped his neck to loosen everything up. She had not always dealt well with the aspects of his abilities, although no cross words had been spoken.

You didn't need words when you occasionally became the other person as a way to communicate.

But she had also become him a few times. It was one of the ways he could know his sanity was intact, because Kathra, or more importantly, Erin, would snap the whip on him pretty hard if he started to slide into darkness.

"Madame," Daniel said as she got close.

He was seated on a mechanic's chair, a low structure that

let these tall women get under and around low things without necessarily being on a rolling board. A'Alhakoth had brought something similar, if smaller.

That she was one of the few women on this ship shorter than him meant that she also had to make daily adjustments.

She pulled up her chair and sat silently next to him, both of them staring at the side of the glass shuttle for a time, this ship being well away from the active parts of the flight deck and the other women working in the distance.

"I spoke with Kathra," she began after a time. "Eventually, I think we're going to Kanus."

Daniel nodded sagely and waited. He was a chef, the very definition of careful patience. Plus, she hadn't asked him a question. Even his depression was not enough to cause him to react now.

"She would like to be done with Sept space forever and possibly the Free Worlds as well," A'Alhakoth continued. "What do you know of the Anndaing?"

"I contain one," Daniel said simply after a long beat.

A'Alhakoth had been inside his head. She understood what that meant on a visceral level, if not intellectual.

"How long ago?" the tiny blue woman asked.

Yes, she understood what he was.

Daniel glanced over at A'Alhakoth and remembered that while she was in her early twenties, her kind matured more slowly than humans. She might be the human equivalent of seventeen or eighteen years old. More driven and focused than even he had been in those days, but Daniel had already known what he wanted to do with his life while she was still searching. Literally, in her case, as she was on a spiritual quest driven by her culture.

"Perhaps a thousand human years, give or take," he replied. "I am translating a book of what appears to be Ovanii poetry and classical literature right now that comes from a slightly earlier era. But the written languages were fairly similar."

"Do you speak Anndaing?" she asked abruptly.

"No," Daniel shook his head. "I could probably listen at regular speed and understand, but I have not practiced enough to speak it. Muscle memory takes time."

They sat for a moment, side by side watching the ship.

"Why?" Daniel asked.

"At home, we speak Kaniea," A'Alhakoth said. "But we also learned Anndaing when the merchants came. In our little slice of space, it is the dominant language. Being able to speak it would be helpful when we got there."

"You speak it," Daniel pointed out.

"Yes, but the others need to learn," she countered. "And I've grown rusty, only speaking Spacer and picking up the occasional swear words in French."

Daniel blushed a little. All the women had taken to cursing in French these days.

His fault.

"Would it benefit you if we spoke Anndaing?" Daniel asked.

He didn't really know this woman well enough to even make educated guesses.

Like the others, he had been inside her head, just as she had been inside his, but he didn't like spying on people. Plus, this came from a radically different physiology and culture than his, regardless of her physical similarity to human.

Four Kaniea generations ago, the Anndaing had decided that the species were finally advanced enough for First Contact. Her homeworld was a complicated amalgam of Iron Age superstitions and neon cities. He'd seen plenty of that from her memories.

"It would," she said quietly.

"Ndidi suggested I ask you something, next time I saw

you," Daniel said carefully, pushing *Doubt* and the others back out of the room so he could think clearly. "Since the Ovanii seemed to use Anndaing letters to write, she wondered if they were from your sector as well, and if perhaps the Kaniea had any legends or history of those people. I haven't been able to find anything here, but none of the Free Worlds maps even show your homeworld."

He paused to let her digest. He was still a stranger, and a *male* one at that, on a ship where all the customs and behaviors he had learned in the Sept Empire were generally wrong.

"I might have," A'Alhakoth said after a moment. She turned to face him. "Why is it important?"

Daniel wanted to brush off the importance with some self-deprecating joke. Pretend that it was nothing more than idle curiosity, but he realized that *Doubt* had cracked the door open and snuck back in when he wasn't looking.

Daniel slapped that fool in his mind and tossed him out the window with a silent curse.

"The Ishtan were pursuing Urid-Varg," he said simply. "Iruoma killed two of them, leaving only four members of the race alive. They were not strong enough to stop me after that, like they had been before. But they will never stop chasing me, in turn. Urid-Varg was more powerful than I ever will be, which was why they attacked now, after waiting so long."

"Okay," she nodded, still uncomprehending, but that was fine.

"They did not die when you chased off the Septagon, A'Alhakoth," he said. "They even managed to escape, presumably when the vessel was damaged. I heard the echoes of their minds before we left."

"But four are not powerful enough to threaten you," she

noted, those horizontal pupils narrowing like a cat laying on its side. "To control you."

"No," Daniel agreed. "So they must find allies."

"The Sept?" she asked, making the same leap of intuition he had.

Confluence of interests. At least he suspected so.

Urid-Varg would have been powerful enough, dangerous enough to possibly take over the Sept Empire had he wanted. Possibly ruled all of human space as a god, like he had the Z'lud and others.

Most likely destroyed humanity, like he had the K'bari.

But the Ishtan might be able to do something similar, if they found the right partner.

Daniel nodded to the young warrior.

"So I am looking for people that might be able to help Kathra fight the Ishtan, and the Sept as well," he said. "She has mentioned turning pirate at some point, a corsair dedicated to a war of liberation against the power of the Sept. I am no longer sufficient in myself to make that happen, but there might be others."

"The Ovanii?" she asked. "If they've been gone for that long, what could they do?"

"Does a stellar species ever go extinct?" Daniel asked rhetorically. "But I'm also less interested in the people and more in their technology."

"Why?" A'Alhakoth asked.

Daniel rose instead of speaking. Gestured her to join him as he stepped up to the strange shuttle and caused a section of hexagons to retract up and down to open a hatch, an airlock of sorts.

She followed him in and looked around with her mouth open, something that her kind shared with humans like Daniel.

"Nobody willing to speak to me even remembers where

this vessel came from," Daniel turned to her and said, carefully remaining several meters away.

The interior of the ship was the same hexagonal pattern, making benches, flight stations, and walls. Water and food were somehow stored inside one of the walls, and could be dispensed, although the food was a gruel that tasted like oatmeal mixed with a touch of honey and a dash of cardamom that came out at room temperature. Healthy, for that flight to safety, but he'd want to add a campstove at some point if he was serious about using this as a transport for any length of time.

A'Alhakoth studied him as much as she did the ship, but that was fine, as well.

"The Ovanii were warriors," Daniel said. "The Anndaing are much more merchants, according to your knowledge and things I can remember. I would like to find a lost graveyard of Ovanii warships somewhere, if such a thing exists."

"What would you do with such a thing, Daniel?"

"I owe the Sept a debt," he said simply, not trying to constrain the growl in his voice at this point. "I was part of the Star Turtle when they harpooned it with the Axial Megacannon. I nearly died. I wanted to die, but I had to get Erin and the others to safety first. After that, Kathra refused to allow me to terminate once I returned to *SeekerStar*, so I am here, and I have needs."

"What needs?" she asked.

"Vengeance."

SIX

AMIRIN PASDAR MET the creatures in a section of the Septagon hastily reconfigured as an alien-atmosphere environment. He would have preferred to have nothing to do with them at all, but he apparently shared an enemy with the creatures.

Ishtan.

There were four of them, representing apparently the last four survivors of their entire species. Thousands of years old at this point, and possessed of a rage even greater than his, if that was possible.

Allies, for now, he supposed, although he was unsure how long that would last. Certainly, they would use him to stalk Omezi's chef to the very ends of the galaxy, if necessary. And made it possible for him to consider such a pursuit himself, even if he still had to build the tools necessary.

The Ishtan had a ship, but it was a primitive, tiny thing compared to modern vessels. Certainly not capable of taking on *SeekerStar*, even with the strange mental powers those being had. That was why they needed the humans.

Why they needed him.

All that passed through his mind as he entered into the inner section where the four creatures lived, not far from the flight deck where they had first landed in the SkyCamel shuttle stolen from Kathra Omezi.

The light in here was off in ways that he really didn't understand intellectually. Darker as well. The smells had an earthiness to them that were alien on a starship.

Amirin Pasdar hoped that he was still himself, although it was hard to tell.

We have not changed you, Pasdar, the strange voice filled his head as he made his way across the darkened room to the human chair where he could sit comfortably. *That is evil itself.*

He was willing to accept that at face value for now, images of white whales in his mind notwithstanding. What of those changes were him responding to things from before the Ishtan and what came later was not a thing he could readily differentiate.

He nodded to the creatures as they rose from their nests and faced him.

Four of them. Snake-like, with spindly arms coming from narrow shoulders and trailing down to long tails. Covered with a pink fur that was heavy and warm. Triangular symmetry down the body, with a mouth that would split into three slices and eyes on each side.

And mental powers, which was what the chef, Lémieux, had apparently used against Uwalu.

He is weaker than Urid-Varg, the harmonious voices continued, obviously reading his mind. *The death of the xxxxxxxxx has also diminished his powers further.*

"The what?" Pasdar asked, confused.

The vessel you called a Star Turtle, the voices replied. *The thing* Vorgash *killed. The human Daniel Lémieux survived and fled. Our life's mission is to end him and make the entire galaxy safe again.*

"The locals have agreed to build for me an upgraded version of *SeekerStar*," Pasdar told them aloud, probably unnecessarily. "It will be without a flight wing, but will be designed to counter such craft. With this vessel, we will be able to continue hounding her, even as *Vorgash* and her support Patrols will return to Sept Space."

He cannot flee far enough that we will not follow, they stated coldly.

Pasdar had joined mentally with the beings twice, so he had some understanding of what that implied. He had watched the creature known as Urid-Varg attack the Ishtan homeworld and destroy it. Listened to most of the species die under the blast of anti-matter bombs.

They could give him a direction that Kathra Omezi had fled, even across the vast light-centuries that might intervene. The creatures had even undertaken to fund a significant part of the construction of the new vessel with resources they had accumulated along their impossible lifespans.

Pasdar had taken to calling the ship *SeptStar*. It would give his pursuit the range to chase the woman across such vast distances. Even as he sent *Vorgash* home with an explanation of the quest he was now pursuing.

For a man who had made a name for himself as a Sardar originally, an officer of an elite ground combat unit, Amirin Pasdar wondered if he was in danger of turning into the legendary fool Sataspes at this rate, originally tasked with circumnavigating the African continent on Earth, and put to death for his failure.

We will explain to your emperor, if necessary, the voices said, still listening. *Such evil must not be allowed to exist in the universe.*

"And when Lémieux is destroyed?" he asked the quartet. "What becomes of the Ishtan?"

We do not know, Amirin Pasdar. Our quest has lasted twelve thousand of your years so far. We are the last.

He shivered at the scale, but Urid-Varg had apparently been on his own galactic quest for power for something more than those twelve thousand, if the dates and scales matched up.

Before humans had first developed iron technology.

"There is much you could teach us," he said, aware that the creatures could read his very soul as he spoke.

It made communication both easier and harder, as he could no longer deflect or lie as he spoke. Amirin Pasdar wasn't sure he had ever allowed himself to be so honest, even inside his own head.

Thus these guardian avengers had already changed him.

Your kind would not welcome it, Amirin Pasdar, they said. *Humans are not yet mature enough.*

Of that, he had no doubt, but Pasdar was also absolutely certain that the mission he was undertaking now stretched every possible allowance his original orders had given him.

Except one.

Stalk Kathra Omezi and break her power.

Whether he killed her or returned the woman to Rhages in chains was irrelevant. No other rebel could entertain the thought that they could escape the Sept, even by fleeing into the galactic interior.

The Sept Empire had made a grave mistake allowing the Mbaysey that option in the first place, when they should have been kept in slavery instead. If he broke her, WHEN he broke Kathra Omezi, others would not agitate to join her.

Or they might indeed join her as well.

These are human concerns, Pasdar. We wish to destroy the chef. If the others resist, you will deal with them as you wish.

Without his power, they are nothing we need concern ourselves with.

Pasdar recognized the dismissal for what it was and rose. The beings claimed that they could not affect him if he was any great distance away, and he accepted that, just as he had accepted their offer of alliance and the funds to keep *Vorgash* on station, buying food and other consumables from the locals at Tavle Jocia while he sent messengers home to Rhages with his updates.

He bowed to them as equals, which Amirin found enlightening in and of itself, as he was a Pasdar of the Pasdar Clan, founders of the Sept Empire itself.

The warship construction would take time, but not all that much, as he was building a smaller and more-heavily armed version of *SeekerStar*. Guns instead of fighters, but he would spin the craft on its axis like Omezi's flagship, rather than rely on gravity field inducers.

His vessel would even mass less than *SeekerStar*, while being more durable, since he didn't need the space of a massive flight deck or the weight of so many fightercraft.

That would give him an advantage in pursuit, as his valence drives would be faster than hers.

Septagon *Vorgash* was an implacable monolith once it got somewhere, able to destroy anything, even Star Turtles, but it moved at a glacial pace and that would let her flee him time and again.

No, Amirin Pasdar would need *SeptStar* in order to run the woman down.

And kill her.

SEVEN

Kathra looked over the mob that was seated in the comitatus dining hall, filling it to the edges. All twenty-two of her warriors. All twenty-two of the leaders from the ClanStars.

It made an interesting symmetry, broken by Daniel and Ndidi joining them after the dinner and desserts had been cleared from the tables.

She stood with her back to the kitchen window now, watching. People on the near sides of the trestles had turned to face her, so she had everyone's attention.

"You have heard the plan," Kathra said as the room fell to silence. "I know some of you have objections, and I would hear them now, in the open, so we can address them. I am your Commander, but I am not a fool."

That brought a chuckle from some corners of the room, and lightened some of the harsh glares from others.

The comitatus were all young women. Kathra's people, as she had made sure she had the loyal ones backing her, over the long years since Yagazie had been assassinated.

Some of these Clan leaders had grandchildren Kathra's age.

Interestingly, those were the ones that she could largely count on to support her missions, as they all had siblings and cousins and friends like Erin's grandma Ezinne, who still bore the barcode tattoo on her face that had once proclaimed her as *property* of a Sept *Vuzurgan*, one of the grand nobles of the Empire itself.

Erin voluntarily wore the same tattoo to remind herself, and others, lest they forget.

It was the younger Clan leaders that might cause mischief. The ones that might not be old enough to really remember the bad days on Tazo, even as the stories were regularly retold.

But some people wished to forget the past in the process of moving past it.

Simisola Ihejirika's chin came up now as the silence returned. At forty, she was an occasional troublemaker, brilliant and capable as a politician, but not a warrior.

Kathra respected the woman, and her place running one of the most successful ClanStars. She had also expected the first complaint to come from there, so she smiled encouragingly.

Best to have it all out now.

"Why must we flee human space?" the woman asked in a deep, authoritative voice.

"Because the Sept have made it clear that no borders will stop them from coming after us," Kathra replied, listening to the emotional grumbling in the room. "At some point, they will catch us if we remain here. If I thought I could draw them away from the rest of the tribe forever, I would, but *SeekerStar* is the only vessel we have that is armed and capable of protecting the rest against pirates."

Most of the emotion in the room today was in her favor, but that was to be expected. The Sept had not treated the women of Tazo in such a way as to win their hearts and minds.

"But you would take us beyond all knowledge, Kathra," Simisola groused.

"No," Kathra countered forcefully. "Only what we already know, having fled the Sept and now the Free Worlds. I have other resources. A'Alhakoth?"

Kathra watched the newest warrior in her comitatus rise immediately, as though she had been expecting the call. But A'Alhakoth was much more intellectual than some of the others, and had been raised in a noble's household, so she understood politics.

Kathra listened as the woman addressed the crowd in a foreign language, speaking several sentences that nobody in the room understood.

Except that Daniel rose now, well across the space, and translated.

"She introduces herself as A'Alhakoth ver'Shingi, daughter of Linga ver'Shingi, a Jarl on the planet Kanus," he said. "She greets us formally and reminds us that her homeworld is Kanus and joined stellar civilization four generations ago when the Anndaing uplifted them. That sector has thirteen intelligent, star-faring species."

A'Alhakoth said something sharply in her native tongue and Daniel replied haltingly.

"Your pardon," he said to the group. "Eleven species. They use a base-eight numbering system for the same reason we use a base-ten, and some of the words are complicated cognates. We will be more technologically advanced than about…half?"

"Half," A'Alhakoth agreed, in Spacer this time. "And there will be friends we can make. It is an older sector, as such things are measured, and the Anndaing have been around much longer than humans have been in space."

Kathra contained her grin as the two sat again, their point made. Simisola and three others were still restive, but most of the rest were suddenly excited at the possibility of trade with new species.

Every ClanStar was a largely self-contained world, specializing in their own aspects of culture and paying tribute to Kathra, even as they traded with one another. The Ihejirika raised lots of chickens and made a thin beer that they exported to the other ships, just as the Okafor raised miniature cattle and made cheese for trade.

These women would have new markets they could tap, and crew they could recruit, as the Kaniea and Anndaing were erect bipeds along the same lines as humans. Perhaps the ClanStars could grow in number and size. Certainly Kathra would stack these women all up against the rest of the galaxy as merchants.

"Forever?" Simisola asked. "How long will we flee the Sept?"

"I can offer you two options, Simisola Ihejirika," Kathra replied. "One, we might run far enough that the Sept cannot find us again, and we can live in peace."

"And two?"

"Maybe we find allies out there, and push the Sept back," Kathra said. "Humans are dense in our sectors, but there are many more aliens out there than anyone understands. They will not wish to live in a Sept collar any more than we do."

EIGHT

DANIEL LISTENED CAREFULLY as A'Alhakoth repeated the story in her native tongue.

Speaking in Kaniea was helping her remember, after something like nearly three years away from home. In turn, he was learning to speak the language as well, and writing all these stories down in Kaniea, rather than just translating.

They were in the comitatus dining hall. It was mid-shift in the afternoon, when his lunch tasks were completed and today Ndidi had not yet assigned him chores for dinner.

Around them, several stacks of paper books waited as well as her datapad and his.

These were simple stories she was repeating. Things you taught your children, but it would allow him to provide Kathra and the others both language and cultural lessons of the new people they were seeking.

The meeting with all the Clan leaders had gone better than Daniel had expected, but Kathra had known those women much longer than he did. Additionally, he had never become any of them. Finally, these women were still on the grand quest for freedom that Kathra's mother had dreamed up to free the tribe more than a generation ago.

The Star Tribe was committed.

A'Alhakoth listened as Daniel repeated the story, nodding and eventually smiling.

"Yes, you have it," she said.

"*Bon*," he said. "How are we coming with the map?"

"I have seventeen worlds listed," she replied, reaching for her datapad. "The directions are only loosely accurate, as I never needed to navigate a ship."

"It is more important that you have cultures and languages, A'Alhakoth," Daniel reminded her. "With your help, we will be well ahead when we arrive, able to talk to both your folks and any Anndaing we encounter."

"They are merchants, you know," she said. "I'm not sure how they will react to a warship in their sector."

"We are a sheepdog," Daniel grinned. "It is the other wolves that must worry, when Kathra Omezi comes for them."

"Do you think she's serious?" A'Alhakoth asked, her blue skin turning darker with concern. "About perhaps recruiting the various nations and species out here to fight the Sept?"

"Perhaps," Daniel equivocated. "Trade is always her preference. But at the same time, I fear that the Ishtan will never rest as long as I am alive. Perhaps not until the gem itself is destroyed."

"Should you destroy it?" she asked, her voice dropping to almost nothing.

She had been him more than once, that confluence of beings that allowed him no secrets from another. It allowed them all a shorthand outsiders would not understand.

"If I thought that would make things better, I would ask her," he replied. "But like you I am sworn to Kathra's service. Her needs. The Star Turtle is lost, but there are other things that I can do to help, such as learning to read Ovanii and perhaps finding one of their worlds."

"It is still war," she reminded him.

"And you were raised as a warrior, A'Alhakoth ver'Shingi," he said crisply. "Spectre Twenty-Three. You are part of our war now, whether you like it or not. That is what comes of comitatus."

"I've never killed anyone," she said, again whispering.

"I have," Daniel reminded her with a pained voice. "Something I would prefer never having to do again. But I will remind you that you wear a pistol on your hip."

"And what if the Anndaing take exception and order us away?" A'Alhakoth asked.

"You would know them better than any of us," Daniel shrugged at her. "I do not believe that the Sept will stop pursuing her, as long as someone can give them a direction. So either she must flee for the rest of her life, or find a place where she can build an armada to fight back. Simple as that. If the Anndaing do not wish to engage with the threat of the Sept, there are other places the Commander can go. Perhaps she will return later to free them from the slavery that Earth will bring. Perhaps not."

"And the Kaniea?"

"Some of you will probably choose to fight," Daniel smiled grimly. "Others will not."

He watched her shiver briefly as she considered the possibility of a war that stretched across star empires.

The Sept had conquered Earth, starting originally in the Persian Highlands of Asia. From there, they had extended their hands in all directions, slowly adding more than half of the human colonies to their ambition. And a few non-human, but the Sept themselves maintained a strict caste system.

Men above women. Humans above non-humans. Bipeds

above some of the more interesting and exotic species Daniel had met.

A'Alhakoth presented as petite young woman, beautiful in her own way, even if she was all blues. Some Sept *Vuzurgan* would seek to add her to his personal harem, given the chance.

Over Daniel's dead body, but that was already their plan, so it would represent his failure, as well as Kathra's.

They stared at each other for a long moment, faces grim, most likely with the same internal conversations.

She rose abruptly.

"I need to pray," she announced in a tiny voice still forged in steel.

"Pray?" he asked.

Daniel had not been in a church save for weddings, funerals, or baptisms, none of them his, in decades. It was an alien concept.

He sought his own peace in the kitchen.

"If I am to kill complete strangers for no better reason than to protect myself, I need to ask for forgiveness now," she announced.

"Oh, no, Spectre Twenty-Three," Daniel replied sharply drawing the woman's head around. "You'll have a reason."

"What?" she asked.

"Protecting the weak from the cruel," Daniel said. "The hungry from the rich. The lost from the conquerors. There is no higher calling than that, with any Gods I have ever known."

She fell silent and nodded.

He watched her go, reminding himself that this alien child was trained as a warrior originally. She was comitatus, in every way that mattered.

And they would all fight.

NINE

CRENCE MIRAY HAD MADE his money by being willing to push the margins on the known map more than the other Anndaing trademasters that he knew. Or their voyagers. Finding that edge, literal as well as metaphorical, when the others of his kind were happy just sailing point to point along the same route, hauling boringly predictable loads on patterns regular enough to plan Eighth-Day Dinners.

Koni Swift, his voyager, was a vessel that had never played by those rules. Since he had taken over as trademaster, they had almost always been at the edges, exploring as much as trading, where both made him and his crew good money.

Anndaing space was a polite, predictable kind of place. Eleven other species in various stages of development, including seven that his people had uplifted when they got there.

Good trade. Good deals.

Enervating as hell.

So he probed the edges.

These sectors were sparsely inhabited. At least these days. Legends of the elders spoke of vast star empires that had once filled this part of the galactic arm, but the few planets that were still inhabited today had been generally reduced to pre-metal development by ecological catastrophes.

Lots of ruins, if you didn't mind so much radiation that you might grow a new fin somewhere. Even the explorer robots didn't last long, cooked by the radiation or attacked by mutant local predators that frequently grew to megafauna sizes.

It was worse than the Ovanii aftermaths he had read about.

Some days, Crence wondered if literal gods had decided to fight a major war through this strip of space. On a star map, accounting for drift, there was almost a razor slash across three sectors. Destruction one hundred light-years wide and several times that long.

"Nightflier, what is our status?" Crence asked, turning to the Anndaing pilot on his left on *Koni Swift's* compact bridge.

"We'll be exiting transit in roughly ten minutes, Trademaster," Jine Riffin replied in a lazy tone.

Like Crence, Jine was larger than average for an Anndaing. They were generally the largest bipeds in the sector, and only the male Kaniea approached their size. Heavier, too, but that was the breadth of body on those blues, lacking the sleekness of the Anndaing's aquatic heritage.

Jine's skin was darker, almost a charcoal gray, rather than the silveriness of Crence's, but there wasn't a better pilot out there for flying into strange systems and mapping them for natives, resources, or trade.

"Everyone make sure to strap your fins down tight," Crence reminded his crew. "We'll be updating old maps today, since nobody has come this way in forever."

"You think we'll find anything worth looting?" Jine asked.

Crence tilted his hammerhead right and left as he considered.

"Doubtful," Crence finally replied. "We're off the normal trade routes that the Se'uh'pal run, out farther to the edge of known space. I presume that they know something we don't, but I also know how lazy they are."

"Lazy?" Jine laughed. "Se'uh'pal? You need to get your fins checked, Crence."

"Predictable, maybe," he countered. "They set their runs based on their own logic, and then run those like they were on rails, never deviating again."

"And you think that we'll find something that's changed since they came through last time?" Jine asked.

"There are legends of mighty things that happened farther out, Jine," Crence replied. "If you'd more closely read the briefing packet I gave the investors ,you'd know that."

"I'm a nightflier, not a trademaster, Crence," Jine laughed. "All that merchant stuff is for you. I just want to fly."

"That you'll do, Jine," Crence smiled, showing off all of his triangular teeth. "We're going into darkness on this one."

"That's why I hired on, crazyshark," Jine laughed.

The rest of the bridge crew joined Jine's merriment.

Crence smiled. The mark of a good crew, a good frenzy of sharks, was the willingness to explore the darkness. He had a good team.

"All fins, stand by for transit to complete," Jine's voice came out of the speakers now, firm and authoritative in ways that most of his friends laughed at. Especially a practical joker like Jine.

Koni Swift dropped out of the transit tube into sidereal

space with less splash than hitting the pool after a long-day's labor.

"Oh, shit!" Jine said a moment later.

Crence was in overall command as trademaster, but it was still Jine's ship to fly. And fight, if necessary. *Koni Swift* had enough guns to protect itself against rogues, pirates, and natives, but it wasn't a warship by any stretch of the imagination. Anndaing didn't build combat vessels unless they had to face another horde like the Ovanii.

Hades, *Koni Swift* was even more dangerous than most of the other voyagers plying the darkness.

A whistle of surprise emerged from Jine's tuna hole.

"What have you got, Jine?" Crence asked quietly, letting the shark work.

"Someone else was here first," the nightflier said quietly. "Whole lot of someones. I'm picking up two-zwölf and change vessels nearby. Completely alien design. Oh, crap."

"Now what?" Crence demanded. "Do we need to get back into transit immediately?"

"Not sure, boss," Jine replied in a tight voice. "One of the big vessels just kicked out two-zwölf more little ones, all coming this way."

"Crap!" Crence agreed.

Had they just run headlong into a pirate base of some sort? This system was marked uninhabited on all charts he'd been able to beg, borrow, or buy. Never been colonized, as far as anybody knew.

Who in hades name was this?

"We're being hailed," Jine said.

"Stand by to transit," Crence replied. "Blind if you have to. We can sit tight somewhere and figure out where we are later. But I don't want to fight anybody today. Open the comm for me to communicate with them."

"Greetings, Anndaing voyager *Koni Swift*," a voice came

over the line. Sounded vaguely Kaniea, with a strange accent underneath. Female, too, which was completely insane, as the females rarely left the homeworld, and even then mostly went to one of the two colonies *Koni Swift* occasionally visited.

But she spoke Anndaing, which meant she wouldn't be completely alien.

Or had at least done her homework, like any aspiring trademaster.

"This is *Koni Swift*," Crence said. "Trademaster Crence Miray directing. Who are you?"

"This is the Mbaysey Tribal Squadron, departing the Free Worlds and the Sept Empire," she said. "Most of my comrades are humans."

Humans? Crence had never heard of the species, but that didn't mean much, with as many worlds as there were capable of fostering intelligent life out there.

"What is your intent, Mbaysey?" Crence asked.

He glanced over. Jine nodded back, all set to trigger the transit drives and jump them somewhere else. Anywhere else.

Someplace the pirates hopefully couldn't chase them easily.

"Truly?" she asked happily. "We've come looking for you."

TEN

Kathra was pleased.

She hadn't planned to encounter anyone in this system, marked on all the charts she had been able to check as uninhabited. Forgotten.

Useless, since the one habitable world had been apparently killed with a bioweapon at some point in the not-too-distant past.

Not enough to wipe out all life, but the diseases had wrought all manner of horrors on the higher lifeforms living on the surface. However many centuries later, the ecosystem was only starting to recover, with evolutionary niches being filled in by whatever species had proven immune.

Nobody would be safe there for probably thousands of more years, unless someone decided to dedicate their life and fortune to repairing and colonizing the planet.

Kathra had no use for planets.

None.

They just tied you down when bad people came, and let them trap you in one place, where an atmosphere wouldn't be enough to protect you. Especially from an Axial Megacannon being fired by a Septagon.

But someone had come here while *SeekerStar* was in-system, possibly looking to do the same out-system mining her squadron was up to.

Thrabo was the last place Kathra had stopped right before she had taken everyone out of Free Worlds space, possibly forever. The stolen Se'uh'pal records she had bought at Thrabo suggested that the vessel on her scanners was an Anndaing voyager. Specifically, a type known as a Cargo-Six for the six standard shipping containers that could be detached, three to a flank, for trade and transportation.

Kathra was a warrior. She could see modifying such a vessel to contain six individual launch bays for Spectres, if she wanted something smaller than *SeekerStar*. Possibly an explorer or a scout of some sort, since the records showed that this class of vessel was usually armed. Roughly equivalent to particle cannon turrets, rather than the heavier Ram Cannons on *SeekerStar*, but comparable to what *WinterStar* had carried.

Even better, the travelers were flying a little shuttle over to her.

That would be a mark of exceptional piloting on their part, to be able to land on the spinning deck of *SeekerStar* with their one, petite transporter shuttle. But the approaching vessel was much larger than one of her SkyCamels, having been designed to ferry one of those six cargo boxes to and from orbit on its back. It simply would not fit into the normal space of one of her shuttles.

Instead, the pilot was bringing the vessel alongside *SeekerStar*'s central hub, where her larger vessel did not rotate to provide gravity, like it did out on the wheels.

She was down here to meet the being known as a trademaster. Erin, Daniel, and A'Alhakoth were with her.

"Docking now," Ife said over the intercom from the bridge behind Kathra. "Not doing a bad job of flying, either."

High praise indeed, coming from a woman like Ifedimma Ogu, who served as bridge commander of *SeekerStar* when Kathra was elsewhere, such as flying in Spectre One. Ife's standards for professionalism were higher than most of the Tribal Squadron could maintain.

These strangers must be good. But that made sense, with a species that had been in space, exploring and trading for several thousand years. And had evolved from creatures similar enough to hammerhead sharks on Earth.

The ship rang with disparate sounds as the transporter came into contact and locked itself to *SeekerStar* with magnets. Neither vessel had similar standards for docking equipment, so the visitors would rely on a soft-seal airlock for now.

Perhaps later Kathra would install an Anndaing-standard airlock and dock for them later. Or modify the flight deck airlocks to handle a vessel that large being hauled inside.

Who knew what tomorrow would bring?

Daniel was hanging almost upside down right now, relative to *SeekerStar*'s spine and bridge. Erin was off by perhaps only twenty degrees. A'Alhakoth stood at her side.

Kathra found it amusing that Daniel wore his darkest blues today, both pants and long-sleeved shirt. It made him almost disappear, compared to the matching tangerine denim that she and the other two women wore.

But Daniel was also the odd-woman out here. The only male aboard *SeekerStar*, at least once the visitors left later. The only telepath.

At least the two of them were both being chased by intractable, relentless enemies. That gave him better reason to belong, besides just being her cook. But he had stopped being merely a cook a long time ago.

Now he was comitatus. But more importantly, he was someone she trusted with her life.

The inner airlock door began to ping and beep as the system engaged. Door blades irised open and a strange smell wafted into the air.

Salty, perhaps. Musky in ways she didn't think she had ever encountered before.

Kathra assumed that it was the smell of Anndaing, mixed with their technology. Certainly, the visitors would be similarly assaulted by the new.

It would put everyone on an even footing, hopefully.

A creature emerged from the airlock. Kathra had seen pictures of the Anndaing, but never put it into perspective. Gray, leathery skin with visible scales that almost glistened.

They were erect bipeds by design. Two legs. Two arms. Five fingers and a thumb that worked close enough to the human design for comparison, if flatter, like it had evolved from a fin.

The head threw all her imaginations off. He had a jaw and mouth like a human, perhaps wider and shallower in a way that would look weak on a human. Nearly lipless, especially compared to her.

Above the mouth was the sensor hammer. Cartilage, rather than bone, it stuck out past the sides of the bone skull like two semi-flattened number four cans of tomato sauce stuck together, with large eyes on the outer portion, the ends canted slightly forward like a rhomboid.

It would give the creature fantastic parallax for hunting, and the black-pupiled eyes were larger than hers, so Kathra suspected that he would see better in the dark than she. Useful in the depths from which the species had originally emerged, countless millennia ago.

A nose with two nostrils was just above the hammer like the blowhole on a Terran cetacean. She wondered if the design was similar to a human whale, with the convergent evolution that had created the hammerhead shark.

Every planet answered the question of biological advancement in its own way.

The creature wore clothing with a distinct military feel to it. Stubby legs ended in leather boots with a heavy tread. Dark gray cloth covered the spots that weren't sheltered with armor plates and occasional joint armor at the flex points. A belt rode low on the hips, with a pistol, a knife, and several pouches for what she assumed were combat gear if needed.

The man's torso was long. Daniel's torso, relative to the legs, was long compared to most of her women. The stranger was as much longer than Daniel.

In addition, when she looked closely the creature's armor looked like larger-pattern scale mail, with each layer a little bigger than the one below as it went up the body, until the ones protecting the collarbones were the size of her palms.

She'd seen a fin on the creature's back when it emerged, swimming easily until it found one of the staples designed to be used in zero gravity. That had armor on both sides as well.

Finally, the helmet covered the rear of the skull, with a flipped-up faceplate that would cover the hammer, the whole being transparent enough to see in all directions.

Kathra assumed that the creature would see like a whale as well.

It came to a rest at a reasonable distance, one boot hooked into the staple and the other cocked and ready to fling the creature across the room into mortal combat if that became necessary.

Kathra wasn't offended. Erin and A'Alhakoth were similarly poised.

Daniel appeared to be relaxed, but she knew better. He

would step into someone's mind at the first moment of danger and do things to them to render the danger nullified.

She had told him not to kill anyone, even with provocation. Pulse pistol bolts were far easier to explain than someone's mind shorting out.

The first Anndaing had a title of Caravan Guard, translated by A'Alhakoth into Spacer. She could tell the creature was a close cousin of Erin. No, actually, probably more like Nkechi, since that woman specialized in grappling and close combat.

Yes, Nkechi's deadly cousin.

She nodded to the creature as he came to rest.

He nodded back and made a sound possibly the equivalent to a whistle.

The trademaster emerged now. He lacked the armor, but wore similar grays. And had not strapped armor or weapons over it, so she could see his outline better.

Exotic and alien, but close enough for her needs. A Vida or an Atter would have been far more interesting to negotiate with, but they already knew humans, from their stations and colonies in the Free Worlds.

The trademaster came to rest on a different staple and studied the four of them for a long moment. His face seemed to smile when he saw A'Alhakoth, a species he should at least recognize.

For the rest of them, that woman's blue was offset by browns and pinks. Kathra wondered if the gray-skinned Anndaing had color receptors, since they had evolved in the depths, but Kathra remembered reading about bioluminescence on sharks and other creatures from the deep.

Now she wondered if he might light up with glowing tattoos in certain circumstances.

The trademaster spoke in a rich baritone that was obviously used to dealing with strangers.

Kathra nearly laughed when Daniel replied and the man flinched visibly.

They exchanged several sentences as Kathra watched.

"His name is Crence Miray, and as Trademaster of the voyager *Koni Swift* he brings you greetings from the Anndaing Merchants Guild," Daniel said pleasantly, turning to face her. "The Caravan Guard is named Alten Rezal, and appears to be something like the equivalent of a Sept Sardar. I have introduced each of you to them as well."

"Invite him to accompany us to the outer decks, Daniel," Kathra commanded the chef with a smile. "We will work better in gravity as we talk."

She listened, but understood barely one word in ten. Still, that was an improvement. And she could imagine being mean enough to transform the entire tribe into speaking Anndaing one of these days instead of Spacer.

If she never intended to return to human space, was a human language even necessary?

The trademaster bowed, gesturing with both flat hands outward in an interesting way, palms up and wider apart than his shoulders. She took that as a good sign and bowed similarly in return.

Moving to the lift was an experiment in social grace. Kathra and to a lesser extent Erin were graceful in zero gravity. A'Alhakoth and Daniel were landswomen. The two visitors moved like sharks, thrusting ahead with such unerring accuracy of vector and direction that Kathra was deeply impressed.

That would come through with their vessels as well. Perhaps she should indeed consider transforming a Cargo-Six into a warscout at some point, if their vessels were as graceful as their masters.

Into the lift, the smell of shark, if that was what it was, was stronger. Richer, like freshly brewed coffee demanding your attention, but doing it in a polite, friendly sort of way, first thing in the morning.

She listened as Daniel explained the workings of the lift, and the need to be feet down as they moved outward into the pseudo-gravity of *SeekerStar*'s spin. Both men seemed amused, so she made a mental note to ask what system they used for ship's gravity.

Sept vessels and TradeStations used Gravity Field Inducers, which were huge and hideously wasteful of power. Sept Patrol vessels used the same, so they tended to be more than half filled with generators and inducers, with barely any space left for crew and guns. A'Alhakoth had mentioned a similar system, but hadn't known any details.

Kathra still could not imagine that Patrol ships were comfortable to live aboard.

SeekerStar and the rest of the Tribal Squadron relied on spin around a central axis, with each ship having a wheel that felt like standard gravity and allowed one to walk in a continuous circle. *SeekerStar*'s three decks also allowed variable levels, with all the Spectres on the outer deck for launching, and the women sleeping on the inner deck, where they were closer to flying.

Quickly enough, the group emerged onto the middle deck.

The two Anndaing were more impressed as they felt gravity under their feet, since the ship turned slowly enough that Coriolis force was largely undetectable.

At least to a human. She wondered if they could sense it.

Kathra felt the need to reconsider every assumption, as she tried to filter it through truly alien eyes and minds.

Because she would need these people, if she truly meant to war on the Sept, one of these days.

ELEVEN

A'Alhakoth had never met one of the Elders, so she was more nervous than she should be. It helped that Daniel was translating, mostly because the trademaster would take them far more seriously if a human spoke.

Kaniea were already expected to be fluent.

She had escorted Kathra and Erin down, keeping a careful eye on the guard, but the man was acting entirely defensively, protecting his principal rather than threatening the humans.

Still, she could tell that the Anndaing were impressed from their body language. *SeekerStar* was still a brand new ship, purpose-built not that long ago. Everything still had that sheen of newness that drips and stains hadn't ground off yet.

They ended up in the comitatus dining hall, which was the social center of the ship, any way you wanted to look at it. The Commander's office would be more formal, but also far too crowded for six people.

Here, they could spread out.

They ended up with the trademaster on one side of the long trestle table and Kathra across from him. She and Erin flanked the Commander, while the one known as Alten sat to one side and Daniel was down the bench a respectful distance, acting as translator and aide to the aliens.

"What is this place?" the trademaster asked, looking around with curiosity.

Daniel glanced at her directly and nodded, so A'Alhakoth answered instead of him.

"The Commander's warriors are called a *comitatus*, Elder," she said carefully. "I am the newest member. We eat here communally, as well as use this space for meetings too large for the Commander's personal office."

"Warriors?" he asked, focusing both eyes on her now, although his peripheral vision was still watching the others.

A'Alhakoth turned to Kathra now.

"Should I explain the comitatus to him?" she asked. "He appears concerned that we are all warriors."

"Yes," Kathra said. "But exercise care in reminding them that we are travelers first, traders second, and only warriors after that has failed."

A'Alhakoth nodded and turned to the trademaster.

"The tribe was made up almost entirely of human women who had escaped a legalized bondage on their homeworld, Elder," she explained in Anndaing. "The other craft contain farms and factories that supply the tribe, while *SeekerStar* guards them. In the recent past, the distant Sept Empire chased us deep into Free Worlds space and attacked us there. The Commander is seeking new lands where the tribe can live and trade in peace. I joined her at Tavle Jocia. Such was my knowledge of the galactic interior, as seen from the Free Worlds, that she chose to explore in this direction."

"Why do they pursue the woman?" he asked.

Daniel leaned forward to get the man's attention now.

"She threatens their male-patriarchal social structure by escaping their predation," he said carefully, working his way into words she didn't think she had taught him. Perhaps once of his ghosts had come to the fore now? "They would make an example of the Commander by breaking the Mbaysey, lest other groups think to escape similarly. Additionally, other powers out there have taken notice of the Tribal Squadron and seek it. Thus we must be armed and vigilant at all times."

"Humans and who else?" the Elder asked, his eyes narrowing in a most-human manner.

A'Alhakoth's pupils were not round, so she would have just slitted them horizontally instead. But they were all well-met alien travelers here.

"They call themselves the Ishtan," Daniel said simply. "This area was once devastated by an entity named Urid-Varg. They think I am his successor and pursue me."

"You?"

A'Alhakoth twitched almost exactly in tune with Erin as the guard, Alten, flinched.

Fortunately, nobody drew a weapon. She still expected Daniel to shoot first.

Or whatever it was he did.

"We encountered Urid-Varg at the edge of human space," Daniel explained with pain and anger in his voice. "And killed him."

A'Alhakoth had never seen an Anndaing express shock physically. The whole of the hammer flexed forward. Not more than half a centimeter, but she didn't realize that it could move at all. The eyes bugged out sideways in a most human, or Kaniea, manner.

His flesh even paled a little, but that was all of his scales flexing outward from the skin underneath.

"How?" the Elder gasped.

"That is not a story the Commander is prepared to share with you at the present time," Daniel said, pausing to translate everything into Spacer for Kathra and Erin to nod. "But the being is no more. I did inherit his vessel, the Star Turtle in which he traveled, but it was subsequently ambushed by a battleship of the Sept Empire and lost into a star's core."

The Elder paused, no doubt thrown off center by the revelation. But he also needed to know that these humans were far more dangerous than they appeared, even as they sought trade instead of conquest themselves.

Kathra had explained to everyone the ethics of the situation, and the need for certain information to be shared, so that the Anndaing and their own allies understood that the Sept might turn this direction.

A'Alhakoth wasn't sure if the Ovanii were more dangerous than the Sept, but the Anndaing had fought the former, driving them either off into the darkness, or breaking them so completely that nobody had heard of them in centuries.

The trademasters could also become warriors, if it was required of them.

"So you bring your troubles to Anndaing space?" the Elder asked, turning to face Kathra now.

A'Alhakoth translated now.

"No," Kathra's response went. "Our troubles drive us from human space, but we are not bound to any planet, so we will trade with any species we encounter. It is the Commander's intent that you understand what human politics might yet come to your space."

The trademaster studied the woman carefully. He rotated his hammer and eyes to take them all in. Alten had not relaxed one iota, but he also refrained from reacting now, aware how delicate things had grown between the two leaders.

One trademaster could not stop the Tribal Squadron. Nor could one voyager.

But they could make the path easier or harder by their words later, being the first to encounter the humans.

Both Kathra and Miray seemed to understand that.

"What trade do you bring?" he finally asked after a moment.

A'Alhakoth remembered to breathe. She translated the question for Kathra, also explaining as she did that such was the traditional greeting between merchants.

"My squadron is largely self-sufficient in vegetables and fruits," Kathra said. "We mine asteroids, comets, and planetary giants for most things that we need, delivering bar stock, sheet metal, and exotic, mostly organic materials to TradeStations, in exchante for meats of herbivores, and advanced electronics that we cannot produce ourselves. We will seek to trade such with whatever worlds we encounter as we continue on this path towards the galactic interior."

"And your warriors?" Miray asked.

"Have you managed such a just and perfect society that piracy is completely unknown, Trademaster?" she smiled. "*Koni Swift* appears armed."

Anndaing laughter was sharper than a human's but similar enough to need no translation.

"Indeed, Commander," he acknowledged with a seated, mirthful bow. "We are merchants who occasionally sail into harm's way. Thus the guns. But your electronics will be radically different than ours. Similarly, I am amazed at your lack of gravplates, spinning the ship instead. It is highly inefficient."

"We have always been a poor tribe, Trademaster," she

replied. "Human technology is more advanced than the Anndaing in some ways, and starkly primitive in others."

A'Alhakoth smiled when the man leaned forward and put both elbows on the table in front of him. The hammer flexed forward and his mouth smiled in that peculiar way of the Anndaing.

"Well, Commander," he said. "Let us bargain."

TWELVE

Daniel was exhausted by the time the aliens were put back aboard their transporter and sent home with a selection of fruits, vegetables, and frozen fish that they could sample in their own labs for allergy issues and taste.

The Commander had negotiated in turn a rough stellar map of the forward sectors, including Kanus and the two Kaniea colonies. While the squadron was not that close, the ships could now sail in a more direct route to get there, as well as to several Anndaing trade platforms and meeting places where they could do more deals.

He turned to the other three and let them see the drain in his face.

At least he hadn't needed to use his powers on them. Nobody was sure what would happen if he did, but they would likely cease to be potential allies if that happened.

"Thoughts?" Kathra asked as they made their way back to the lifts.

"The potential remains good," Daniel said. "I listened mostly to the trademaster's emotions. Generally, he stayed positive, once we got past the bits with Urid-Varg. The potential for trade with a new species factored high, as did the sorts of things he could learn from our technology, as well as what he might want to sell us later."

"And the Sept?"

"I suspect that they discount the danger of a Septagon, since I doubt that they will see one in our lifetimes," Daniel said. "But if they get into Free Worlds space at some point, that might change. Personally, I wonder if we've triggered the larger confrontation between the Sept Empire and the Free Worlds that everyone has been expecting. Has the war already started behind us?"

Kathra paused as the lift doors closed and they began to descend back to the ring.

"Part of my mind wishes that we could turn back and take *SeekerStar* to raid the edges of Sept space, just to teach them better manners," Kathra said. "On the other hand, we have a duty to the tribe to protect them. Having just convinced them to leave human space perhaps forever, it would not do to go back on that."

"How much should we tell the Anndaing?" A'Alhakoth asked. "Or the others, like my people?"

"The truth," Kathra answered. "Perhaps not all of it, but if you tell no lies, you don't have to remember them later. We are traders escaping an oppressive regime of humans, and looking for a quiet place we can live. Nothing more. But also nothing less."

Daniel nodded. The Sept could not chase them this far in a Septagon, and he doubted that even their present anger would cause them to commit the level of Patrol forces necessary to maintain a logistics train this far beyond their borders.

It was the Ishtan that he feared. Not that they could take him. Even having lost some of his strength when the Star

Turtle died, he figured he was the equal of the remaining four, at least from a mental standpoint.

But who would they seek as allies, knowing that they were overmatched?

He had nightmares of a Sept/Ishtan alliance. They would not seek to conquer the Sept Empire, as Urid-Varg would have, but at the same time, they could do much to threaten the rest of the galaxy if they saw Daniel as an evil that must be destroyed.

Should he just destroy the gem for good? Cast it into the fires of a star as a way to finally let his ghosts go to their final rest, whatever that was?

Several beings surprised him by stepping forward in his mind as they rode outward.

One of them quietly reminded him of a book of Ovanii poetry and drama that he had just translated, when it would have been lost forever otherwise.

Forever?

The being nodded, so perhaps the Ovanii had been destroyed after all. If you broke their armadas and let the survivors integrate into a larger galactic whole, Daniel supposed that it was possible for a species to die out.

At least an entire culture.

"You've gone quiet," Kathra said, stirring him to come back to the surface.

"Thinking quietly depressive thoughts," he said simply. "Wondering at the Ishtan and the gem and what I should be doing with it."

"And?" she pressed.

"My ghosts remind me of the good I can do as well." Daniel looked up at the giant woman, looming so tall over him.

"As would I," Erin spoke up suddenly, after being silent for so long that he had almost forgotten the woman was with them. "The tribe exists because of Daniel Lémieux. Several times over. And I require you to continue."

"Require?" he asked, turning to look at the dangerous woman with the barcode tattoo on her face and the metal replacement for her lower right leg.

Erin surprised him by smiling now.

"You still haven't opened a restaurant somewhere on a planet and taught Ndidi how to run a bistro," she laughed. "I've seen that in your mind."

"Are you ready for me to train yet another chef?" Daniel laughed back at her, teasing the woman. "I would need to place her on a planetary surface for at least two years, if that was my task. You'd be back to eating stew and cornbread with every meal."

He appreciated the shudder of horror that ran through Kathra's long frame.

"No," she commanded definitely. "You will have to locate me another Golden Diamond-rated chef to replace you first. Then, perhaps, I will be willing to talk."

Daniel wanted to argue with her, but he could see the mirth in the back of her eyes.

Wishing for unicorns, as his grandmother would have called such a demand.

As the elevator door opened, Daniel turned to head back to his cabin, unneeded for another hour or so, barring emergencies.

Kathra stopped him with a hand on his arm before he got more than a step. The others watched from a discreet distance.

"You can also translate human poetry and philosophy into Anndaing, you know," she said simply.

Daniel stopped cold. Kathra smiled, nodded and departed the other direction, trailed by the two women.

He could. All this time, he had been trying to find value in giving Kathra the information she needed.

But he could also bring the better parts of human culture to the places they were headed.

Shakespeare. Lao Tzu. Locke. Socrates.

But Daniel knew exactly where he'd start.

With a cookbook.

THIRTEEN

CRENCE CONSIDERED things as he finally returned to his own bridge.

"Jine, you ready to start reading their map data into our system?" he asked, turning to look at his pilot.

"Are we sure this isn't some elaborate practical joke?" the man asked. "They've listed nearly a thousand inhabited worlds, broken down into what they call Free Worlds, mostly closer, Sept Empire farther out, and a number of new colonies every which way."

"Which is what she promised us, in trade for a map of the three main Anndaing sectors and five more around them," Crence replied with a flex of his hammer.

"The trade potential is stupendous!" Jine exclaimed. "Both in cultural goods, but also technology, both ways."

"Not all will want to trade with us," Crence reminded the nightflier. "Plus, there will be requirements for factories at both ends capable of turning out the sorts of replacement parts necessary for things to work. That will take time."

"And we'll get filthy, stinking rich on the licensing deals

and maybe financing for such things, just from being in the right place at the right time," Jine said.

"I will remind you, yet again, that we might have set out to open new markets, rather than trying to make our margins on the old ones," Crence smiled. "There is still risk involved, especially if the Mbaysey have enemies that might be coming after them."

"So do we race home immediately?" Jine said. "Or do we press deeper and travel to one of these weird TradeStations they described?"

Crence grimaced. Jine smiled back at him.

The nightflier had hit the exact crux of his dilemma. They could not be two places at once.

He owed it to the Merchants Guild to brief them with everything he had learned, but in doing so, he immediately lost his first-mover advantage. Others would quickly load up with everything they thought they could trade and run like hell for human space.

He'd still have an advantage, as long as he was able to recruit translators out there, since he knew what to ask for.

Did Commander Omezi have crew she might be willing to let him recruit? They would need to be bilingual, which perhaps limited him to the two he had met, the Kaniea A'Alhakoth and the human Daniel.

Crence smile wickedly.

He would invite one of them aboard *Koni Swift* as an ambassador to the Merchants Guild. A teacher who could add another language to his vessel's current list, so that when they were ready to head to human space, he would be able to communicate with those folks immediately.

Plus, it would give him the opportunity to see the strangers at close quarters, and learn what kinds of people they were.

"Open a communication line to *SeekerStar*," Crence said boldly.

Jine was in the process of moving *Koni Swift* away from the human vessels. Less of an immediate threat, either direction, especially considering that all those tiny vessels appeared to be one-shark combat fliers, highly maneuverable and over-armed for something so small.

None of them threatened *Koni Swift* individually, but twenty of them could overwhelm his vessel quickly. It would be worse if the massive warship known as *SeekerStar* chose to be hostile.

Crence thanked his ancestors that he had the luck of the star gods on him, to have encountered a new culture, and the first ambassadors he ran into were friendly.

Running in fear from someone else, if Kathra Omezi's story was to be believed, but any significant threat to the Anndaing Merchants Guild would possibly trigger the Call to Armada for the first time since…

When? The Ovanii?

No, the passage of Urid-Varg, when that creature had intelligently decided to avoid Anndaing space and eventually destroyed the K'bari instead. Thus this very swath of destroyed systems in a broad stripe several hundred light-years across, when the Armada had finally joined with others to oust that bastard.

Urid-Varg had been eventually driven from known space, disappearing from cognition with that monstrous vessel of his.

Destroyed? Was that possible?

The human Daniel had proclaimed it with such sincerity that Crence was tempted to believe him.

But how? And was it possible that Daniel had been the one to do it? Such had been suggested, since he claimed to have inherited the Urid-Varg's vessel before it was subsequently lost.

If it had been.

Crence knew serious doubt.

To believe anything else would be to suggest that these humans were dangerous enough to be a threat to Anndaing space all by themselves.

"Crence, I have someone on line, speaking Anndaing," Dane Roguez got his attention, seated opposite Jine.

Crence opened the line for everyone to hear, rather than digging out the headset. His crew needed to know about this, if not why.

"Greetings," he said. "This is Trademaster Crence Miray. To whom do I have the pleasure of speaking?"

"This is A'Alhakoth ver'Shingi, speaking for Commander Omezi," the Kaniea woman replied in a confident voice.

"I have a subsequent proposal to make to the Commander," Crence said, marking this as a new stage of negotiations, the previous round having been apparently fruitful for all involved.

"We await your wisdom with joy, Elder," she said with what he suspected was a smiling, polite sarcasm in her voice.

Crence nearly laughed. Slathering it on a bit thick, perhaps, but this woman also knew how to handle the situation in delicate ways that the humans would lack, at least until they learned.

"Given the broad range of new developments and options possible before us, it behooves me to take a message directly to Ogrorspoxu, to the MasterHall of the Anndaing Merchants Guild itself," Crence said. "Such a meeting as ours is larger than one trademaster meeting another in deep space."

"Such was one option we anticipated, Trademaster," the young Kaniea replied carefully.

"I would inquire with the Commander if she had a bilingual crew member that would be willing to accompany *Koni Swift* to Ogrorspoxu now, as an Ambassador, in order to make a more complete report of your culture, your message, and your needs."

The way the line went dead suddenly told Crence that someone had muted the connection, probably so that they could explore all the ramifications of the gift-fish he had just dangled out there like he was an angler.

He smiled and leaned back into his chair. They were likely to be a while, but he would not be offended. The worst thing she could do right now would be to offer a swap, where one of his people joined her vessel, doing the same thing.

It was unnecessary, since they had two speakers now, but it would also give Crence yet another fin up on all those poxy bastards back at Ogrorspoxu.

His grin seemed to be infectious, from the smiles coming back to him from Jine and Dane. But they'd spaced with him a number of times, and understood some of the twisted ways his mind worked.

Careful merchants tended to be successful. Crazy ones occasionally got rich.

He was known to throw the bones down on occasion.

"The Commander asks for the duration of such a mission," the Kaniea youngster came back on line. "As well as the most efficient means by which such an ambassador might be reunited with *SeekerStar* later, Elder."

Oh, good one, young lady. Assume that I'm going to more or less dump them with the folks back home, and then run for deep space and the Free Worlds as soon as it would not be insulting to everyone involved.

With a bilingual crew in hand.

He felt a maniacal laughter threaten to bubble over.

"While the details themselves will be subject to Board

Members beyond my immediate control, I believe I can pledge the honor of the Guild that a transport would be put at your ambassador's disposal. I presume that Kanus is likely your first serious stop?"

"Such is our plan, Elder," she said. "Please stand by while I translate."

Again, mute. He couldn't even record the conversation over there and begin to break down their tongue. At least it wasn't tonal in nature, so he could do much with written text, he presumed, once he learned pronunciations.

But Crence was hard pressed to remember the last time he'd had this much fun with a translation.

Now, who would he send over, if the woman in charge offered him a trade?

FOURTEEN

K ATHRA NODDED as A'Alhakoth finished her translation.

Kanus made the most sense, from the several hundred worlds the trademaster had offered for her map of human space. It would allow her newest comitatus member a chance to visit her home again, and give Kathra the option of finding more like her.

Neither the Anndaing nor the Kaniea were as sexist as the Sept, but the Kaniea were still a little primitive in such things.

Only by being born the daughter of a Jarl had A'Alhakoth been trained and educated as she was.

At the same time, there would likely be more women out there Kathra could recruit, both for the Clans as well as the comitatus, possibly. Kaniea women that might have a chip on their shoulder.

Kathra smiled.

"Let him know that we have understood his offer, and that I need time to communicate with my crew before proceeding," Kathra said. "That way he's not waiting. We'll call him back when we have an update."

A'Alhakoth dutifully translated the message and then Ife cut the line.

Ife turned to Kathra with a smile on her face.

"Should I call him to the bridge, or did you want to meet him in the dining hall?" the woman asked.

Kathra glared at her, but Ife was invulnerable, it seemed.

"If we go to Kanus, that practically demands that A'Alhakoth be aboard *SeekerStar*," Ife said simply, grinning ear to ear. "That leaves Daniel as the most obvious candidate, if we can be assured that those silly merchants can protect him from whoever wishes him harm."

"He can take care of himself, you know," Kathra said. "But yes, confirm that he is in the hall or ask him to join me there. Ndidi probably has him cutting vegetables by now."

Kathra turned to launch herself toward the hatch.

"Ife, you're in charge for a while, or grab Erin if you need something," Kathra said with a laugh. "A'Alhakoth, you're with me."

They found Daniel waiting for them out front, rather than back in the kitchen itself, chopping up a large tray of carrots and potatoes on his left into a bowl on his right.

"Ndidi did not feel she could spare me, even for the Commander," he grinned as he looked up.

"She might have to," Kathra glanced around, but it was just the three of them at the moment.

Someone would probably wander in for a snack at some point, but that was a comitatus prerogative, anyway.

"Oh?" Daniel asked, still chopping without looking down.

Kathra was certain she would lose fingers trying something like that.

But Daniel was an expert. She sat across from him, with A'Alhakoth beside her.

"The trademaster went ahead and asked for an

ambassador to the Anndaing, as I suspected he would eventually," she began. "Someone to accompany him directly to their main world aboard their vessel, to meet with his Board. He would then, I presume, drop our ambassador there so that he could beeline to someplace like Thrabo, in Free Worlds space, to start making trade deals before anyone else, with the added advantage of learning languages along the way."

"I see," he said, but it looked more like a placeholder than an agreement.

"My preference is to keep A'Alhakoth with me, so that we can draw on allies on Kanus," Kathra continued. "Would you be interested in visiting their world? What was it called?"

"Ogrorspoxu," Spectre Twenty-Three spoke up. "Not their homeworld, because nobody knows where that is, but the closest you'll get to a definition of a perfect planet, according to legend."

It seemed that Daniel had given the idea much thought already, because he nodded.

"Yes, that would be a good idea, for a number of reasons," he said.

"Such as?" Kathra asked, surprised that he so readily said yes.

Comitatus, yes, but this went beyond that. At least she thought so. The rest of her women might have different interpretations.

"The Ovanii," he said. "They were a star tribe, much like the Mbaysey in their day, but they were raiders, rather than explorers. Eventually the Anndaing and their allies broke the Ovanii, but they must have had interesting ships. This core world of the Anndaing is probably a good place for me to do research. And find more things to translate, since I have access to a number of willing accomplices, eager that their stories not be lost. I would also like to know more about the K'bari."

"My concern is the Ishtan, Daniel," Kathra countered. "If they can track you, you will be far removed from what we can do to protect you."

"You could send someone with me," he grinned. "Iruoma would be a good candidate, since they will never control her again. Areen is also a possibility. Joane is probably the nerdiest, when it comes to learning new technology."

"I could also send Yejide," Kathra smiled slyly, watching Daniel's eyes get large for a second. It felt good to tease him occasionally. "Remember, Daniel, you have no secrets from me or Erin."

His mouth opened to say something, but nothing came out. He tried again with the same result.

Kathra turned to A'Alhakoth instead.

"You will never repeat this conversation," she said simply, watching the woman's slit pupils open large as well, before she nodded.

Comitatus.

"Yejide has had a crush on Daniel since the beginning, but been unable to act on it for a variety of reasons," Kathra explained, dropping her voice down, just in case someone besides Ndidi was in back helping prep food. "It eats at her, but she is just as stubborn as Iruoma in her own ways."

A'Alhakoth turned to Daniel and smiled innocently.

"So, you'll seduce all of us at some point, if I just patiently await my turn?" she asked in a smiling voice.

Kathra felt her jaw drop open. Daniel's face went white for a second and then turned a color of beet red she didn't know *Rabics* like him were capable of.

"No secrets, Daniel," she smiled, reminding him. "I have been you, just as you have been me. I might have peeked, but it is obvious that you didn't. Thank you."

Kathra hadn't really considered the Kaniea woman from that angle.

Most of the Mbaysey were homosexual, only taking pleasure from other women. Being eighty-five percent of the entire tribe, and all of *SeekerStar*'s crew save Daniel, made that a necessity, if a woman sought release. But the Kaniea clung to a more primitive, binary model, men and women living in roughly equal numbers, in a society tilted somewhat towards a patriarchy that was slowly breaking down as modernity caught up with them.

A'Alhakoth would see Daniel as someone she could take into her bed, if she chose. Just as she had all of the comitatus to work with as well.

Kathra just laughed.

"Consenting adults," she reminded both of them of her rules. "And not a threat to the good conduct of the ship or the comitatus."

Daniel sputtered, but nothing intelligent came out.

Interestingly, he never once stopped cutting, nor managed to cut himself in the process.

Finally, he did put his knife down and drew a deep breath in.

"Any of the Spectres you have mentioned would be welcome, Kathra," he finally said. "I doubt that I would need an entire harem, in spite of what Urid-Varg thought was appropriate. But I do look forward to what my ghosts and I might learn out there. This was one of the K'bari worlds that were destroyed by Urid-Varg."

"I know, Daniel," she said, sobering. "And it will help all of us who are Mbaysey, which includes you."

He nodded in recognition, but had nothing more to say.

Kathra turned to A'Alhakoth, catching the gleam of merriment in the woman's eyes.

"Let us go do a deal with our trademaster," she smiled back.

FIFTEEN

Pasdar stared out of the porthole in his office and smiled briefly at the vessel that had quickly taken shape under his guidance and with the input of his new allies.

SeptStar, shortly to be flying his flag, with a small crew of the most elite sailors he and his aspbad, Hadi Rostami, had been able to identify from the masses available. Amirin Pasdar was just sad that he would not be able to bring Rostami with him, but *Vorgash* would need an aspbad like him to make it home.

Not that anyone in space represented a physical threat to a Septagon, but the man would be facing one of the *Vuzurgan*, the Grand Nobles of the Sept, if he was not called before an *Andarzbad*, one of the Emperor's Councilors, to explain the disappearance of a naupati like Amirin Pasdar.

Pasdar had split his time over the last month supervising construction of the new vessel and writing up all the reports and information that Rostami would be carrying home.

More likely, one of the Patrol vessels would be loaded up with as much food and consumables as they could haul, and race well ahead of the rest of the fleet. That would give his leaders time to consume his message and plan accordingly for when *Vorgash* made it home.

But not enough time to stop Pasdar.

Amirin considered what it would do to his reputation, to hare off on this wild chase, when he could have simply returned to Sept space having driven Kathra Omezi entirely from the human sectors of the galaxy. But that would be a failure he was unwilling to admit, as he looked up from his desk and studied the nearly-complete warship in the near distance.

All Omezi had asked was freedom for her collection of perverted women from the men of the Sept Empire. Escaping into the alien darkness would probably grant her that.

He would not allow it.

His orders were already being stretched in terrible ways, but he was still within the letter of them, using the resources of his new allies, both human and Ishtan, to build a vessel capable of chasing the woman.

You will not escape me, Omezi.

He put his pen down and flexed his hands and shoulders from the tension that had taken root.

It was entirely possible that he had crossed some line. Emotionally. Psychologically. Mentally.

But she would not defeat him.

Once already, *Vorgash* had been chased from the field of battle by Kathra Omezi. That alone was worth chasing her to the gates of hell and beyond.

A Septagon, defeated by a pack of primitive women from Tazo. Nearly destroyed in the process.

He would have her head on a stake to present to the Emperor before he returned home. That much he had sworn.

A knock at the hatch caused Pasdar to swear under his breath as he checked the clock.

How much time had he spent daydreaming of his revenge?

He opened it to admit Rostami.

The man entered, sat without comment, and waited, his face composed.

Amirin knew that he had let himself get out of control and fought to bring everything in his mind to heel. Normally his aspbad spoke without prompting or reservation in the privacy of this office.

They stared at each other for a long moment.

Finally, Rostami stirred.

"Should I go instead?" the man asked simply.

Pasdar considered it, wondering if he had let his emotions get completely out of hand.

How crazy had Amirin Pasdar gotten, with such rage in him?

"What do you see when you look at me?" Pasdar asked in a voice that sounded like a creature emerging from a swamp.

"I fear that you are not the naupati who took us across the border into Free Worlds space, Amirin," Rostami said. "Something has changed in you, in a bad, black way."

Pasdar leaned back in his chair and stole a glance at the ship in the distance.

For the briefest moment, it turned into the giant, white whale of legend, at least to his subconscious. That frightened him even more than he realized.

He had been ordered to chase Kathra Omezi and break her so-called Tribal Squadron. Nothing could stand before a Septagon, but there was also nothing in the galaxy that could not outrun him, so anything he would have tried would be a long, stern chase.

Only by building *SeptStar*, in the same yard as *SeekerStar* and with access to the very blueprints of that ship, had he taken a step that would ensure his eventual success.

"Yours does not have to be the hand that holds the harpoon, as long as the whale is slain," someone said.

It didn't sound like Rostami's voice, and the man's face betrayed a curious confusion when Pasdar turned back to him.

"What?" Pasdar demanded.

"I did not speak, Amirin," Hadi Rostami replied.

Pasdar drew a deep breath.

Amirin Pasdar had walked right up to the edge of a cliff and had been prepared to leap off it.

To his death. Socially, if not literally.

It would be better for him to return to Sept space and find his center.

Then perhaps he should cause a new fleet of such *SeptStars* to be built. They were faster than Patrols by a significant margin. Cheaper to build, since they did not rely on gravity field inducers.

Only in their fragility did they betray themselves, as a Patrol vessel was much more durable and tough. But a *SeptStar* was far more heavily armed, as a result of all the space freed up.

"Yes," Amirin Pasdar said aloud. "We need to change. I will return to Sept space with *Vorgash* and prepare for whatever follow-up you will need, Hadi. You will take command of *SeptStar* as soon as the builder trials are complete, and then begin your quest. We will build at least two more secret, forward operating bases on our way home, so that you have a place to return to."

"We will find her," Rostami promised earnestly. "We will destroy her."

"I wonder if that is necessary," Pasdar mused. "If you hound her mercilessly, and you can with this design and a few freighters to keep you resupplied from Ardabil or the other forward bases, then you can cause her squadron to eventually disintegrate. They are civilians, not warriors."

"And your friends?" Rostami asked.

"They will act as bloodhounds, leading you to the cook, who will be at Omezi's side," Pasdar said. "They are entirely alien, but I find a pureness of vision in them. I wonder if that is part of my own insanity, when you must live in the shadows at this level of Sept culture."

"They will infect me as they did you?" he asked.

"It is entirely possible," Pasdar replied. "But they care only to see the cook destroyed, so while they will drive you, they will not lead you astray."

"Then perhaps you can return to yourself, once we are away," Rostami smiled.

Pasdar nearly snarled back at the man, but then he understood how much of his new behavior was possibly driven by the Ishtan and their single-minded, apparently-deathless pursuit of the cook and his forbears.

Nothing Amirin Pasdar had done over the last two months would damage his career or social standing, when it was made known at the Imperial capital at Rhages.

As long as he shaded a few things in obscurity.

And ordered Rostami to chase Kathra Omezi down in his name.

SIXTEEN

DANIEL STUDIED the scrutinizer device Joane Obiakpani, Spectre Five, was carrying. It reminded him of a smaller version of the boxes his custom dress shirts had been packaged in from the tailor, back when that was a thing.

Back when Daniel had cared about such things.

Seven centimeters thick and wrapped in black leather to protect the metal and give it friction in your hands. Twenty-one centimeters wide by nearly thirty long, it was heavy enough that it came on a strap you hung around your neck, so it could dangle at your side.

Portable scanner capable of being programmed to identify and analyze a number of things, including a small compartment at the top which you could open to insert something larger than a gumball but smaller than an orange.

It would hopefully keep them both alive.

The rest of the boxes around them in the landing bay were the reason they needed a scrutinizer in the first place. And the reason Daniel hated camping.

Not the glamorous kind, where you drove or flew up to a tent or yurt someplace and relaxed, but the type where you put everything in a backpack and walked somewhere without roads, reception, or decent take-out food.

When you had to carry all the food you would eat, so it had to be simple, light, and rather bland. Cornmeal and wheat flour. Egg replacement mix. Dehydrated meat. Equally dehydrated sauce.

Pedestrian cooking that involved throwing things in a pot, adding water, and bringing to a boil.

There was no art to it. No soul.

On the other hand, nobody could even begin to predict how long they would be away from *SeekerStar*. There was no way to carry enough food, in any form, for two humans.

They would bring consumables for a week or so, and already have worked their way slowly through Anndaing food options, using this portable scanner to make sure neither of them were accidentally poisoned or intoxicated along the way.

It helped that A'Alhakoth's metabolism handled most human food well. She actually had fewer allergies than some of the other women in the comitatus, when it came down to it.

Something of his pique must have communicated itself to Joane, as she looked up at him and smiled, that gap between her front teeth drawing the eye down from the poof of hair she always managed to keep looking good, even after stuffing it under a flight helmet.

"Maybe you should take some seeds?" she grinned.

Daniel scowled up at the woman standing there. *Up*, like he did most of the comitatus.

She was just as immune.

"Thought about it," he grumbled. "But that requires all manner of soil bacteria be introduced into their ship, in addition to what we'll be bringing personally. Plus whatever they'll have that will infect the soil in return. And I could only bring enough for perhaps one or two pots, so we'd have the choice of tomatoes, peppers, or perhaps squash. In a few months."

She shrugged. Before Daniel had come along, the comitatus hadn't eaten nearly as well. A poor tribe focusing on getting enough nutrients into young, growing bodies so that they could turn out to be big, strong women like Joane. Or Kathra.

Actually having food that was a pleasure to eat was something that he had done to spoil them, when all it used to take was the occasional trip to a TradeStation for dinner.

At least he'd ruined them for poor cooking. It was a good thing Ndidi was going to be better than him, one of these days.

Kathra and Ndidi approached now as other women started loading boxes and gear into the SkyCamel. Erin was already aboard, doing her preflight and unwilling to allow any other woman to fly Daniel over.

The two of them had a most complicated relationship, but it worked. Erin had had to pull rank on several other women in the comitatus for this duty today.

Daniel paused to make sure he was ready to face the aliens when he arrived. Dark pants. Long sleeved shirt. Heavier, button-up overshirt, since nobody ever kept their vessels as warm as the Mbaysey did.

Under it all, the bodysuit that he had inherited from Urid-Varg after he had killed that *salaud*. And the gem, resting comfortably at the top of his breastbone. It might look like it had been embedded, and nobody but Daniel could remove it from him while he was alive, but it was just attached.

He liked to think of it as a symbiont, rather than a parasite. The ghosts in his mind as a result of its presence were generally helpful.

Beside him, Joane was wearing the current uniform of the comitatus, courtesy of a massive sale of fabric at a Sept TradeStation years ago.

Heavy boots to mid-calf designed for planetside terrain as well as station treads. They were a rough, matte brown that didn't require stupid amounts of time and effort to keep clean, mostly because the Commander didn't believe in lining all the women up for regular inspections.

The comitatus these days wore long pants tucked in to the boots and made from a reasonably heavy denim they had found at Soomi, someone closing out nearly one hundred long-bolts of the stuff, all in a soft orange somewhere midway between sand and flame. Daniel had called the color tangerine when he first saw it, and that name had stuck ever since.

Jackets worn on other ships were the same material, lined and then waterproofed, because every damned TradeStation has thermostats controlled by men and kept three to five degrees cooler than Kathra kept *WinterStar*. Black pullover shirts under the jackets stood out against the brightness of the fabric.

Like the rest of the comitatus, Joane had a bolter pistol strapped to her thigh, available in a hurry if she needed to take someone down with a compact particle projector fed by ammunition disks.

Kathra wore an identical outfit as she approached, including the pistol. Beside her, Ndidi had taken to wearing the same sorts of dark colors Daniel preferred in the kitchen, where they did a reasonable job of hiding stains and you didn't need to stand out.

Drawing attention to yourself was for your cooking. Nothing else mattered.

"Try not to get lost out there," Kathra teased with a smile as she came to rest near them.

It was an old joke between the two of them at this point.

"See what you can do to improve my harem while I'm gone," Daniel grinned back.

He was the only male aboard *SeekerStar*, ninety-nine point whatever percent of the time. Urid-Varg had originally chosen to take the Mbaysey as his hostages because that sick *salaud* had wanted to have an entire tribe of women as sex slaves.

Daniel never regretted killing him. The galaxy was a better place with that *branleur* in hell.

"I will be expecting at least two new recipe books upon your return," Ndidi interjected with a grin on her face.

"Two?"

"One filled with all the Anndaing things you learn," Ndidi nodded solemnly. "And the other from whatever interesting folk you find when you get there and they find out you can cook."

"I shall keep you apprised of my progress," Daniel replied dryly.

The group laughed.

"Joane, your job is keeping him alive," Kathra said, her voice growing far more serious now. "We're going to Kanus to trade and recruit, but I need the Anndaing merchants on our side. And we'll presume that the Ishtan can still track Daniel until someone delivers me the rest of their heads. Or at least their soul gems."

Joane nodded. She was a quiet woman at the best of times, which made her an ideal traveling companion for an introvert like him.

"So what do I do if they make us an offer of more ships, and crews for them?" Joane suddenly asked, smiling again.

"Unless you plan on starting your own clan with your own ClanStar, make sure they're warships," Kathra teased.

"Not ready to start making babies," Joane countered.

"Too many of you trouble-makers around that I need to keep out of harm."

Daniel chuckled along with the women.

That was one iron rule in the comitatus. No mothers. If you wanted babies, you retired from the flying and fighting, so that the tribe didn't end up with orphans.

Not many of the women sworn to Kathra had ever made that ultimate sacrifice, but she had no flexibility on that one matter.

Daniel wasn't sure what it would mean in a few years when both Kathra and Erin went to the sperm bank at the same time, set to raise cousins that would be the next generation to protect the Mbaysey. He'd never imagined, back when he took a job as her personal chef, that he'd be here that long.

Now he wasn't sure he would ever leave.

Ndidi did not surprise him when she hugged. Like him, she tended to touch. And like anybody who spent time in a kitchen, it was always safe touch, because someone holding a knife or a hot pan who objected would teach you better manners quickly.

Kathra did surprise him with a similar hug, leaning down from her tremendous height to wrap her arms around his shoulders. It was like he was ten again, since she was an entire head taller than he was.

"We will do you proud, Kathra," Daniel said as they separated.

"Just be safe," she replied.

He nodded. As long as he had the gem, there were painfully few things in the galaxy that threatened him.

Besides his curiosity.

SEVENTEEN

CRENCE HAD RETIRED to his cabin after they had gone through all the ceremonies of welcome for a visiting trademaster coming aboard *Koni Swift*. Daniel wasn't such a person, but he was both more and less, so Crence figured that it would all balance out.

Nobody would be able to accuse him of insulting such an important trade ambassador when they got to Ogrorspoxu, even if the man had immediately headed down to the kitchen with his assistant to inspect and taste everything.

Humans were as omnivorous as Anndaing, but relied more heavily on roots and dried vegetables for their nutrition than his kind did. Still, Jine was plotting the sort of high-speed run to the capital that would get Daniel and Joane there before he accidentally poisoned them.

At least he hoped.

On the desk in front of him, Crence studied the collection of odd coins he had traded Kathra Omezi for as part of the many side deals they had done before departing. No doubt, she was equally interested in Anndaing currency and doing something similar, but when trading tons of materials, everything was usually done on a barter system. Things you could get here and sell or trade for a profit over there.

Coins were for crew experiencing shore leave on a station.

Kathra Omezi had let him know that she had no more Sept Crowns, but the notes he had taken contained a full breakdown of how such things were valued against the Free Worlds Guilders he had.

Crence especially liked the bit about how the Free Worlds had initially settled on a system based on fours, rather than the ten fingers that they used, or the twelve of Anndaing. It let them completely derail negotiations with the Sept Empire, because things never ran evenly.

There was something utterly amusing to baking such a practical joke permanently into your economy.

One Guilder had a picture of the Free Worlds logo on one side, and an engraving of an animal called a sloth on the other. Good for a beer or a slice of argha.

A Four Guilder coin had large, predatory bird on the obverse called an eagle, and could buy someone dinner and a beer in a nice dive.

Eight Guilders was a boar. Twenty-four on the human's base-10 system was a tiger. Ninety-six was a snake. Three hundred and eight-four was a unicorn. Seven hundred and sixty-eight was a dragon.

Truly rude. It spoke well of the Free Worlds. The Sept was apparently a rigid, decimalized economy that didn't take well to non-humans.

Crence had caught undertones, even through translation, that Kathra Omezi would eventually be seeking allies to help her push back against the Sept. He still wasn't sure how she would do that, with an entire squadron of unarmed transports around her, but she had struck him as capable of doing such a thing.

And someone had supposedly killed Urid-Varg.

Worse, done it in such a way that they didn't immediately brag about it to the entire galaxy. Did the humans not understand what that monster had been?

Granted, after the K'bari and their allies had finally turned on their god/emperor, he had vanished, fleeing into the darkness faster than the pursuing squadrons had been able to chase.

But a great deal of time had passed, if he only reappeared in human space in the last few years.

Where had the monster gone?

A knock disrupted his ruminations.

"Come," he called.

Dane opened the hatch and slipped in.

"The two ambassadors are done in the kitchens, Crence," he said.

Crence gestured the shark to sit and studied him.

"How's Mase doing?"

That got a grin.

Mase Jacksanch, the kitchenmaster, was a fussy old fish, tasked with keeping things simple and running for the thirty crew members of *Koni Swift*.

"Daniel did not challenge his professionalism nor his credentials," Dane laughed. "Not directly."

"Not directly?" Crence perked up.

"There was a brief explanation of what a Golden Diamond was," Dane chuckled. "And how the human came to be the personal chef for the human woman Commander Omezi. I suspect there will be a bake-off, probably about the time we reach Ogrorspoxu."

"Should we have Jine plot a slower course home?" Crence grinned. "Give Daniel and Mase time to work out their communications, and let Daniel learn about Anndaing food?"

"Televise it on pay-per-view?" Dane sat up sharply, hammer flexing forward.

"Might make the biggest possible splash around," Crence teased.

"Our stock values would go through the roof!" Dane gasped. "Should we issue more, grant the two humans some serious options with a good vesting schedule, and use that free money to finance our run into human space with as much stuff as we can carry?"

"I'll make a trademaster out of you yet, Dane," Crence smiled. "Plus, if Daniel's any good, he'll have to practice on the way home, so we get to experiment with something more interesting than casserole and stew."

"I wondered why you didn't complain about taking the human woman's primary cook as our ambassador," Dane replied.

"That was only part of it," Crence let himself grow serious again.

"Oh?"

"Daniel's interested in the Ovanii, Dane," Crence said.

"So?"

"So a human should have never even heard of the Ovanii," Crence said. "Even to the Kaniea, they would only be distant legends. And yet he treats them like a thing. Part of the research he wants to do at Ogrorspoxu is to find out more about them."

"Why?" Dane's hammer twitched forward and back with a confused rhythm.

"I don't know," Crence said. "But remember, they claim to have destroyed Urid-Varg, Dane. These humans. By themselves. Not with the aid of the entire species amassing tremendous warfleets, like when the Anndaing have called the Armada."

"How could they do that?" Dane leaned forward now.

"That is the reason I wanted the cook," Crence explained. "There were hints that he did it himself. Alone."

"Urid-Varg?" the shark's hammer was flexed as far forward as it would go.

The obscenity that he whispered under his breath was one that Crence mirrored in his own soul.

"What *are* humans?" Dane asked.

"That, my friend, is a very good question."

EIGHTEEN

A'ALHAKOTH WAS PLEASED to be headed home, now that *Koni Swift* had departed for the Anndaing capital. It had been several years since she had seen Kanus, and she was beginning to think that she might have finally started to grow up.

Humans grew and aged faster than Kaniea. They might be considered an adult as early as sixteen, where she was only now barely reaching that state at twenty-three. But then again, humans only lived for perhaps eighty to one hundred years, depending, where she might see two hundred, since the genes in her family were known for great age on both sides.

But she would not be returning as a Kaniea seeker, even if her quest had been successful.

She was comitatus. A member of an elite, human, warrior band made up entirely of women. Mother would be appalled. Father, knowing him, amused.

Kaniea society would split right down the middle if pressed, between the conservatives pining for the days before indoor heating and plumbing on one hand, and the progressives who looked up at the night sky and wondered what might be out there.

And who they might find.

It wasn't a generational thing, since her great-grandsire had been young when the first Anndaing Contact Ambassador landed and brought them into the modern age. But perhaps there would be two cultures for a time, until the stodgy ones finally got over themselves and admitted that being able to watch a comedy vid from the comfort of their warm bed wasn't a sign of moral decay.

But she was going home. At least temporarily.

Did she want to remain longer, when the Mbaysey moved on? A'Alhakoth didn't know.

She checked the clock and decided it was close enough. She would have language lessons today, teaching the comitatus Anndaing and a little Kaniea. The latter was more common on Kanus, but everyone with any aspirations to depart the planet or work with any of the aliens was bilingual.

In a way, she supposed that was the easiest way to mark the cleavage through Kaniea society. Whether or not you got jokes that Anndaing told.

She had never really understood it in such stark terms before, but there it was.

Father and three of her four brothers were multi-lingual. Mother only spoke Kaniea, as did her brother Goli and her sister E'Elbarth.

Most of the women A'Alhakoth knew didn't speak Anndaing, come to think of it. She could remember discussions with Father about why he insisted, and would not allow her to stop.

Had he seen her future?

And when looked at that way, how many other women would be even capable of running away with a group of alien women? Many men would volunteer immediately, especially with the possible romance of war, but Kaniea men were raised on ancient, martial glories.

Kathra Omezi only wanted women as her warriors.

A'Alhakoth entered the dining hall with a smile, noting that she was still far too early for the group who would be practicing conversational Anndaing with her.

Too many nerves and too much twitchiness driving her today.

Ndidi was putting out what smelled like fresh brownies on the serving table. A'Alhakoth was drawn by the smell.

Kaniea didn't have the same reward receptors in the brain as human women did for chocolate, but A'Alhakoth did have a sweet tooth, especially with fresh cacao grown on the Zalman ClanStar.

Ndidi smiled at her as A'Alhakoth took a bar, still warm from the oven.

"Thank you," A'Alhakoth said.

Ndidi studied her for a long moment, as though the woman had Daniel's ability to look inside someone.

"Everything okay?" Ndidi asked.

A'Alhakoth froze for only a moment, but they both noticed it.

"Sit," Ndidi commanded.

Kathra's new chef was tinier than any of the rest of the Mbaysey on this ship, but still half a head taller than A'Alhakoth. Daniel's size, almost exactly, which was apparently about average for a human woman, while he was small for a man.

A'Alhakoth was too used to home, where she was average, at 153cm tall using the human scale, and the men in her family were average for males at 183cm. Kathra would tower over everyone, as would much of the comitatus.

That was going to be interesting to watch.

"How are you handling things?" Ndidi asked carefully.

A'Alhakoth started to reply, but realized that the woman had already seen past all her evasions.

She opened her mouth, and then closed it without speaking. Took a bite of brownie bar to buy herself some time.

Ndidi studied her while she did. At least the human woman seemed sympathetic.

"I wonder who I am," A'Alhakoth finally managed, hoping it made sense.

Ndidi smiled and chuckled.

"Then you're doing fine," the human woman said warmly.

"I am?"

"It's called growing up," Ndidi continued. "There is a you who left Kanus three years ago, but she's not the woman coming home today."

"No, she's not," A'Alhakoth replied, seeing the truth of the words.

"Are you going to remain with us?" Ndidi asked, cutting right to the heart of A'Alhakoth's misgivings.

"I want to," she said.

"But?" Ndidi pressed.

"I realized, just now, how few Kaniea women might be interested in even traveling into space at all, let alone doing something as serious as joining the Mbaysey," she said, reaching inside to study that knot of vertigo and fear that had formed, something she had never dealt with before. "Or the comitatus."

A'Alhakoth knew a sudden rage at herself. She was a warrior, as Father had insisted she be trained, in spite of her expressing other wishes as a child.

But she could not see any other avenue where she might

have been as happy. He had understood her, better than she had.

"I am a second daughter," A'Alhakoth said fiercely. "And I come from a large family, with five older siblings. My parents are both Jarls, one of the lower ranks of the nobility on Kanus, but I still wonder how many such women the Commander might recruit."

"Any who are good enough," Ndidi said. "And wish to come. Perhaps only one Kaniea will."

"But…"

"Are you afraid of being alone?" Ndidi asked.

A'Alhakoth considered that thought. Compared it to the knot in her chest.

No, that wasn't it.

She shook her head.

"Children?" Ndidi asked.

A'Alhakoth nearly passed out at the strong surge of emotion.

"Yes!" she gasped. "The Commander will have very few slots for Kaniea men. And all of those on the ClanStars, where they will be required to do labor many will find beneath themselves, unless Kathra recruits from the peasants and yeomen."

"And you, like the others of the comitatus, will want children eventually," Ndidi nodded.

"Will I have to depart, in order to mate?" A'Alhakoth's rage finally found that center that had depressed her.

All the other comitatus could take for granted that they could go to the sperm bank and select for the characteristics they desired. Doubly so if they personally knew the donor and he had already proven himself as a valuable member of the tribe.

"I doubt it," Ndidi said. "While I haven't spoken to

Kathra on the topic, I'm sure she's given it thought. Maybe that's why she's starting here."

"So I could find a male?" A'Alhakoth asked.

Ndidi laughed.

"Knowing Kathra, she'll hold a series of competitions and pick the top dozen to make contributions to the bank, for you to use later as you see fit," Ndidi said.

A'Alhakoth felt all the breath rush out of her lungs. A competition? Her, the subject of a challenge for Kaniea men to compete over?

"Really?" she squeaked, still amazed. "Me?"

"You're comitatus, A'Alhakoth ver'Shingi," Ndidi's voice turned deadly serious. "Only the very best will even be considered."

NINETEEN

Hadi Rostami sat at his new command station on the compact, almost claustrophobic bridge of *SeptStar* as the clock counted down. He could not call it a Command Node, like he had commanded from *Vorgash*, as there was no Great Causeway here, where he and Pasdar could pace, above those twenty men, who had commanded the thousand who commanded the three hundred thousand that made up a Septagon.

He was only taking sixty-eight men with him directly. The seven women brought along as sex-objects did not count, except that they had to be fed and housed. In addition, there were two freighters attached to his independent command, hauling supplies and replacement parts. Those would be his lifeline to the forward operating bases that would keep him in the field as he sought Kathra Omezi.

Seventy-five then, technically, plus four.

He did not understand the Ishtan. Amirin had allowed the creatures into his mind and been changed, so Hadi had kept them at a more polite distance.

But he was also not the great warrior-commander that a former Sardar like Amirin Pasdar was. Nor was he a member of one of the Seven great clans that had originally banded together into the Sept, first conquering Earth, and then moving on to take human space.

Hadi Rostami was a scholar, masquerading as a naval officer. A bureaucrat. Many would seek to insult him by using the term, unaware how important those folks truly were.

Feeding the three hundred thousand men of a Septagon was an exercise in logistics that showed on a daily basis what utter amateurs some of the greatest so-called commanders in human history really were. Logistics had destroyed Napoleon and Hitler, just as it had shown Wellington and Patton to be the better men.

A single battle might be won on heart, but an entire war is won on boots and bread. Septagon *Vorgash* was among the best in the fleet for that reason.

So Amirin Pasdar, possibly the greatest warrior-commander alive right now, had sent his bureaucrat out to chase down his greatest enemy.

Because logistics works both ways. You cannot flee if you must stop to forage. And if you break up into smaller elements, forcing a single pursuer to choose his prey, you weaken yourself as the final confrontation approaches.

Kathra Omezi could not break away from her squadron without leaving someone vulnerable, a lone calf. So she would be hindered by them.

Hadi would use that knowledge as he planned.

The clock was nearing zero.

SeptStar, like its prey, was a central pillar of a vessel, around which a ring was hung at the waist. The ring spun to supply the illusion of gravity, but both vessels had their command nodes on the central hull, in zero gravity.

But it did not feel right to give this command seated. Even more so because the three men with whom he shared this bridge were seated ninety degrees apart from each other, around the circular hull.

Hadi unbuckled and rose, holding on with his toes to a bar set for this purpose. Already, he had been forced to change the standards of uniforms for his new crew, as such bars and other devices damaged the polish on leather boots. They wore cloth straps around their boots now to protect the polish, and removed them when they rode down into gravity. Eventually, he might have to locate an expert who could supply his crew with better footwear, as he and his men moved beyond the rigid structures of the Sept.

He reached down and triggered the switch to allow his voice to reach every corner of this vessel, including the weirdly-lit suite where the aliens resided. He would deal with them later, but this was a human task now.

A *Sept Imperial* thing.

"All hands, this is Aspbad Hadi Rostami," he said calmly, listening to the echoes in the room. "Our day is at hand. Septagon *Vorgash* has tasked us with completing the mission that they cannot. Bringing the Mbaysey to heel. Or destroying them, if they refuse. The Naupati has chosen you men as his instruments of justice, of all the possible sailors and warriors on *Vorgash*. We will make him proud, just as we will bring glory onto our Emperor."

Hadi paused to take a deep breath and let his words settle the men.

"Navigator, your course has been laid in," he continued after a moment. "Initiate."

"Initiating breakaway," the man replied formally. "All systems nominal. Valence drives charged."

"Make your jump," Hadi ordered the man.

SeptStar leapt out of the universe.

Somewhere, with a team of deathless hounds leading him, he would run Kathra Omezi down.

And destroy her.

TWENTY

KATHRA STUDIED the planetary system below her from the bridge of *SeekerStar*, looking over Ife's shoulder, at least metaphorically. In zero gravity, they weren't even on the same plane.

Kanus. Home of the Kaniea. Birthplace of A'Alhakoth ver'Shingi, now known as Spectre Twenty-Three.

The start of a new phase in Kathra's life and the lives of the entire Mbaysey.

On a projection of the explored galaxy, with Earth and Rhages centered, Kanus was a simple dot clear out on the edge, towards the base of the arm containing those two worlds. Not all that close to the center of the galaxy as such distances went, and emotionally it was forever away from where she'd come.

And this was just the start. A world on the nearer edge of Anndaing space. Part of their trade empire, except empire was the wrong word.

Trade Confederation, perhaps. A place where eleven species lived and traded with each other, plus however many strangers might wander in from the edges of the maps.

Humans had probably made it at least this far at some point. They were like that.

But they might have come as lone merchants or travelers on a ship, rather than an entire tribal squadron come to trade and explore. To seek the sparsely inhabited systems where they might mine the giants for gases, the asteroids for metals, and the comets for water.

All without ever setting foot on a planetary surface.

Kanus maintained an independent Customs Union with the other systems, but used modern, Anndaing vessels. Modified versions of the transport that Crence Miray had used to come aboard *SeekerStar*. Some were armed. Others were pure rescue vessels to assist a ship in distress.

Nobody had ever seen anything like one of her 'Stars.

For one, the Anndaing used a gravity system vaguely similar to the human one, but apparently smaller while still much more efficient. Kathra had not yet determined if the next vessel she built should have one.

On the one hand, a ship could be compact and more durable, since it didn't have to spin like a top. On the other hand, those would be complicated parts that needed to be replaced on a regular basis, bought from some Anndaing ally's factory.

It would also tie her down and make her dependent on someone else.

SeekerStar only needed fuel derived from those gases they mined, and minerals left over from planetary formation. And physics.

Kathra did not need anyone else, except to provide the tribe with the vast amounts of grains that could be more efficiently grown on a planetary surface, letting the ClanStars focus on exotic and interesting things that they could trade amongst themselves and send as tribute to the other ships.

"Everyone behaving?" Kathra asked the room.

"So far," Ife replied, grinning. "Most of the squadron is hard at work on the edge of the system, escorted by about half the comitatus. They know not to embarrass you today. And the locals are no more twitchy than one would expect, with twenty-seven alien ships that just showed up on their scanners broadcasting an Anndaing trade request."

Kathra nodded. Smiled even. From here, everything was just points of light in the distance, set against the darkness. Even the Anndaing TradeStation in the near distance was nothing more than a slender column, which alone marked it as something outside the normal.

Sept stations tended to be flat cylinders connected together on the level, like clover leaves. This was a top rather like *SeekerStar*, with perhaps forty levels, all of which had docks.

Not that *SeekerStar* could dock with something like that, but the two were darkly mirrored.

"And the station?" Kathra asked.

"Waiting for you to fly over and say hello," Ife nodded.

"Good enough," Kathra decided.

She kicked off and headed aft quickly. The ride down to the flight deck was the longest part, and then she was aboard Spectre One and launching into the gap.

No SkyCamels today. Tomorrow, most likely, once there had been conversation to establish rules and rates.

Eleven Spectres flew in a formation that only looked random to an outsider, with her and A'Alhakoth being escorted by the other nine.

"Spectres One and Twenty-Three, preparing to land," Kathra said in Anndaing as she approached the large bay.

It would hold one of those transports easily enough, so she could have stuffed two more fighters in here, given the skill of the pilots, but Kathra wasn't showing off today.

Best to keep a few secrets, just in case.

Inside, the deck was simple steel, so the magnets in her landing gear would hold her in place quite well. She still rotated on her gyros before setting down, lining the nose of her craft up with the bay door.

And the guns, as well, just in case there was a need to blast her way out of here later. Kathra doubted it, but she was an alien on someone else's station, in their system, and had only A'Alhakoth's three years out-of-date memories to go on.

And whatever lies that grinning shark had sold her for a pocket full of magic beans.

She laughed to herself as her Spectre settled.

The bay door closed and she could hear and feel atmosphere begin to fill the volume.

At some point, she would need to upgrade at least one SkyCamel to mate-dock instead of taking up a full repair bay, but she might just buy one of those transports instead, depending on how expensive a mechanic might be to hire for it.

Out and up, Kathra emerged from her top hatch at the same time as A'Alhakoth did. Locked her hatch. Climbed down the ladders to the deck.

They wore tangerine today. And pistols, diplomacy be utterly damned.

We are comitatus. You make way.

But she smiled as she met the young Kaniea woman midway and started across to the main hatch where a party was no doubt waiting for her.

Cycle through the airlock, marveling at a system where they irised open silently.

Kathra emerged first.

The hallway had something of a crowd, but she could see big, blue men politely holding folks at a distance. Closer, two

Kaniea males, a female, and an Anndaing, all dressed in what looked like formal robes to Kathra's eye.

Everyone was shorter than her. Significantly. Half a head or so for the men. The tiny woman was A'Alhakoth's size.

Kathra stopped at a polite distance and bowed her head, feeling Spectre Twenty-Three doing the same on her left wing.

"Greetings and welcome to Kanus," the Anndaing said carefully, returning the bow in the same manner that Crence Miray had done.

"It is my exquisite pleasure to visit the home world of one of my comitatus women," Kathra replied, watching the Kaniea pupils slit hard in surprise at her linguistic abilities.

As if she hadn't been working her ass off for this very moment since she identified her next goal.

"I am Morgan Wilzae," the shark said. "Trademaster In Residence. This is Dola Masumi, Ambassador, and his deputies, Evgi Wallicki and Ae'Alreth Zarrani."

"I am Kathra Omezi," she said formally. "Commander of the Mbaysey Tribal Squadron and leader of the comitatus. A'Alhakoth ver'Shingi, Spectre Twenty-Three."

More bows. The Kaniea had a history similar enough to humanity that they shook hands, a custom once designed to show you weren't holding a blade in it.

Even the Anndaing joined in.

Quickly, they were moved to a large room dominated by a table, except that this was not a dining hall. Looked like a space permanently dedicated to meetings.

Part of Kathra was appalled at the hideous waste to have such a space, but she also recognized that Kanus did not face the daily crush of poverty of a poor tribe hiding and fleeing in space.

This was what wealth would look like.

If she survived the next round of adventures and problems to grasp it.

The Kaniea across from her looked apprehensive, but the trademaster was possibly a close cousin of Miray, from the smile on his face and the way his eyes studied her.

"We met the vessel *Koni Swift*," Kathra said as everyone got settled. "Trademaster Crence Miray bartered with us."

She pulled an Anndaing coin from her pocket, placed it on the table, and left it at that. The Anndaing wrapped up so much behavior inside such a term because it conveyed a level of trust and civilization between well-met strangers.

"And they did not choose to accompany you to Kanus?" the Ambassador asked carefully.

Kathra felt confident at this point that she spoke enough of the tongue for polite, casual conversation, but A'Alhakoth leaned forward to translate now. Things were going to get technical and complicated.

"We did a deal with them," A'Alhakoth smiled. "A line of credit drawn on the Anndaing Merchants Guild Bank, against the services of two of our ambassadors that they are currently transporting to Ogrorspoxu."

Kathra smiled politely at the two different ways that information was received. The three Kaniea were all surprised and perhaps pleased at the news. The Anndaing's hammer flexed forward so far that she wondered if it hurt.

"Ambassadors?" he asked after a beat just long enough that maybe the others had missed it, but not Kathra. Nor A'Alhakoth.

Time spent educating human women and trading information and goods with *Koni Swift*'s crew.

"The Commander's chef is fluent in Anndaing, in spite of being human," A'Alhakoth said into the gap with just a hint of a smile. "That allowed the Mbaysey to come directly to Kanus now, instead of calling on Ogrorspoxu first."

The shark's eyes swelled outwards so far that Kathra wondered if they might indeed pop out of the sides of his hammer.

"And you intend to trade here as your first stop?" Morgan Wilzae asked, perhaps a touch breathless.

As in, just how wealthy might the Trademaster In Residence get, if friendly aliens suddenly showed up here with stories, materials, and needs? And brought the entire trade sector to town to do deals?

Kathra smiled. It was something that human, Kaniea, and Anndaing shared, so he would react.

"It is my hope that Kanus can become something of a base of trade operations for us, at least for a time," Kathra said for A'Alhakoth to translate, watching the reaction on the four faces. "We are generally a nomadic tribe, but it is my understanding that humans are exceedingly rare in this slice of the galaxy, so we will trade. Perhaps purchase advanced technologies. And recruit."

"Recruit?" the Ambassador spoke up now, perhaps a shade put out.

"The Mbaysey are not just human," Kathra said. "Even my comitatus, the women warriors sworn to me life and soul, include a Kaniea now. The various ClanStars at the edge of the system contain seven species, although we are more than ninety-seven percent human at present. That is not necessarily a permanent condition."

"What is your goal?" the man asked, eyes narrowing.

"Exploration," Kathra replied. "Then trade. We chose not to remain part of the Sept Empire, a human thing, nor the Free Worlds, which is a multi-species political organization between here and the Sept Empire. What lies beyond you, closer to the galactic core? I might wish to find out."

She watched that information settle in on all four of

them. Saw the way faces reset into different alignments as they began planning.

With any luck, she wouldn't need to run any deeper into the galaxy to escape the Sept or the Ishtan. She could just maintain the tribe here for a generation.

Not that Kathra believed that for a moment.

TWENTY-ONE

As a visiting Ambassador, Daniel rated a suite of rooms comparable to what the Trademaster, Crence Miray, had aboard *Koni Swift*. While he retired there in the evening to read, living there all the time would have been too much, even for an introvert like him.

Instead, he tended to spend much of his time in the dining hall, just as if he were still aboard *SeekerStar*. The trademaster had a small library of actual books, printed objects rather than electronic files on readers, so Daniel had just continued on his earlier task of translating.

Here, however, he was taking an Anndaing history book and translating it into Spacer, with a little French thrown in for good measure. Crence was going to get a copy, along with whatever else Daniel had done by that time.

Including a book of Ovanii poetry.

Daniel had chosen the book in front of him because it was history, but it was still more a volume on general trade than a review of the Ovanii or Urid-Varg. He could probably fill in everything they ever wanted to know about the Conqueror if he chose, but that wasn't happening today.

And the Ovanii barely rated one paragraph.

At least there was information about the K'bari.

The rise of a trade confederation rivaling the Anndaing. Centuries and more of trade and conflict as the two sides largely carved out sectors of space for themselves and drew reasonable lines on maps.

Again, Daniel knew more, just because he had a book he had already translated. And written from a K'bari point of view. And a K'bari ghost in his mind.

A shape settled across the table from him. Unlike the trestle tables on *SeekerStar*, these were rectangles that would seat six, but you had to push them together for more, and then risked banging your knee on a leg when you sat.

Daniel looked up from his homework. The shape had been too big and noisy to be Joane.

Crence Miray sat across from him. Trademaster of the ship, which was roughly the equivalent of a captain or aspbad, depending on how you wanted to translate the relevant cultural concepts.

Daniel closed his book and studied the shark. It was too early for the daily lessons in conversation. And it was just the two of them right now.

Crence looked around once with those wideset eyes on that interesting hammer, but they were alone. For now.

There was no threat emanating from the man, but Daniel reached out with his mind to listen to the shark's emotions anyway. Two weeks away from *SeekerStar* just meant that he'd have one hell of a time getting back to Kathra if things went wrong right now.

Or the Ishtan showed up.

Not that he couldn't get ugly if he had to.

"Trademaster," Daniel nodded, resting his elbows on the table.

He liked the Anndaing man.

"Daniel," the shark replied with a quick smile.

Daniel waited, unsure what the man was up to. He chose not to peek.

"I wanted to ask why you had such a fascination with the K'bari and the Ovanii," Crence finally said quietly.

"But?" Daniel asked.

"But I'm more concerned about how you can translate those two languages," the trademaster said. "The K'bari have been gone for a long time, the Ovanii even longer."

"I could say that Urid-Varg made it possible," Daniel replied, finally understanding what had brought Crence to him today. "But that raises even more questions than it answers, doesn't it?"

"Especially as you claim that Urid-Varg is destroyed," Crence said.

Daniel understood the look in those eyes now.

Trojan Horse. A simple, wooden statue, according to ancient legends, that was brought inside the walls of Troy, where men emerged and opened the gates from the inside, allowing the Hellenes to destroy the ancient city.

Given the number of centuries between the events described and them being written down in any format Daniel had always assumed a bad description of a siege tower covered with horse hides and wetted down to protect it against burning oil. Plus the image of a long, upright neck with a platform for getting over the walls would look remarkably like a horse, seen from the side.

But the outcome was still the same.

Troy sacked and her people hauled away in slavery by the warriors pledged to Agamemnon and Menelaus.

"You fear that I am another Urid-Varg," Daniel said simply. "And that you are hauling me directly to the heart of the Merchant Confederation where I am a poisoned apple."

"I would have perhaps dressed it up in prettier finery, but

yes, that is close enough," Crence said. "What are you, Daniel Lémieux? And how did you kill Urid-Varg?"

Daniel chuckled.

"Actually, I beat the *salaud* to death with a fire extinguisher," he said with a smile. "Afterwards, he tried to conquer my mind, like he had so many others, but we had surprised him, and his plans eventually failed. But not before he did things to me that I cannot easily explain."

The shark had grown perfectly still and quiet. His mind still had a flavor of fear mixed with threat, but nothing Daniel was concerned about.

Whatever Crence might think to do, Daniel was still faster.

But he dared not merge identities with the Anndaing. Crence was male, at least enough that he could probably use the mind gem in ways that Kathra and her women would never be able to. The man would learn secrets, and then perhaps be infected with the sorts of greed that would make him want that power for himself.

It didn't matter that he might make excuses about greater goods. Daniel was still the only man he could remember who wouldn't want to be a god given the opportunity.

But he'd already been there. That Golden Diamond was as close as a normal human could possibly get to that level of adulation and respect and fear.

"Afterwards?" Crence whispered. "After you had killed him?"

"He was twelve thousand years old, Crence," Daniel said. "There were things he had done to ensure that death might only be a temporary inconvenience, in ways I won't bother to explain right now. He was not prepared for humans in general, and Commander Omezi in particular. He is truly dead now, but I bear his touch, and will until I'm dead. That includes memories of languages so old that they have been forgotten."

"Ovanii and K'bari," Crence nodded.

"And others," Daniel said. "I do not have any of Urid-Varg's immense power for evil, but many of his memories."

"And the ones that hunt you?" Crence pressed. "The Ishtan?"

"Urid-Varg's mortal enemies," Daniel said. "They would wipe out any taint of his existence, and were terribly offended that I didn't just choose to die at the time."

"So what will you do at Ogrorspoxu?" Crence turned the conversation beyond Trojan horses now.

"Talk money with greedy bastards like you," he laughed. "And then send you to Thrabo or Tavle Jocia with a list of cargo guaranteed to make you rich if you get there first."

Crence laughed along with him.

"*If* we get there first?" Crence asked.

"That isn't the most likely outcome?" Daniel smiled. "You land at Ogrorspoxu just long enough to hand me off to someone else, then practice your human Spacer language lessons before anyone else can catch you?"

"Maybe," Crence grinned, his hammer tilting up a little at both ends.

"After the excitement dies down, I will ask for a library card," Daniel continued. "There are books I want to read, and will translate into human for you and everyone else."

"It is a long journey to human space," Crence noted. "Across that dead zone that once represented K'bari space."

"And there will be monsters," Daniel said. "Human and otherwise. But the Free Worlds will welcome you, and the Sept can go piss up a rope for all I care. They are Kathra's enemies, just as the Ishtan are mine. Specist *salauds* intent on conquering all human space and then subjugating the rest."

"What does Commander Omezi want?" Crence asked.

"To be free," Daniel said. "To get there, she intends to find the best technology any culture has to offer, in order to build herself a ship that can push the Sept back. And anyone else that threatens her."

"The Ovanii were fierce, deadly warriors in their time," Crence mused.

"So I gathered," Daniel nodded. "That is why I want to know more about them. The Anndaing overcame them with raw numbers eventually, but perhaps they have something to teach Kathra, even after all this time."

"Have you brought your war to my threshold?" Crence asked, turning serious. "Threatened the peace of the Anndaing with a human issue?"

"No," Daniel retorted. "They were always going to find you eventually. The Sept Empire cannot stop expanding, or they will drown, like sharks on my worlds or your distant ancestors who still relied on their gills. Kathra has given you a century or two advanced notice that they are coming, so that you could prepare for them."

"And her?"

"She's going to fight them," Daniel said simply. "I'm going to help."

TWENTY-TWO

Hadi Rostami did not enjoy visiting with the creatures Pasdar had met when *Vorgash* had killed the Star Turtle, but they were necessary to this mission. More than necessary.

Fundamental, perhaps.

So he took himself around the wheel to the space on the upper deck where they had been installed. Unlike *SeekerStar*, *SeptStar* only had two decks on its ring, and those were not required to maintain a flight squadron of up to sixty fightercraft.

SeptStar was smaller, lighter, and faster through jump as a result.

And the Ishtan were leading him to his prey.

He approached the hatch to their environment, colder and darker than the rest of the ship. The door opened and he entered.

Unlike *Vorgash*, they had a small space here. Four couches around the outside of a medium-sized room, with space to pace if they needed. Slither, maybe?

Additional food had been packed for them, but they

could process human sustenance well enough. A steward delivered four trays twice per day.

Hadi walked to the center of the room and took his seat on the human chair that had originally been added for Amirin, before he came to his senses and sent others off to die in his place.

Die?

Hadi considered that a highly likely outcome. Not a given, but a warrior prepares each morning to make his death a glorious, hard-fought thing, and then he can face it without reservation or fear on the day when it finally arrives.

Hadi Rostami had no fear.

Nor should you, the voices said. *You are not our enemy. You are an ally who will help us rid the galaxy of evil.*

Hadi shrugged.

"An ally of convenience, perhaps," he replied, unwilling to lie, even with these creatures in his mind.

Convenience because you are fruit flies compared to Ishtan, they harmonized. *The youngest of us is fourteen thousand of your years old. We are the last.*

"What will you do when the chef is destroyed?" Hadi asked. "What happens to the last of the Ishtan, when the last mission has been completed?"

We have given this much thought, Hadi Rostami. Humans risk becoming like Urid-Varg, given access to the knowledge we hold.

"I would agree," he nodded at them. "The Sept would conquer the Free Worlds and then move on. The only question is how many cultures and species they might destroy forever before they fell."

He sensed almost a hiccup of surprise from the four beings. As though they had been expecting the naupati and forgotten that not all men were the same.

Were Ishtan just pieces of a common whole, without individual identity?

You are closer to the truth than you might imagine, Hadi Rostami, the voices filled his head. *Ishtan is a single being, even as it is composed of individuals. We are less than we were, but we still are.*

He shrugged. After this much time around them, he wasn't all that surprised by the revelation.

Your thinking on the Sept betrays disloyalty to your cause, but also a deeper understanding of the arc of empires than that of Amirin Pasdar.

"Empires of conquest breed resentment," Hadi replied, thinking back to his historical studies. Warriors always focused on tactics and strategies, rather than logistics and the construction of stable bureaucracies that outlived emperors. And even ruling houses. "Both the Chinese and the Byzantines forged stable structures not reliant on a *Great Man*. And they gave outsiders both reason and opportunity to join. That fostered loyalty to an ideal, rather than any particular individual. The Sept ideal sees gradations of power and privilege. It will eventually fail."

And yet you support it, they noted.

"I am Sept," Hadi replied with heat, almost surprised by the depth of patriotism his own words churned up. "That fall will occur long after my time, and in the meantime I work to strengthen the structure, that it might yet improve for others drawn into our web. That it might change into something lasting."

Inwardly, he studied himself with a jaundiced eye, but could detect no hint that the outsiders were manipulating him.

We are not, they chanted abruptly. *These are your thoughts, perhaps subsumed ere now by your loyalty to the person of Pasdar. In such betrayals of the Sept ideal, you do perhaps represent a human future that the Ishtan might assist. But such an occurrence would require many generations of human lifetimes to come to pass.*

Hadi nodded. In that time, Sept would evolve or fall.

Hadi Rostami would be forgotten, except as perhaps a footnote suggesting that his mission to bring down the Mbaysey was a success or failure.

Long after his time.

Long after your time, they agreed. *But the mission is well begun. We see the shadow that the cook Daniel Lémieux casts in his passage. We will bring you to his destruction, even though we must rely on ephemeral humans and their tools to achieve.*

Hadi shivered at the concept of ephemeral as the Ishtan conveyed it. They had sworn to live forever, if that was what it finally took to destroy the creature known as Urid-Varg. Twelve thousand years later, they had lost two in combat, but the other four still chased.

They were weaker now than they had been before, but the chef was a pale shadow of Urid-Varg, from what they had shown him.

And Hadi would bring the whole might of the Sept with him to destroy the Mbaysey.

Soon.

TWENTY-THREE

CRENCE STUDIED the logs and the charts from the privacy of his office. *Koni Swift* was getting close to Ogrorspoxu now, but he wasn't sure how he felt about that.

There were no easy answers to the complexities that the humans had introduced into his life.

A rap at the hatch was followed a moment later by Dane opening it.

The shark entered with a small tray of something in one hand. Four disks, each about the size of Crence's palm and not as thick as his fin. Each was a weird golden-brown in color, with a dusting of something brownish-red across the top.

The smell that accompanied him into Crence's office was sweet and compelling.

Dane sat the tray on the desk and took one of the disks in his hand, followed a moment later by taking a bite out of it.

"Daniel has failed, yet again, to kill us all," Dane announced as he chewed. "Mase, however, lost this round."

"What are they?" Crence asked.

"Daniel calls them snickerdoodles," Dane said. "Some sort of dense sweetbread with a really rich, complicated set of flavors going on."

"And nobody has died of poisoning?" Crence asked as he reached for one and studied it.

Still warm from the oven. He broke off a piece and sniffed it. Yummy and earthy in ways that shouldn't appeal to a sea-based creature, but he took a bite.

It was quickly evident why Mase was on the losing side of this round, whatever he'd made. This snickerdoodle thing was *good*.

"We yet live," Dane nodded.

"You do realize that he can't kill us all until we get him to Ogrorspoxu and land, right?" Crence teased, just to watch Dane's eyes bulge suddenly with the faintest hint of panic.

He took a bigger bite of the treat.

"He wouldn't," Dane gasped. "Would he?"

"You've been nice enough to the human that he saves you for last?" Crence laughed. "They do eat meat. Anndaing might not qualify as cannibalism to a human."

Just watching Dane's hammer twitch made it worth it. The sputtering from the shark was a bonus.

"Did Mase get the recipe?" Crence asked.

"Well, yeah, but it required the last of the weird stuff Daniel and Joane brought with them from their ship," Dane said. "From here on in, he's cooking with our supplies."

Crence nodded.

"We'll be at a human planet soon," Crence reminded the shark. "If we can pick up bulk raw materials, we could introduce new foodstuffs into Anndaing culture at one hell of a profit. A truly ambitious shark might figure out how to grow all the ingredients and bring them someplace like Ogrorspoxu. It's not just technology that might make us rich."

Dane nodded and grabbed the third disk.

"Which reminds me," he said around a mouthful of cookie. "Joane was asking about our tech. Nothing bad, mostly just what things were and how they worked, but I got the feeling she's also pretty good as a mechanic. We've got what, four days left?"

"Give or take," Crence agreed. "Jine's yet to calculate the last few jumps, but I haven't told him to push or lag, either. Why?"

"So did you want to let Joane apprentice with some of the maintenance?" Dane asked. "I got the impression that she wouldn't push, but also wouldn't say no. We friendly enough?"

Crence went for the last cookie before Dane got greedy. The shark could be like that.

And he was right back to the top of the conversation he had been having with himself before the interruption.

How far did they trust the humans? Daniel had provided very concise and glib answers to most questions, except *how* Urid-Varg had gotten himself into a position where a small human could beat him to death with a fire suppression cylinder and live to tell the tale.

Or what the touch of that *salaud* had done to the human afterwards.

After the Conqueror was dead.

Was Crence bringing an infection to the heart of the Anndaing Merchants Guild, even accidentally?

Joane was even less known than Daniel, but she barely spoke Anndaing, and then with a thick accent. His human was barely good enough to talk to her about much of anything beyond the basic pleasantries.

Crence could see hiring a few humans first thing when he got to wherever he was going, just to sit around and talk with his crew.

Possibly a new assistant cook for Mase, while he was at it, as long as the person knew how to make snickerdoodles.

He leaned forward and flexed his hammer upwards just enough to make his point.

"Don't set her to fixing anything critical," he decided. "About what you'd do with any rookie who didn't know their fin from their tail. Keep them friendly and keep us safe. Once we get to Ogrorspoxu, they'll be someone else's problem, at least until we get back from human space."

"Understood," Dane said, sobering as the implications sunk in.

The humans were still relative strangers, even if they had been model traveling companions.

And Daniel had too many holes in his stories to make Crence feel safe.

Balance that against the potential for enormous profit, especially if Anndaing grav systems were really that much better than what humans had. *SeekerStar*'s guns appeared to be more powerful than anything a ship that small should be able to mount, so maybe the humans were better at mayhem and warfare.

Welcome to the life of a trademaster.

TWENTY-FOUR

Joane was no mechanic. She was the first to admit that. Adanne and the others were much better at taking things apart and putting them back together again. At the same time, those ladies were just mechanics, rather than comitatus warriors. They didn't generally know which end of a pistol was the dangerous one.

Joane was the nerdiest of the warriors, and the killer among the mechanics.

She grinned that they had her cleaning kitchen equipment today. She'd been a *probie* before this, probationarily welcomed until she could prove herself worthy of remaining. And assigned the scut duties nobody else wanted because they had someone that such things could be dumped on.

Like *SeekerStar*, *Koni Swift* ran pretty much completely on electrical systems powered by the ship's generators. In essence, they used resistance to generate heat for the stoves and cooking tops.

Earlier, she had helped dismantle and clean one of the local units that heated and circulated warm air through vents to all the rooms contained within this set of the ship's frames. Technology that was ancient, only because nobody had really bothered to improve on it in forever.

She was working with Dolon Marquez today. Shark of all trades, as it were, since he was mostly a stevedore moving cargo around, as well as the ship's medic.

And principle handyman when it came to fixing mechanical things.

One of Mase's stoves was acting up. They had assigned Dolon and his new assistant to fix it. Or rather, Dolon had handed her a reader loaded with servicing instructions and grinned at her.

At least there were no flammable gases involved, if she did something wrong. And Daniel had cheated along the way, although she was never about to tell those boys that.

One of the advantages of being able to merge with Daniel, before they had gotten here, was that he had taught her to read Anndaing at a working level sufficient for a non-scholar leaving school at the end of her teen years.

Not good enough to write poetry in Anndaing, even if she managed to find the inclination, but fine for reading an exploding diagram and technical steps to take a stove apart.

"Three wrench," she said, as she got the big panel off and looked inside.

Just because, she leaned back and made sure that the fuses to this side of the kitchen were off.

Measure twice, cut once.

Dolon handed her a metal thing that she could call a wrench. More or less. Octagonal head raised and requiring something like a socket tool to open.

Stupid threads were backwards, but she'd put that down to barbarity on the part of folks that had been in space before her species discovered electricity.

Joane stuck the thing in and started backing out bolts.

After tightening the first one accidentally.

"So," Dolon asked in a breezy tone for a shark. "You a spy?"

"If I am, they forgot to tell me," Joane replied with a grunt as she got the bolt out and handed it to him. "Why?"

"You can read stuff better than someone we picked up on a street corner," he pointed at the reader on the deck between them. "Can't speak well."

"A'Alhakoth had us doing conversational stuff, but Daniel handed around a few books," she lied easily. "Figured we'd need it when we got to Kanus. Finding you folks midway just made it that much faster, since we could trade for good maps. I was looking forward to meeting her kin, but I'll be last now."

"Yeah, but you'll be the prettiest girl at the dance when we get to Ogrorspoxu," he grinned.

She turned and fixed the shark with a cold, hard smile. Daniel had warned her. Kathra, too.

"I don't like creatures with a penis," she said bluntly. "Even weird ones like yours. Especially weird ones."

He stopped and screwed his mouth sideways almost like she would. The hammer kind of slanted down.

"Oh," he managed. "How does the tribe survive?"

"We've got a freezer," she grinned at his confusion and discomfort. "Put it in the centrifuge and separate out boys from girls if you want to make sure you only have daughters. But I'm not ready to retire from flying and the comitatus."

"So none of your kind like boys?" he asked, shocked a little now.

Like he'd never actually met a real lesbian before. She looked in the memories Daniel had gotten from A'Alhakoth, but it was no more uncommon among the Kaniea than humans.

Anndaing might be different. She'd have to let folks

know when she got home.

"There are a few of the women who are open-minded enough," she smiled and purred at the shark, rather enjoying his disquiet maybe a little too much. "But Daniel was the only male aboard *SeekerStar*. There are a few on the ClanStars, but we protect them from doing anything dangerous. Most are farm husbands or teachers."

"Protect?" he seemed to gasp.

"Oh, yes," she smiled.

Joane was afraid she might have broken the shark's mind, as he just sat there and blinked at her, so she backed out three more bolts and lined them up on the deck beside her. Reaching in, she pulled the panel out and handed it into Dolon's unresisting hands.

The smell that came out of the compartment told her everything she needed to know, even before she looked.

Something had burned out and arced across a section of wiring, blackening it and getting things hot enough that the current probably fluctuated when cooking.

Good way to ruin snickerdoodles. Lucky for her and everyone else that Daniel had used the other stove.

Mase might demand a recount, since he'd been using a broken tool.

Shucks, more cookies. Or something.

She leaned back and pointed.

One advantage of a hammer like the Anndaing had was that he could stick one end of it inside a piece of equipment like this and see better than she could from out here.

"Manual says medium gauge wire," she offered as he extracted his hammer. "Thinking we should use the heavy stuff instead. Might want to consider moving up your replacement cycle, too. If you're getting wiring faults like this, might be worth the expense to replace before something goes really bad."

"I'll let Crence know," Dolon managed, rooting around in the tool box and handing her a spool of wire with a blue sheath.

Joane measured a run and cut herself a strip, reaching in to clip the bad wire out and sniff it. Cooked, good. Lovely fresh smell of ozone.

"So what are you doing to do at Kanus?" Dolon asked as she worked.

"Maybe stop running," Joane replied. "The Sept Empire has been after us, off and on, for nearly my whole life. Be nice to find a place where we can take the time to live in peace and maybe get rich."

"Crence said that your boss suggested they'd come after you," Dolon said hesitantly.

"No, they'll come after you eventually," she corrected him. "We're just here now."

"Why?"

"You aren't a human male a little lighter-skinned than Daniel," she growled. "Persian Sept first. *Rabic* next. *Anglos* after that. Then everyone else. And that's just humans. Males rate higher than females, regardless of species. Aliens are at the bottom, in layers based on difference from basic human morphology. A Se'uh'pal woman would be at the very bottom of the list, as would an Anndaing one, when they got far enough out here to say hello with their Axial Megacannon."

"Really?" Dolon asked.

"That's why Kathra wants to find a place for the tribe to be safe," Joane turned to face the shark from close enough to bite him.

"Why's that?"

"So she can go spank those bastards," Joane said. "With whoever she can recruit to help."

KANIEA

TWENTY-FIVE

A'Alhakoth was suddenly twenty again, looking ahead at the end of her childhood and plagued by visions of a so-called witch who told her that she would travel up and out farther than any Kaniea ever had before.

Even she doubted that the old woman had expected what had happened next.

The SkyCamel was busy landing on a field her father had specifically designated for such a thing, even though he had only ever seen Anndaing shuttles arrive. A'Alhakoth had offered to fly, and been overruled by Erin, not that she was surprised.

Any other outcome and Kathra's second in command might have missed the trip. Here, she could be part of it, especially since Father would never allow Erin to remain with the SkyCamel while welcoming alien visitors, and his own youngest daughter, to his estate.

Kathra grinned at her from across the shuttle bay as the landing gear settled. It was as though the Commander could see what was going on in A'Alhakoth's mind, but then she,

Kathra, and Daniel had merged several times as they planned this, so perhaps Kathra Omezi could.

Coming home was awkward. Doubly so since the Mbaysey had no home except what they carried with them, the rest abandoned on Tazo and not missed in the least.

"We're here," Erin said from the pilot's station as the engines shut down.

The tall woman unbuckled and turned to face them as she and Kathra rose. Erin had chosen a pair of short pants that showed off her mechanical right knee and shin while not slowing the woman down one bit. Combined with the barcode tattoo on her cheek, her tall mohawk, and her lighter-brown skin compared to Kathra's nearly black flesh, and the woman looked completely alien, perhaps formed into a biped form for the convenience of traveling with them.

It would make a powerful statement to the Kaniea they were about to meet. Even if it was just her parents.

Already, A'Alhakoth felt something like an alien on this world, so far had she come from the still-child who had left.

Kathra smiled at both of them, all three women wearing the flame colors of the comitatus today. She made a point of drawing her pistol and checking it, so A'Alhakoth did the same.

Again, violence was of such a low probability as to be practically impossible, but Kathra Omezi took nothing for granted, and expected her women to do the same.

Erin being here, dressed so fiercely, made more sense when considered that way.

Finally, the three of them came to stillness, like that wisp of fog just as the sun began to warm things.

"Shall we?" A'Alhakoth asked.

"You lead, Spectre Twenty-Three," Erin said.

That brought it home. She was alien.

A'Alhakoth ver'Shingi was no more. She was Spectre Twenty-Three in her heart and soul. One of these women.

The people coming across the field to greet them now were just the Kaniea who had birthed and raised her.

Spectre Twenty-Three felt her shoulders come back and her head come up.

She moved to the hatch, checked through the boarding window, and popped it open, smelling her homeworld for the first time in so long that she had almost forgotten that scent.

Emerging, she saw a crowd gathering, although nothing so formal as a party or a mob. No, this was just all of her old neighbors and friends joining her family to welcome their youngest daughter home.

She stepped down onto the soil of her heart and smiled. The locals began to clap and hoot.

Father emerged from the mess of people, with Mother on his arm as he escorted her into that open space reserved by unconscious command for the aliens.

Like her.

He was finally aging, the lines around his eyes and mouth growing deep enough that they could not be ignored. Both parents had hair fading down to the color of the sky, that brighter blue that so many hid underneath dyes, but her parents left natural.

A'Alhakoth stepped close and smiled, seeing them now through adult eyes. She turned sideways as Kathra and Erin stepped out.

The crowd fell silent.

"Linga ver'Shingi, Father, and Ch'Caani ver'Shingi, Mother, it is my great pleasure to present to you Kathra Omezi, Commander of the Mbaysey Tribal Squadron, and Erinkansilemi Uduik, her Second-In-Command of the

Comitatus to which I belong now," A'Alhakoth gestured. "Kathra, Erin, my parents."

The two women stepped close and shook hands with the smaller Kaniea. Erin was a shade taller than Father. Almost everyone on the planet would look up to Kathra. Mother was just the tiniest bit shorter than her youngest child as Ch'Caani engulfed her in a hug.

A'Alhakoth felt tears as Father joined Mother and held her.

It was good to be home.

Quickly, Kathra and Erin got introduced to the rest of her family. Alla, who would inherit the estate and Goli who surprised her by even being here, the man being of the conservatives who were still offended that the Anndaing had ever arrived. Sister E'Elbarth, gravid with her first child. Kilra and Trelga who still seemed trapped in that period after school and before adulthood had begun.

All the husbands and wives would be presented later, along with cousins and any relative on good enough terms with Father to be invited to meet true aliens. And possibly get involved in the off-world trade.

After the brief salutations, Father led them into the Longhall.

The banquet and celebration lasted well into the night, with revelry, chatter, and music that comforted A'Alhakoth, while at the same time feeling alien to her, after even such a short time among the humans of the Mbaysey and their long-lost-but-not-forgotten African roots.

She was not even required to fend off any marriage proposals, but she chalked that up to the long letter she had sent down to Father when *SeekerStar* had arrived in orbit.

What man wanted a wife who would not bear him children any time soon, as she was sworn into foreign service for an alien warlord?

The night wound down. Father politely threw out the last of the talkers well past his own usual bedtime, leaving her, Erin and Kathra at the long table with Father and Alla, a spitting image with fewer lines around the eyes and hair that had not lost any color or luster. Any stranger meeting Alla on the streets would guess him to be Linga's son or nephew on the first try.

Even their attire marked them as different, with the two men in greens and the women looking like fire demons from hell.

Spectre Twenty-Three smiled at the image.

"What?" Kathra asked with a similar smile.

"Fashion," A'Alhakoth answered. "Until this moment, I had not made the association that being dressed as we are, we fit the ancient image of the ifrit from the southern deserts, terrible demons who take the form of women and lure men and caravans to their doom."

"It did help with any lingering ideas of proposals for alliance," Father leaned forward and laughed. "They will be interested in my status, but certainly you have cured them of any silly ideas that they might be able to control you."

"What fools still had that notion?" Alla spoke up now, merriment twinkling in his eyes at such a lively and effective evening.

Alla would take over more and more of Father's duties, which probably included finding suitable spouses for Kilra and Trelga, especially now that they would be in high demand for strategic marriages.

Assuming Spectre Twenty-Three did not bring shame down upon her house.

"So what are the first steps towards alliance, Commander?" Father asked, suddenly serious and sober in ways he had not been when others had been around to watch.

Kathra grew serious as well, as though sloughing off a cloak. Erin was the same way, although she had embodied fierceness all night as a way of making Kathra look less likely to kill you and eat your heart.

Not unlikely, mind you, but Erin would probably still do it first.

"Trade," Kathra said. "We have been advanced a line of credit on the Anndaing Merchants Guild, for sending Daniel and Joane to Ogrorspoxu. The ClanStars have been over-producing everything they could, partly because we were not sure how long it would take to get here, and partly so that each of them had goods for whatever merchants we happened upon. The Tribal Squadron itself is nearly full of all the metal stock and exotic materials we could mine from a variety of planetary systems along the way."

"Such has Spectre Twenty-Three told me, in about that much detail," Father replied, nodding to her as one of Kathra's people instead of his daughter.

For a moment, A'Alhakoth felt a spike of cold dread in her stomach at being frozen out, but then she realized that he was treating her as an adult. Someone capable of messing up their own life, although the choices she had made so far had turned out better than she had ever expected.

"For obvious reasons, we have a soft spot for trading with House ver'Shingi, if possible," Kathra continued.

Father nodded and turned to Alla, seated on his left.

"Decisions I make today will bind you in turn," he said with all the gravity of a stern patriarch A'Alhakoth could not remember growing up. But he had also spoiled her when he could and pushed her into roles and expectations that were so at odds with the rest of Kaniea culture.

But they made her happy. And him.

A'Alhakoth let that thought warm her. She was happy. The comitatus was her home, at least until, like the others, she desired children and retired to flying SkyCamels, or perhaps serving as a deck officer on *SeekerStar* under Ife's command.

"Understood, Father," Alla said, just as seriously.

Father studied the four of them slowly, seeking something in the various faces seated around him, but A'Alhakoth wasn't sure what it was.

"We have generally been happy within the limits of the ancestral estate," he said. "With what trade we might undertake with Anndaing merchants and others who come along, but largely we have worked with locals who were the middlemen, rather than participating directly."

He paused, again seeking something, but he must have found it, because he smiled ever so slightly now.

"As my daughter has joined your house, Commander, I believe it behooves the rest of us to become more engaged in commerce, if only to put our resources at your benefit when dealing with others who might be less scrupulous with the Mbaysey," he said.

A'Alhakoth felt her breath catch. Father was really going to jump into the modern age with both feet?

"My second son will, of course, be mortally offended," Father continued with a wry smile the others shared. "But Alla, you are welcome to explain things to him, and he is welcome to go off in a huff to some monastery in the mountains. Whether or not he chooses to sell off his shares in a new trading company I cause to be created will be something I leave to your generation to sort out."

He turned to her now and smiled, almost like Death itself.

"All of your generation," he said.

A'Alhakoth nodded, aware that she had truly become an adult in his eyes, at least as far as business was concerned.

Alla had always been the big brother who took her with

him when he was off having adventures. Goli was always the stern one who tattled on her to their parents or nannies when she did something wrong. E'Elbarth was probably the closest to Goli in temperament and outlook, but all she ever wanted was to get married and raise a big family on a big estate somewhere, and she had married into another House that might be allies in Father's new venture.

"You are sure, Linga ver'Shingi?" Kathra asked, her own voice deep and serious now as well. "A'Alhakoth explained some of my issues in her letter. I know, because I read it before she signed it. But you will also inherit those issues as my ally."

"We share Spectre Twenty-Three, Commander," Father smiled. "Kaniea culture does not have such a thing as a comitatus. At least not yet. However, if we treat her as married into the Mbaysey, then yours just becomes another House with which I am bound, and my neighbors, short-sighted fools that most of them are, will be able to understand at least that much. They need to welcome the future, for it has arrived."

A'Alhakoth nodded at those sage words.

The Mbaysey's arrival would be probably almost as big a cultural and social shift on Kanus as the first Anndaing ship landing had been.

All because of her.

TWENTY-SIX

Daniel hadn't been sure what to expect when he arrived at Ogrorspoxu, but he would have been wrong, whatever he expected.

But then, this wasn't like First Contact was a weird, unexpected thing to the Anndaing. They were forever roaming and meeting new people. Like the Free Worlds, the Anndaing Merchants Guild encompassed hundreds of world and eleven core species, in addition to whoever happened to wander along, like the se'uh'pal, who made the Anndaing look like amateurs when it came to going anywhere and trading with anyone at any time.

A'Alhakoth had originally made it to Tavle Jocia on a Se'uh'pal ship, but Daniel was hard pressed to remember where their homeworld was. When he asked his ghosts, he got one of the few unanimous responses, when everyone shrugged at him together, like wheat blowing in a field on a summer day, just before harvest.

Ogrorspoxu didn't shrug at him, but also didn't treat his arrival as all that great of a thing. Daniel had to wonder if the Se'uh'pal equivalent of the Anndaing Merchants Guild had kept most of human space secret, or at least obscured, from anyone else, while bringing the occasional human goods from beyond the pale.

Hopefully, his arrival here wouldn't mean Se'uh'pal assassins in his future for increasing their competition. Being murdered by a creature roughly A'Alhakoth's size that reminded Daniel of a bipedal rabbit sounded too much like a cartoon, or the start of a bad joke.

He found himself cooling his heels in a small waiting room, with assurances that Joane was in the next one. He'd undergone a quick medical exam, but that was mostly just to compare to the medical records he had brought with him from *Koni Swift* and *SeekerStar*, showing him to be in good health. None of their machines would be calibrated to handle humans, at least not yet.

Daniel grinned that he and Joane might become the future baselines for Anndaing space.

Talk about confusing, when other humans came along, and the men were her size and the women his. He grinned at the general rudeness of it all.

The door opened and an Anndaing woman entered. Apparently, the white longcoat that doctors wore transcended cultures, for reasons Daniel had never explored, but it did.

"Hello, Daniel," she said, taking the other seat across from him.

At least he was finally dressed. Not bored, because he could always talk with whichever one of his ghosts felt like sharing memories or knowledge with him. But at loose ends.

"Hello, again," Daniel replied with a smile.

"So you are an ambassador from the humans?" she said, checking her clipboard.

"The Mbaysey," he corrected her. "A nomadic tribe of humans. No one person can speak for even a majority of my kind at present."

"I see," she said as she checked something with a pen. "And the rest of your tribe traveled directly to Kanus?"

"One of our crew is Kaniea," he reminded her, although it felt more like they were just checking all the stories he had shared earlier, looking for lies and evasions now. "By sending me here directly, *Koni Swift* could save time on their next departure, especially since I was already fluent and could communicate."

She nodded mostly to herself from what he could see. Her hammer was at rest.

"Well, you appear to be in excellent health, and your papers and credit are in order," she replied, handing him the booklet that he had been issued. "I see no reason to keep you or your companion. There are some folks waiting out front to talk with you. Crence Miray and a friend."

Daniel nodded and rose as she did. He was official now, a documented Ambassador who existed in their various systems. Plus, he had gotten paid an officer's daily share as crew on *Koni Swift*, so he had some money of his own, in addition to the line of credit Crence had arranged for Kathra to do things. Not enough to get stupid, but certainly enough for beer.

He wondered if Crence would be off-planet and headed out-system by sunset, just to get that much of a head start on anyone else wanting to trade into human space that wasn't a se'uh'pal.

He kept that thought to himself as he exited the room and found Joane already chatting in stilted Anndaing with Crence and another shark who wasn't as big or bulky.

Daniel came to rest a proper distance away and bowed just enough to show off what he had learned from A'Alhakoth and Crence.

"Daniel Lémieux, Ambassador from the Mbaysey," he

said politely. "You've met Joane Obiakpani, known to the Commander as Spectre Five."

"Wyll Koobitz," the stranger replied with an equal bow, pronouncing it almost exactly like *while* to Daniel's ear. "Representative from the Merchants Bank."

Ah. Important people, then. Merchants Bank was as close to a government of all the Anndaing as you could get with a group of interstellar traders operating across such a broad swath of space and not limited to any one planet's legal system. Especially when not everyone involved was Anndaing.

"I have arranged a meeting space for us," Koobitz continued, gesturing down the hallway. "And Crence has made arrangements for you at a local hotel for a week, while everyone figures out what the next steps are."

"Please," Daniel gestured, falling in behind the sharks with Joane and the quick grin she shared.

Daniel hated meetings. Especially when they weren't held in dining halls. But he also understood that he was Kathra's personal representative in this, the first male ever accorded the privilege.

Possibly the last one, as well, unless someone truly impressed her on some future date, but he couldn't speak for all those men who had foolishly not chosen a career in the culinary arts.

Pleasantly, this didn't even feel like an inquisition, as they ended up in what Daniel would have called a salon, rather than a conference room. Several comfortable-looking chairs upholstered around an open space, decorated in various colors. Side tables holding what looked like magazines, as well as a device to call for a waiter or something.

Rugs on the floors deadened the noise, and someone with a good eye had hung paintings on the walls. There was even a view out a window down into an interior courtyard filled with plants and a pond, which was all the more impressive when he remembered that they were aboard a station in geosynchronous orbit of the capital city below.

A pitcher on one table looked like water with ice.

Daniel gestured and confirmed.

Probably safest, since anything might be poisonous when you crossed species lines and got into someone else's biochemistry.

"I have read the executive summary of Crence's encounter with the Mbaysey," Koobitz began as they all got settled. "It appears to be rather elaborate, considering what he normally files, so I found myself both pleased, and concerned. How might the three of you allay my fears?"

Daniel found it amusing that Crence Miray looked almost as sheepish as Joane did, but for different reasons. She was reading the surface context of the words. Crence had gone deep and saw where the other man was about to start asking pointed and possibly hostile questions.

Daniel wondered how close the two men were as allies and friends at this moment. Much would hinge on how quickly Koobitz would allow *Koni Swift* to run like hell for Tavle Jocia with fresh cargo even now probably being swapped for the goods Crence had been hauling before.

"And please don't waste my time with whatever song and dance you were thinking about," Koobitz continued. "Especially you, Crence."

At least he was speaking without any heat to his words, so Daniel leaned forward and got Crence's nod.

"We supplied *Koni Swift* a detailed map of human space," Daniel said. "A cultural map, as I understand such a term from him, touching on trade needs and capabilities as Kathra Omezi was able to identify them in her years along the edge of the Sept Empire and then deeper into Free Worlds Space."

"I see," the man said, leaning back.

Probably he did see now. Such a map would be incredibly valuable, but every trademaster would have access to it, just as soon as she logged in here on Ogrorspoxu and updated her files, or met a ship that had been here after today.

Crence Miray and *Koni Swift* would have just as much of a lead as they could get from now, loading new cargo based on that map. And the fact that Daniel had recorded a number of conversational training videos with Joane. Those were also being uploaded now for common use across Anndaing space, where he and she would get an ongoing royalty monthly for as long as they were in use, but Crence and Dane spoke passable Spacer now, as long as you didn't mind an accent that split the difference between Algeria and Ogrorspoxu.

Money would talk, and Crence Miray had the vocabulary to trade.

Koobitz turned to Crence now, flexing his hammer forward a little and zeroing his eyes down on the other shark.

"Just how soon until you filed for departure, you old pirate?" Koobitz asked.

Apparently, Anndaing could blush. It was weird. The gray face took on a bluish tinge, the hammer drooped at both ends, and the nose flared open.

"I thought so," Koobitz continued, turning to Daniel. "You are currently scheduled to remain here for a time, Lémieux. His departure will not be a problem?"

Daniel started to say something, but Crence interrupted.

"Having the reasonable expectation that Daniel could not make binding trade agreements with the Guild, I might have promised transport for them to Kanus," Crence said with a sheepish smile so at odds with the cutthroat shark Daniel had just spent the last two weeks talking to that Daniel looked at him. "We would need to send an accredited

Ambassador to Kathra Omezi to talk, so I figured he and Joane could catch a ride then."

"I see," Koobitz replied so dryly that Joane chuckled, so she had been following things quietly. "And I shouldn't be offended enough at you right now to send *Koni Swift* to Kanus?"

Now Daniel laughed. It was like watching a comedy vid, so they must have been doing this for his benefit.

"Someone will get first-mover advantage with *SeekerStar*," Crence pointed out. "No reason it can't be you, or someone you wish to reward. I plan on running straight through Thrabo to a place called Tavle Jocia, which is apparently a major shipyard world at an interior trade crossroads in Free Worlds space."

"Shipyard?" Koobitz perked up.

"Indeed," Daniel inserted himself. "Commander Omezi recently commissioned a new vessel there, the ship known as *SeekerStar*, which is now her flagship."

"What are human vessels like?" Koobitz asked pointedly.

"I am the wrong person to ask," Daniel answered honestly. "Being merely a chef by training. However, *SeekerStar* was built to rotate a ring around a central hub, to save the expense and effort of gravity field inducers. If I understand some of the conversations, *Koni Swift* is more advanced in certain areas, and less so in others. Trade that merged the two into a new whole should thus benefit both sides."

"And this Sept Empire your Commander is apparently fleeing?" Koobitz asked. "I noted in one of the appendices that something called a Septagon apparently appeared deep in Free Worlds space and attacked *SeekerStar* nearby, destroying the vessel known as *WinterStar* in the process. What is a Septagon?"

"A dedicated, human warship based on a seven-sided

structure," Daniel let his face get serious as well. "Each of the facings is thirty-two hundred meters wide. From the tip of the bow to the flat of the engine wells is just over seven thousand meters. The core is seventy decks tall, with several towers in various places above that. It has a normal crew of three hundred thousand sailors. And an Axial Megacannon that is powerful enough to destroy anything they meet."

There was a long pause. Kathra had included all those notes, but Koobitz hadn't read deeply enough into the report to get there. At least not yet. Daniel expected that to change by this time tomorrow, especially the part where specist humans in command of city-destroying beam weapons, with a proclivity for orbital bombardment, might be headed this way.

What else would you like to know?

"Oh, and they fly incredibly slowly, due to all that mass that the valence drives must move," Daniel added. "Plus, feeding a fleet of four hundred thousand people requires a significant and complicated logistic chain, which is why Kathra Omezi decided to thumb her nose at them and head in the direction of Kanus, where there is a hope that we might find a place to live for a time. And allies when those *salauds* from the Sept finally decide to come after her."

"How soon is that?" Koobitz asked.

"I'd like to die of old age first," Daniel said. "But the Emperor of the Sept has not asked my opinion on the topic. I am here to establish some level of diplomatic relations, encourage the Anndaing Merchants Guild to talk to the right people, and let *Koni Swift* go off on a trading adventure to the Free Worlds without me, where presumably they will begin gathering intelligence for the Guild so you can make better determinations, and do so early enough to act, instead of merely reacting."

He paused just long enough to let those words sink in before he continued.

"Personally," he said, "I would like to find a library or college where I might be able to do some more research on the K'bari and the Ovanii. The former because of what Urid-Varg did to them when he passed. The latter because I translated a book of Ovanii poetry that we found on Thrabo, and want to know more about the species and their history with the Anndaing."

Crence had already heard the story, but the other shark just went blank, his hammer dropping and pulling forward in confusion, his eyes blinking too rapidly.

"You speak Ovanii?" Koobitz sputtered.

"No, I read it," Daniel corrected him. "And a number of other languages, based on things no human should know, but which were left to me when Kathra Omezi finally destroyed Urid-Varg."

"I thought you said you killed him," Crence spoke up.

"I did, but that was just his body," Daniel replied. "Kathra killed his soul when he came back for me."

A longer pause this time, as both sharks processed that tidbit.

"How many languages can you read, and possibly speak, Daniel?" Koobitz asked in a sidelong way, like he was afraid of the answer.

"More than is probably healthy for me," Daniel retorted. "Find me Ovanii histories and things, and I'd be happy to earn my keep translating them and whatever else you might have lost over the centuries."

"And rent him a commercial kitchen," Crence slipped in. "He's a fantastic chef. Even Mase shut up eventually and conceded defeat."

"I didn't think it was possible for Mase Jacksanch to shut up," Koobitz stated plainly.

Daniel and Crence smiled together. Joane chuckled.

"And you, lady warrior comitatus?" Koobitz asked. "What is your need?"

"I am here to evaluate your technology for the Commander and keep Daniel from being alone," she said simply in Anndaing. "And kill anyone that threatens him."

Not the way Daniel would have phrased it, but it did a good job of getting the point across.

Daniel was here representing the merchant options for Kathra.

Joane was here for when negotiations failed and warfare became the only answer.

TWENTY-SEVEN

Kathra decided that she might actually like living in this sector of space, given time. The view out her cabin window alternately showed the primary trading station and the blue and green marble below her.

Linga ver'Shingi had carried through on his threat/promise and established a small but promising trade office on the primary station, treating her like a relative by marriage, which was probably about as good as Kaniea society could deal with the comitatus right now.

How soon until other houses decided to offer up their own daughters to possibly join the comitatus? Kathra would not relax her standards for membership, but there was no reason not to let them try. She had always planned to recruit some to expand the Clans, once she felt safe enough from *Vorgash* and his friends that she could.

No Septagon would be able to come this far, except at the head of an armada so great that other species would eventually record its passing in their own histories.

And she would hopefully have so much warning that she could either flee, or recruit sufficient forces to help.

The Sept were a linear beast, at the end of the day. *Vorgash* had surprised her and Danial at Tavle Jocia, but they had come hunting her and the Turtle specifically. Presumably they had built some sort of network of forward bases, just to be able to reach that far into Free Worlds space.

Hopefully, someone at Tavle Jocia had drawn a similar conclusion.

To do something similar now would require an enormous effort, since she had gone completely beyond the end of any map she could find in Free Worlds space. Someone would have to bribe the Se'uh'pal for better sailing directions.

Hopefully, that meant that they could never find her again.

Except that she didn't really believe that. The Ishtan had found Daniel, and not the Turtle. Had forced Daniel to lead them to the Turtle so that they could destroy it, and then him. Even reduced by a third, she suspected that they would be able to find him again, once they had more allies.

How long did they have, her and Daniel, until trouble came again? And could the Kaniea or the Anndaing stop them when they arrived?

Nothing she had seen could stop a Septagon. Well, that was untrue, upon reflection. Spectre Twenty-Three had been perfectly willing to fly the shattered remains of *WinterStar* into the side of the beast like a harpoon. That would have done massive damage, especially if her old warship had managed to somehow explode. It had been threat enough to cause *Vorgash* to flee.

Kathra rose now and exited her cabin, still too wound up to consider sleeping. Nights like this, she frequently would pick a direction and walk long ways around the deck a few times until she was finally tired, or at least relaxed.

A quarter of the way around, she ran into Erin, walking

towards her with the same saunter to her step. They met midway and stopped.

"Can't sleep," Kathra said as Erin started to open her mouth.

"Me, neither," the other woman replied.

Erin turned and they started walking.

"I'm worried about Daniel," Kathra admitted in a low voice.

Erin knew the truth. As much as Kathra had a sister, it was Erinkansilemi. They had no secrets at this point, all the more so because of Daniel and his abilities.

"You cannot be two places at once, Kathra," Erin reminded her.

Kathra stopped walking so suddenly that Erin had to turn around.

"What?" Erin asked.

"Why not?" Kathra asked.

Erin blinked. Opened her mouth to speak, and then closed it again.

"What did you have in mind?" Erin asked quietly.

"The Ishtan were tracking Daniel," Kathra said. "Probably they were able to see that gem, since Urid-Varg took it from the most powerful of their kind before he killed most of the rest. They cannot find us here, except by asking travelers. That gives us time. But they could come out of a jump wherever he is, with whatever allies they have recruited, and ambush him."

"And you don't think Daniel could take care of himself?" Erin smirked.

"Not against the Sept," Kathra snapped. "Or a Free Worlds pirate in Ishtan pay. Big guns could batter him to death while he fought against the snakes trying to take over his mind. He knows that. Presumably the Ishtan do as well."

"What about the being in two places part?" Erin asked now.

"The Sept are only after me because I am the leader of the Mbaysey," Kathra said, starting to walk again. Erin fell in beside her, thumping on the odd strides because she hadn't worn her boot. Just the metal heel. "The rest of the Mbaysey are not safe, with me here or gone."

"They'll get up to mischief without you around," Erin noted.

"Will they?" Kathra countered. "We have a relatively safe place we could trade. An ally by marriage in A'Alhakoth's father. On top of that, the Anndaing and others are aliens who are not likely to be viewed by the Sept as anything but monsters if they make it this far. Even the Kaniea would be suspect, since they are blue."

"What do you propose?" Erin's voice got reserved.

"Concursion," Kathra said. "Leave most of the tribe here while I take *SeekerStar* to wherever Daniel is and make sure he is safe. And then keep him with us in the future until the Ishtan are no longer a threat."

"You are not leaving me here with the old women, Kathra Omezi," Erin growled.

Kathra grimaced. Of course Erin could read her mind.

"Who, then?" Kathra asked.

"Iruoma is fierce enough to deal with those whiny farts," Erin laughed. "But she was with Daniel before and would be no more willing to remain behind than I am."

"It cannot be anybody in the comitatus," Kathra decided. "None would forgive me, if we ran into trouble and had to fight without them."

She fell into silence and thought. Erin knew her well enough to do the same.

They walked.

"Perhaps, it is time for the Clans to grow up," Kathra finally said.

"How so?" Erin asked, matching her stride for stride.

"We will not return to the land here," Kathra said. "But Anndaing space might be a good place to establish some sort of permanent base. A TradeStar, if you will. Or a CityStar, if we could find the money and expertise to build such a thing."

"TradeStar?" Erin asked, her face twisted sideways in confusion.

"A ClanStar in more or less permanent station here," Kathra said. "Perhaps the forerunner to a TradeStation-sized ship that could waddle along with us like a Septagon when the whole tribe moved on, one of these days."

"And the growing up part?" Erin pressed.

"If I need to be gone for an extended period, the twenty-two clan elders would need to make decisions as a collective. Enough of them are still fiercely loyal to Yagazie's dream that I don't have to fear a revolution in my absence, I don't think. Grandma Ezinne is not the only woman who still has a tattoo on her face."

Erin absently touched the barcode on her right cheek. The one that was an exact duplicate of her grandmother's, the infamous Ezinne. The thing that had once marked the old woman as *property* of a Sept noble, a *Vuzurgan*.

"And Linga ver'Shingi?" Erin asked.

"What happens if we turn him into a Trade Factor the likes of that fat bastard that built *SeekerStar* for us?" Kathra asked. "Isaev, without the shitty parts of his personality."

"How big are you dreaming, Kathra?" Erin gasped.

For the first time in a while, Kathra heard something other than gruff determination in Erin's voice. Awe, perhaps.

"It was not enough that we escaped Tazo," Kathra said. "The Sept sent assassins to kill Yagazie for that and put me in charge well before I was ready. They did not stop when we fled Sept space. They will not stop now. We need allies who can help us when they come this far into the galactic interior, or who can come to the aide of the Free Worlds when the Sept inevitably starts to push on their border."

"So we're done fleeing?" Erin growled.

"We are," Kathra nodded. "I would like to take the war to them. But I will need a lot of support to do so. That includes the whiny old farts on the ClanStars. But it also includes a Kaniea Jarl named Linga ver'Shingi, and whatever others Daniel and I can find."

"About damned time," Erin said.

Kathra nodded. She had been fleeing from the Sept for her entire life.

She was done running.

TWENTY-EIGHT

Crence walked into this last meeting with great trepidation in his hearts. Wyll had basically demanded a few minutes, back on the station, even as *Koni Swift* was stowing the last finfull of boxes that he hoped would make him rich.

More rich. Crence Miray was already one of the most successful trademasters of his generation. He could not rest on that, however.

His pups would never want. Their pups would not, if his children had even half the success he had enjoyed to date, and that was before Kathra Omezi.

But Crence Miray wanted to leave a mark on the galaxy that would still be here in ten thousand years. When pups born then might bear his name as a talisman of luck and honor.

Hopefully not for being the biggest fuckup in Anndaing history. He had no doubts that his arriving on the doorstep at Tavle Jocia would set in motion a major realignment in trade across this entire quadrant of the galaxy.

Humans, as far as Omezi had shared with him, only saw that gap of uninhabited star systems that were still marked

K'bari on his own maps, and thought that perhaps nothing lay beyond it. No great civilizations, ancient by human standards. No masses of civilized worlds hungry for new goods.

The Anndaing were just as guilty, as the K'bari had effectively blocked them for so many generations, and the memory served as something of a psychological wall even today.

Crence Miray and *Koni Swift* would shatter that delusion.

What would happen then?

All these thoughts chased themselves back and forth in his hammer as he opened the door and found Wyll Koobitz already seated and a steward standing nearby, ready to take drink orders. A plate of fried squidlings sat on the low table between the two chairs, missing a few already.

Wyll held a goblet of fermented boullo juice in one hand as Crence approached.

"The same for me," Crence decided, pointing to Wyll's glass.

If the boss was drinking alcohol tonight, then hopefully it was a social event, and not a dressing down.

Crence sat and the steward exited. The room was similar to the one earlier, with only two chairs and greener carpeting.

Crence studied Wyll's face and grabbed a squidling.

"I suppose you were already aware that the Guild Council cannot be gathered fast enough to stop you," Wyll said in a droll, severe voice that still had a touch of humor under it.

"The thought had occurred to me," Crence managed as an evasion.

Wyll could pull rank right now and order him to stand down until the Council dragged his fins up in front of them for a formal hearing.

"I am less worried about the Sept," the Banker continued. "My staff read the necessary parts over the last several hours and conclude that their threat should best be measured in years and perhaps decades, even if they decided tomorrow to invade us."

Crence nodded. He'd talked to Daniel and Commander Omezi extensively on the topic, even going so far as to buy a small tablet device from her, after which Omezi had filled it with a variety of notes on the Sept from her own records.

That woman had a hatred for the ages. Crence was just glad she had seen him as a potential ally and not a threat. *SeekerStar* could have annihilated *Koni Swift*, had she been of a mind.

Wyll took a drink and munched on another squidling. The steward returned with a second glass and left the bottle when he departed.

"What is Daniel Lémieux?" Wyll Koobitz asked in a hard voice when they were alone again.

Crence took a sip and let the sweet, smoky taste linger on top of the salt from the squidlings. That question had kept him awake several nights on the trip home.

"More than human, and less so," Crence offered. "Joane Obiakpani is what she appears: a gruff, technically-minded warrior. Slowly learning Anndaing, with a Kaniea accent that is evolving as she spends time with my crew and later with her people. Tough and stubborn, but alien and on edge around us for that reason."

He paused, looking for the words.

"Daniel talked and acted like an Anndaing merchant or scholar from the first moment we met him," Crence continued. "He claims that Urid-Varg tried to take him over, in ways he will not elaborate, but that Kathra Omezi did kill the *salaud* eventually. Daniel was changed anyway, at least to some extent. Again, he will not explain, but he does indeed read Anndaing, K'bari, and Ovanii like a native. I don't know anybody who can read the old Ovanii texts."

"Is he Urid-Varg?" Wyll asked.

"If he is, he is playing a game with tides so long that they might not come to crest in my lifetime," Crence answered. "I think that Urid-Varg did do things to him to make it possible for the man to become his servant, but failed before he could finish. Perhaps some shard of the conqueror lives on in Daniel, but he certainly hasn't shown the kinds of power or threat that would have made me want to space him."

"And now you wish to leave?" Wyll pivoted.

"Tavle Jocia represents a trading coup of the first order," Crence reminded his boss. "As well as the opportunity to catch the Free Worlds off-guard and gather enormous amounts of intelligence on them. We only have Omezi's word on things, and Daniel's, but they would not have given us this much data to work with if they really had something to hide."

"And the Sept?"

"Again, Commander Omezi and Daniel, and even Joane, consider them a threat to the civilized galaxy that must be resisted," Crence said. "They say that non-humans are not particularly welcome there, but merchants are less hassled. Perhaps, when I return, your bosses will want to finance a mission into Sept space. The Se'uh'pal are apparently ubiquitous, so maybe we hire them to haul some of our people there undercover to inspect things and see what truths we can find."

"I dislike the thought of another war coming," Wyll grimaced and took a sip.

Crence stole two squidlings this time.

"Do the humans suspect the shape of Anndaing space?" Wyll asked.

"I don't think we qualify as a conspiracy, Wyll," Crence

countered. "Just a form of government that is uncommon in human space, although Daniel suggested that it existed in the distant past on their own homeworld. It is unlikely that we would have to send the Call to Armada yet. If nothing else, our logistics train to attack a Sept world would be just as long and tortured as theirs to come here. It is more likely that we might do something in the meantime to surreptitiously help the Free Worlds resist Sept aggression."

"What would Kathra Omezi do, if she had no other hindrances?" Wyll asked.

And Crence finally understood the purpose behind a private room, less than an hour before *Koni Swift's* scheduled departure.

"Fight them," Crence answered, drawing on similar conversations with the woman before she left, and Daniel since. "Plausible deniability?"

"Freedom fighters are just another shark's outlaws and pirates," Wyll quoted the old scholar. "If one batch of humans want to inflict damage on another batch of humans who might later be a threat to the Merchants Guild and our worlds, we should perhaps investigate the possibilities of everyone fighting over there, before we have to fight over here."

"So I should take a hard, straight run to Tavle Jocia?" Crence asked, understanding that there were many things unsayable at this point, even among their own kind.

But he'd gotten wealthy by handling some of these odder jobs quietly for the Guild.

"And straight back here, regardless of the transport options presented, unless you can convince someone to come to Ogrorspoxu."

"Loaded up with whatever books, videos, and intelligence-bearing materials I can haul," Crence nodded.

"Just so," Wyll nodded. "I will continue to study Daniel

Lémieux, as well as send someone to Kanus to get a better understanding of Kathra Omezi and her humans. It is not necessarily a gift tuna we should discount, but keep your fins upright, understanding that tomorrow might be the beginning of a new era in Anndaing history."

Crence nodded. He'd felt that same way the instant he scanned more than a score of completely alien vessels in the middle of what should have been nowhere.

He snagged the last two squidlings before Wyll could get them, pondering his future. And everyone's.

What trouble would the humans bring?

What trouble was he facing?

But more importantly, how much wealth could he acquire in a single lifetime?

TWENTY-NINE

DANIEL HAD to agree with Crence Miray on at least this much. Ogrorspoxu was a paradise of a world, at least the capital city where he had landed.

The city of Therly sat at the mouth of a great river of the same name as it debouched into a bay so large that it had looked like a sea in its own right when the shuttle had been bringing him and Joane to the surface. Mountains with a gap at the mouth of the bay blunted the effect of tides and storm, so the three days he had spent here in this hotel with the fantastic view of the bay reminded him of a small pond somewhere, like glass in the morning until the breezes finally ruffled the surface a little.

The Anndaing had treated him like visiting royalty, so he presumed that Crence Miray and Wyll Koobitz had been impressed enough with the tales he had spun. Most of them were truth, with just some important parts left out. The parts that might get him killed by his new alien friends.

He had a suite. Him in the big bedroom, with Joane in one of the smaller ones that was only the size of the comitatus dining hall on *SeekerStar*. His felt large enough to land several Spectres comfortably. Both of them were relaxing in the main room this morning, watching the rising sun slowly cast city shadows onto the water.

Even the food had been excellent, as they finished nibbling on an early brunch, but Daniel had been able to spell out for the kitchen of the hotel exactly what he and Joane liked and how to prepare it after their time aboard *Koni Swift*. That had helped.

The only thing he was really missing was fresh eggs from a chicken, but the sharks had nothing similar in their pantry, so he had told them the mix of basic chemicals they could use to get a similar effect on grain to make it rise from a flatbread into the kind of loaf he preferred.

Culinary revolution, one chef at a time.

He checked the wall clock for the local time and realized that their visitor would be along shortly. Daniel rose and stretched, pulling everything tight and trying to look a little less rumpled than he probably felt.

He'd given up formal and glad-handing when he walked away from the restaurant. Anyone else asking him to return to those ways would have gotten a piece of his mind, but it was Kathra.

Enough said.

A fin rapped on the outer door. Joane moved to answer, grinning at him as she did. No one could possibly be fooled into thinking she was just a harmless observer. Especially not when she was armed and refused even polite suggestions that her pistol was unnecessary in Therly.

Daniel didn't bother mentioning what he might do to a potential assassin. Better as a surprise.

"Ambassador," Joane bowed and genially waved Wyll Koobitz into the suite.

The shark had arrived alone today, instead of in the

company of some of the folks that had come previously, who never had questions but just silently observed.

Daniel assumed they were spies for other factions in the Merchants Guild who needed to be assuaged as to what was going on.

He got the shark seated and poured a mug of something more or less equivalent to hot tea. Perhaps a weak, sweet coffee. Hard to gauge without actually putting the leaves into the scrutinizer that Joane habitually kept with her.

Daniel hadn't cared enough to know, and didn't ask Joane if she had.

They made small talk over pastries that were the first steps away from sweetened flatbread into perhaps the world of scones. Daniel had a meeting scheduled with the head chef of the hotel later in the evening to expand that shark's repertoire.

"How may I be of service today, Wyll?" Daniel finally asked, having completed the requisite meandering.

Wyll responded by reaching into his jacket and pulling out a chip.

"I visited the academy library and found you some reference material," he said.

Daniel nodded and pulled out an Anndaing reader tablet he kept in a nearby drawer. The form and function was almost identical to one he'd brought with him from *SeekerStar*, but the internals were so radically different that they'd just gone ahead and given him a second one for local technology.

Joane had one as well, but didn't spend nearly as much time staring at hers.

He plugged the chip into the side and brought up a file listing.

Daniel looked at Wyll sharply.

"Seriously?" he asked.

"An interstellar culture might fade out, but a good library never loses anything," Wyll nodded. "Some things, however, do get misplaced from time to time. We were hoping you might be able to magically read some of these files. I don't even know the character set two of them are written in."

"Roahrt and Z'lud," Daniel answered carefully. "The Ovanii will be obvious, because they use your alphabet, and the K'bari is still fresh enough that you should have scholars who can read it."

"Yes," Wyll agreed. "How is it that you know the other two, Daniel Lémieux?"

Daniel stared at the shark for a long moment. He felt Joane tense, ever so slightly, but she would not initiate violence. Wyll, however, wouldn't even make it out of that chair before she tackled him, if it came to violence.

Daniel reached out with his mind and touched Wyll Koobitz. Not sufficient to read anything, but so that he could catch the emotional signature of things roiling underneath.

They had just walked out onto thin, spring ice, the two of them. But Wyll Koobitz had intentionally provoked it.

Daniel wondered what sorts of security systems were monitoring the room right at this moment. And how quickly teams of armed killers might come through the doors, windows, and possibly even walls.

Wyll Koobitz was a power in the Merchants Guild, regardless of what stories he might tell alien chefs.

"Before she killed Urid-Varg, the conqueror had been preparing me to be his next vessel," Daniel replied carefully. It was not a lie he could be caught out in later, even as he left out key bits, like the gem hidden at the base of his throat under his clothing. "Part of that includes access to…not *his* memories, as I had no memory of being Urid-Varg, but the other beings that he had, let us call it *ridden* for now. I can occasionally access their memories of being alive, for lack of a better way to describe it. A number of them were K'bari. And there are also many Z'lud, considering how long he ruled them. Because these people chose to aid me, I can read Ovanii. One of them was also Roahrt and I can see the letters on this screen side by side with the Spacer and the French I know. Perhaps an odd mix of the two, but enough that I can translate them."

"But you are not Urid-Varg?" Wyll's voice got tense.

"Urid-Varg is dead," Daniel scowled. "I beat his body to death. Kathra killed his mind."

"How?"

Daniel did not move, aware that Wyll Koobitz would not be pushing this hard by himself. Armed warriors who were confident that they could overcome both him and Joane were nearby. When Daniel listened, he could hear them, poised right at the edge of his perception.

Many of them.

"He had a device," Daniel explained, sliding closer to the truth than he had before.

But Kathra needed these people as allies. Friends, even. A safe port for the Mbaysey.

"A device?" Wyll asked, unconsciously leaning forward, mug apparently forgotten in one hand.

"It contained his mind, if you will," Daniel said. "He had transferred himself into some sort of computer program when his original body died, twelve thousand human years ago. I am just a chef, so please don't ask me how he did it. But killing the body of his host did not kill that device. The thing called to me, and began to transform my mind into a receptacle he could take control of, even though we thought he was dead. I have the memories of the others, at least before each of them was taken in turn. Kathra blasted the thing with a pistol identical to the one Joane has, and freed me. And believe me, she is far less trusting about such things than the Anndaing."

"So you are no longer human, per se?" Wyll asked tightly, his hammer flexed forward and eyes zeroed in on Daniel.

"Not just human, I suppose," Daniel corrected him. "I can read K'bari, Z'lud, and Roahrt, however slowly. I've actually gotten pretty good at Ovanii, only because for such a martial culture, they had such interesting poetry."

"Really?" Wyll asked, perhaps deflected enough that he didn't pursue Daniel into the web of evasions he had just laid out.

"Indeed," Daniel agreed. "I think I uploaded a copy of that original book. I know that Crence had a copy and was supposed to file it, but as it was love poetry from a dead species, it might not have gotten much attention."

"You said dead?" Wyll asked.

"I presume dead," Daniel nodded. "The K'bari had memories of the Anndaing defeating that people so resolutely that they vanished from K'bari history at a certain point. We have often wondered, Kathra and I, if an interstellar species can go extinct, or if they just fade to irrelevance after long enough that it doesn't matter."

"And you're interested in the Ovanii?" Wyll asked.

They'd already gone over this before, but Daniel realized that they were either concerned enough to do something to him and Joane, or close to deciding to help them.

"*SeekerStar*, for all its martial capabilities, is not a warship," Daniel said. "Yes, it is far more heavily armed than most craft that size, and carries within it Spectre gunships that are also dangerous, but a Septagon is a force of nature that cannot be directly resisted. And Patrols come in swarms that one must usually flee. But the Ovanii built warships designed for direct combat on a regular basis according to their own stories."

"They did," Wyll agreed, himself giving off waves of evasion, but Daniel did not dive directly into his mind. Not yet, anyway. "They were, in their time, a terrible scourge of piracy upon the Anndaing, before we broke them."

"Yes," Daniel nodded. "Kathra Omezi would like to be able to go do terrible things to the Sept, for reasons that I included in my various notes, and Crence no doubt elaborated on himself."

"And only the Sept?" Wyll asked.

Daniel could hear the breakthrough in the shark's voice now. The triumph, if he could call it that.

"The Free Worlds would have been our home, had that been allowed," Daniel replied, still wondering at the use of *our* in that context, but he was Mbaysey now. Nothing would ever change that. "A'Alhakoth ver'Shingi gave us a new option hopefully so far away from the Sept that we would be safe after they proved that they would violate Free Worlds borders just to come after us. Crence just happened to be in the right place during the week we were at that place, and could meet him. He cut months off the journey and let us go directly to the worlds and people we needed to meet."

"And having met them?" Wyll pressed.

"I am a researcher, Wyll," Daniel said. "My job is to find Kathra Omezi the tools to protect her people, and maybe go back with her someday and do terrible things to the Sept. Her job is to insure the survival of the Mbaysey itself, so more interesting questions will probably only be answered when you ask her yourself."

Daniel did lean back now. Wyll was relaxing, so perhaps they were past the crux.

He was really looking forward to introducing Wyll Koobitz to the Commander.

THIRTY

Kathra studied the twenty-two faces of the Clan leaders, seated around her in the comitatus dining hall. Her own women were here as well, lacking only Daniel and Joane from the last such meeting, the one before they had chosen deep space.

"And that, my friends, is what I feel is the best plan for us, at least for the present," she finished her explanation. "We will leave the rest of you here and go retrieve Daniel."

Titilayo Okafor stared at Kathra for a long moment as the others fell silent and waited. Nobody wanted to be the first to argue, but Kathra had no doubts that such was coming.

"If they can track him and not us, are we not better off in the long term, if he is away from the Tribal Squadron?" Titilayo asked.

It was not a hostile question, at least on the surface, but several women growled or gasped in response.

"It is a good question," Kathra replied to the room, looking at the various clan leaders seated here. "And the correct answer is that we might be able to hide from the

Sept for many years if they had all of deep space to seek us."

She paused, letting her face fall into something terrible for them to behold. Not rage, but perhaps not far short of it.

"But he is Mbaysey," Kathra continued. "Should we set a precedent where someday it might be a better choice to abandon a ClanStar? And more importantly, Daniel is comitatus."

"He is a male," someone on her right shouted in an angry voice.

Several others agreed noisily.

"Yes, he is," Kathra said to that side of the room. "That should tell you a great deal about the value I place on him as a person. Daniel might be more important to the survival of the tribe than any of you."

She got a number of rude responses to that, but all lacked heat. The Mbaysey did not leave their own behind. While the comitatus was sworn to die in her service if necessary, they would also ride to the rescue of one of their own.

And Daniel was as much a part of those women as Joane.

Nkiru Okeke rose from where she sat in back. Tiny, as the woman went, she was also among the oldest of the clan leaders, as most chose to stand down when they reached a certain age, unwilling or unable to continue to execute their duties. Nkiru had not been ground down by her seventy years.

Kathra wasn't sure the stone existed that could grind Nkiru down.

"Why did you really send Daniel to Ogrorspoxu, Kathra?" the woman asked, staring this way with penetrating eyes. "You could have sent *Koni Swift* as your messenger and bade the lords of the Anndaing come to you here. Or sent any other of the comitatus. Why him?"

Kathra stared at the woman. Yagazie had considered

Nkiru a dear aunt in her own time, although Kathra did not have as close a relationship with the woman as her mother had. But Nkiru would be one of the leaders of this council if Kathra Omezi left them to Concursion.

Or did not return.

"We need the Anndaing as allies," Kathra replied. "Sending them an ambassador shows politeness on our part. But you are correct, any of the others could have gone in his stead. He had a second mission there."

"What?" Nkiru asked.

"Research, for a much longer-term goal of mine," Kathra replied. "At some point, it will be necessary to fight the Sept. They have made it clear that even the Free Worlds are not sufficient to stop them from chasing the Mbaysey. Trying to bring us to bay. By coming this far, we have only delayed their retribution. We have not stopped it."

"And what will Daniel be able to do?" Nkiru asked as the women around her waited silently.

"I've asked him to find me a warship," Kathra said. "Something that we can use to take the war to the Sept. They could only chase us as far as Tavle Jocia with hidden bases that will eventually become the foundation of a full invasion of the Free Worlds. All of you know that the Sept will not rest until all humanity is under their yoke."

That point scored home, as many of the woman barked their support.

"At some point, even that will be insufficient for their dear Emperor at Rhages," Kathra continued. "They may never rest, once they discover how many aliens are out there for them to conquer and oppress. How many Tazos do you think they would have if they were truly masters of all they survey?"

The woman were getting raucous now. Even the youngest tribe member born on a ClanStar had been raised with tales of their old reservation. Most of these women actually remembered it well, although Kathra had only vague memories.

But Tazo was the past. *SeekerStar* represented at least a slice of her future.

Nkiru raised a hand to calm the mob and waited while her peers settled.

"Yes," she said, staring at Kathra and even surprising her by agreeing.

The rest of the room let out a similar sound of surprise that it might be over that quickly.

"However," Nkiru continued before anyone could speak, "you must remain here, Kathra Omezi. On this I will not budge."

Kathra felt her chin come up, in spite of being nearly a head taller than the older woman.

"Why is that, Nkiru Okeke?" Kathra asked, striving mightily to restrain her sudden rage at this woman who proposed to set bounds on the Commander of the Mbaysey.

"Because we could lose all of the comitatus and not fall," Nkiru replied. "Lose *SeekerStar* and whatever other vessels and pirates you recruited to help us fight. But you are the Mbaysey, Kathra, and you do not have a daughter who might someday lead us. You lead because we chose to follow, but you are also Yagazie's daughter, and filled with her fire. Without that, the Mbaysey are just a bunch of old women."

Kathra was astounded at the woman's sheer audacity to suggest such a thing. But she could see sudden nods and fierce smiles on many of the other women.

Even Erin did not smother her grin quickly enough, but then her own face fell as she realized that she might have to give up flying and fighting as well, if she truly intended to raise a sister to Kathra's child.

The whole universe would change overnight. Areen,

Kam, and Joane would be senior among her comitatus at that point. Plus, Kathra would have to recruit many aliens to her side and her cause.

Could she just become a queen, seated safely someplace safe like Kanus, while the others went out and fought her wars for her?

Nkiru's smile promised exactly that as the only acceptable outcome to the twenty-two clan leaders facing her now, faces drawn sharp and taut.

Kathra drew a deep breath and let the feeling of helplessness wash over her and recede, like waves on the surface of an ocean supposedly did. She had brought the Mbaysey to this moment, asking these women to make sacrifices.

It was their prerogative to demand sacrifices from her. Forty faces studied her now, awaiting that moment when the future emerged from its cocoon.

"No," Kathra said.

"No?"

"Not yet. The comitatus have always been warriors," Kathra pronounced. "If this works and Daniel is successful, then I will need women, and perhaps even men, who can become aspbads and even naupatis. They may come from within your ClanStars, so I will charge each of you with finding them among your own. And I will charge the entire Mbaysey with recruiting more of them."

"But?" Nkiru asked, picking up on the subtleties in Kathra's voice.

"But first I must go and bring Daniel home safely," Kathra replied. "After that, I will return here for good and we will prepare for war."

THIRTY-ONE

Daniel rode in the rear of a luxurious ground car, humming across the blacktop surface as they entered the starport and began to wend their way through the larger ships back towards a far corner of the vast reservation.

Joane did not fidget, but he could feel her excitement from where their thighs touched. She nearly vibrated with energy, and even smiled occasionally.

Had he not known better, Daniel would have thought she was under the influence of some fantastically interesting pharmacological compounds. Kitchens were notorious for various substances ingested to get you going, slow you down, or lift you off the surface of a planet.

He had not generally participated, if only because being an Executive Chef left one so little time to actually turn off from the job. You were always planning future meals, dealing with catastrophes, soothing fragile egos, or banging heads together to get people to behave.

Finally, he couldn't take it anymore, so he turned to her.

"What?" he asked simply.

Her grin was infectious, in spite of her general nerdiness most of the time.

"Boneyard," she giggled simply, as if that said it all.

Maybe it did for her, but Daniel was lost.

"Boneyard?" he asked.

"A place where they store dead starships, Daniel," she said primly.

"I am aware of our destination, Joane," he let her smile embrace him. "Why are you like this?"

"We're going to be surrounded by dozens, hundreds of old ships, from across who know how many cultures and eras," she expanded. "One of them might give Kathra the tools she needs to finally go teach those Sept bastards some manners."

"And?"

"And you don't know a damned thing about ships, in spite of everything else," she laughed. "So I get to be in charge of where we go and what we look at."

Daniel thought about it. Made sense. She'd been relegated to a secondary role for much of this trip, hobbled to a certain extent by the initial need to learn the language and culture he'd already had imprinted on his soul. And by the fact that he was the one who was Kathra's Ambassador.

But now she would become Kathra's Engineer. He could see that making her so uncharacteristically bouncy today.

It was a good thing that the two of them were alone in the rear of the vehicle, as the driver had never lowered the partition once they got in. Daniel didn't even know if the driver was male or female. Up until now, they had mostly dealt with male Anndaing, but he'd been given to understand the flakiness of such an outcome, where Crence's senior crew all happened to be male, and much more than half of Wyll's staff.

Female Anndaing looked remarkably like the males.

Smaller and perhaps sleeker, but they didn't have breasts or any outward sexual characteristics to differentiate them, like humans did. And he'd never dived deep enough into the research to tell.

The car rolled to a halt next to a ship that was parked with no close neighbors, clear out at the edge of things, with the boundary fence just beyond it.

"We have arrived," the voice came over the intercom, letting Daniel and Joane know that nobody was getting out to open the doors for them.

As he opened the door, Daniel wondered if there was even a driver, or perhaps the vehicle was automated, or driven remotely. The doorman at the hotel had opened their door to let them in, thinking back.

The Sept did not allow that level of automation. All vehicles were under sentient control at all times. Partly, a level of trust that being aboard made you a better driver. At the same time, overpopulation required that people have something to do, rather than just sit in front of a screen, mindlessly rotting their brains—or worse, plotting revolution.

Daniel emerged into the afternoon sun, already cooling as a breeze was suggesting a storm front in the offing. Joane was right behind him, wearing her jacket.

Kathra always kept the ship nearly eight degrees warmer than the air around them at this moment. Daniel thought he could see his breath.

He studied the vessel as a crewmember emerged at the bow and started down the ramp to the ground.

The Anndaing built standard ships, even as individualized as they got. Modularized, perhaps, with various options being assembled at the factory, or allowing a trademaster to swap out sections later easily as an upgrade package.

This was what they called a Cargo-2. Two big cargo pods at the center running parallel with the spine, each six meters tall, eight wide, and twenty long. The pods sat next to each other in cradles loaded from the outsides.

He had seen the Cargo-1 that was the original basis for the design, half as wide with a single pod for a belly on a shark. The front of the ship was living quarters for the crew, along with the cockpit, with a catwalk running down the spine above the pods and connecting to the engines and engine room at the rear.

Because it was Anndaing design, instead of a beak for the cockpit like a human ship would have, these vessels had a hammer, usually with a bridge to the right and a matching room to the left that could be anything, depending on the owner. Daniel had seen plans for various ships that listed the left hammer as an observation deck, an office, the trademaster's cabin, and even a detachable, mini-cargo module for hauling extra material.

Daniel nodded as he finished studying the vessel. It was well founded and clean looking in ways that suggested a classic car, rather than a beater being held together with cloth tape and bondo like a few of them he had seen in his time.

He turned to the Anndaing approaching, recognizing her from yesterday.

Raja Zoodrah, Trademaster of the Cargo-2 *Windrunner*. She had come to the hotel the day before to meet them briefly, but only as part of a larger group as Wyll had been moving quickly to do something. Daniel had gotten the impression that the circle of people who knew the truth was still relatively small.

Why, he didn't understand. At least not yet.

Trademaster Zoodrah stopped and bowed. Daniel and Joane returned it.

"Your personal gear, what there is of it, is being delivered from the hotel shortly, along with the rest of my cargo," she said with a smile. "Shall we go aboard?"

Daniel nodded, but let Joane take the lead. Shortly, she would be the expert. Maybe he could go back to being a chef and occasional translator of old books.

Up the ramp, his original impression of the ship was borne out. *Koni Swift* had felt like a hard-used but much-loved vessel. The kind of thing you flew on a variety of missions and eventually either took in for a major renovation, or wore it out and sold it to the next owner to repair.

Windrunner had been kept almost pristine inside, in spite of being over a century old. Daniel was almost surprised not to have that new ship smell in his nose as he emerged from the airlock.

At the top of the ramp they stepped into what would have been a mud room, were this a house on a planet somewhere. Space suits in various sizes and constructions, but all for Anndaing by shape. He and Joane could use one of the soft suits if they had to. It would just have a much wider faceplate than he needed.

Except that on the end were a pair of newer ones that looked like they had been made especially for humans.

Raja noticed his surprise and smiled.

"Wyll found you a couple of standard Kaniea male suits," she said. "Daniel's has been adjusted down to fit his arms and legs, but Joane's is just out of the box."

Daniel touched the one with the shorter legs. He'd been scanned, at least visually, for this close a fit, even if he didn't need such a thing to survive in deep space.

Not that he was going to tell them that. He had made it a careful point while on this planet to strip both layers at once when he needed to take a shower, putting them both back on again later while not revealing that silly lime-green and white suit that refused to take on any other colors, regardless of how hard he tried to change it.

Urid-Varg had been possessed of an utterly terrible fashion sense.

"This way." Raja led them through the nearer of two hatches on the left side of the room. This would be the rear bulkhead on this level, with another level above it and then the catwalk hallway above that.

The room on the other side of the hatch took Daniel's breath away. If the interior of *Windrunner* was carefully clean and precise, this was the epitome of luxury such as the highest lords of the Sept might demand for their travels.

The carpet under his feet looked deep enough to have its own tides. The walls were covered over with wood strips a little wider than his two hands together, stained in different shades and cut from different parts of different trees from the textures. Three-meter ceilings in here let the room feel airy, as did the various lights on tables, in corners, and recessed overhead.

The furniture looked hand-crafted, from the table with wooden chairs to the upholstered sofa and cushy seats formed around what looked like a fireplace.

Daniel did a double-take at that last bit.

"It puts out heat, runs one of the most effective holograms I've ever seen, and will fool anyone," Raja said. "Makes things homey. Wyll picked out this particular pod for you, based on things you told him."

"What other options did we have?" Joane asked.

"Chrome and steel, seascapes, and jungle," Raja laughed. "Assuming modern bordello wasn't to your tastes. This one had the best kitchen, and I've been told you are a pretty good cook?"

"He is an award-winning chef," Joane laughed. "Who misses being constantly in the kitchen, spoiling us."

"Well, my crew is only four, so we have a tendency to casseroles or frozen meal packs," Raja replied. "If you want to make dinner occasionally, be my guest. An ambassador pod like this has a better kitchen than I do forward. Plus, you've got this whole thing to yourselves, when normally we'd haul at least one finfull of staff and fill the second pod just with their stuff. Our spare pod had nothing in it right now except a few crates of food and books, from what Wyll told me."

"I can explain more, once we take off," Daniel said. "Like you, I have a feeling that there is more going on than we have been told."

"Well, let's finish the tour, then you can let me know any last minute things you need," Raja said. "At that point, we're about two hours from liftoff, according to the most recent updates from Wyll, and then I can haul you wherever it is we're going."

The pod had two decks, with an oversized sleeping chamber supposedly for him and six more for assistants. He and Joane took the two closest to the spiraling staircase, ignoring the decadence in back, as they were still larger than either of them had aboard *SeekerStar*. Extravagant restrooms upstairs and downstairs, in addition to the utter decadence reserved for the ambassador. Salon. Kitchen. Dining nook.

Far more space than Daniel needed or even wanted, but Wyll was treating him like an important personage, so presumably all of this was intended to be communicated to Kathra at some point. Were they preparing to aid her in her quest, or fattening her up for a slaughter of some sort?

They ended up in the kitchen downstairs, the three of them. Daniel checked the pantry and cooler units, making sure he understood everything that was stored as what he and Joane could safely eat.

"Everything good?" the trademaster asked as he finished up.

"It is," Daniel said. "Rather looking forward to cooking again."

"And our mission?" she asked. "Secret until orbit?"

Daniel nodded, but kept his mouth shut. He had a chip from Wyll Koobitz with a recording for him to play once they cleared the atmosphere and were ready to cross the stars. Presumably, it would contain coordinates for Raja Zoodrah to get him to the place Joane called her boneyard, where so many old ships and dreams had gone to die.

Hopefully she wasn't afraid of ghosts.

THIRTY-TWO

A'Alhakoth rapped on the frame and stuck her head into the office. It felt alien to her, but Kathra rarely closed that hatch, and expected her women to intrude like this when they had a question or concern that needed to be addressed.

If this had been her Father, she would have had to be so much more formal.

Kathra looked up and smiled.

"Good afternoon," the Commander said. "Come in."

A'Alhakoth did and sat in the seat on the left automatically. Erin was always on the right when she was here, so every other woman had gotten into the same habit.

They were alone, the two of them.

"Problem?" Kathra asked.

A'Alhakoth had worked herself up to this, but it was still hard to actually say. Kathra Omezi was not that much older than she was, but A'Alhakoth still felt like she had only just escaped childhood.

This was her Commander.

But Kathra insisted on openness inside the comitatus,

even before Daniel had made it possible to truly share one's inner self with the others.

"*SeekerStar* will be departing for Ogrorspoxu tomorrow," A'Alhakoth began.

Kathra nodded, both elbows resting on her desk and watching.

"I would prefer to accompany you," A'Alhakoth managed.

"You do not wish to spend the time with your family and kin?" Kathra asked in a careful voice.

"My family will be departing on *SeekerStar*," A'Alhakoth replied, surprising herself with the depth of her emotions on the subject. "Those remaining here are merely distant kin to me now."

"Interesting," Kathra said.

They both waited, possibly for the other to flinch first.

A'Alhakoth felt like turning into an asteroid at this point, just lurking in the darkness until the sun itself burned out.

"I get the impression that you do not see this as a reward for excellent service," Kathra finally spoke. "I have no one better suited to dealing with the Kaniea and Anndaing locals and speaking with my voice."

"I am aware of that, Commander," A'Alhakoth answered. "But I am sworn into your service, expecting to fight and perhaps die for you if necessary. Comitatus."

"And you don't want to be left behind," Kathra concluded the thought for her.

"I doubt any of us do," A'Alhakoth smiled. "This is personal."

"Personal?"

"We are here because of my luck in encountering Erin and Daniel at Tavle Jocia," she said. "In providing an option you have never expected, when you needed to seek friends beyond the Free Worlds. In being able to open doors quickly here and possibly provide the Mbaysey a place they might reside for a time before moving on."

"But not a home?" Kathra asked intently.

"*SeekerStar* is our home," A'Alhakoth replied. "Concursion is our place. Kanus is just the planet where I was born, before leaving to find my adult self. Linga and Ch'Caani are the parents that protected the child A'Alhakoth."

She paused, looking for the words.

"You will never live on a planet again," A'Alhakoth finally said. "Even a TradeStar or CityStar would travel with us, taking us to new star systems, showing us new sights."

"Not many of the women understand that," Kathra admitted. "Most think that Kanus will become a home base for the Mbaysey."

"If so, that is a thing measured in months, not years," A'Alhakoth nodded solemnly. "I've seen your memories and dreams. I know the truth. Maybe not as well as Erin or Daniel, but Mbaysey means forever sailing in the darkness between stars. I do not wish to be left behind, even for a short stretch. Certainly not if something happens to all of you and I am all that remains of the comitatus. I should not be the one they turn to, as your successor."

Kathra laughed. It was warm and friendly, rather than harsh and biting. A'Alhakoth felt it comfort her.

"You are harder, tougher than any of those women, A'Alhakoth ver'Shingi," the Commander said now. "I would stack you up against Nkiru Okeke or Simisola Ihejirika. Old age and treachery would still only carry them so far in the face of your will when you set your mind to something."

"Acknowledged," A'Alhakoth said. "But I had hoped that there might be someone else, someone not comitatus, that you could designate as your voice."

"None who are not comitatus, Spectre Twenty-Three,"

Kathra said sharply. "That is part of what makes you what you are. Daniel and Ndidi as well. People who have met the standards I demand, in order to share my table and speak with my voice."

"And the treacherous, old ladies of the ClanStars?" A'Alhakoth asked.

Kathra actually smiled, which warmed her.

"I doubt that they would select you as the new Commander, if something happened to the rest of us at Ogrorspoxu," Kathra said. "But that is a responsibility you must be prepared to accept, A'Alhakoth. The Mbaysey is more than just me, just as it continued after we lost Yagazie to a Sept assassin."

"And when you return for good and ground yourself to have a daughter?" she asked.

"And Erin as well, unless I miss my guess," Kathra nodded. "Then our world will change more drastically, especially if we find a way to take my war back to the Sept. Until then, you have seen more of my mind and my plans than anyone remaining, so you will be able to make decisions with a better understanding of what I would have done."

"That includes building up a sperm bank of Kaniea males against future need?" A'Alhakoth asked.

"Absolutely," Kathra nodded. "You will not be the only Kaniea to join the Mbaysey, I expect, but the males will remain on the ClanStars and the factory ships. Only the women might qualify to fly on *SeekerStar* with us. They will need the same sort of future that I have. If Anndaing or others ask to join us while I'm gone, you won't have Daniel, but any candidates will go to a ClanStar anyway."

"And if I end up having to build a new comitatus?" A'Alhakoth pressed.

"Don't relax your standards, once set," Kathra turned serious. "I have only ever had forty-seven women, including all the ones who have retired to start families. That's of the thousands I could have picked from. Erin lost a leg and is still the top of the pack. With friendly planets and sectors to recruit from, we could possibly get *SeekerStar* to the point where I had to build sixty more Spectres to fly off this deck, plus add people like Ndidi and women or even men who might command warships we build to fight the Sept. And make no mistake, when I return, that's the plan. I am relying on you to start the process, because I will need someone to get inside their heads before we have Daniel, so we can know who to accept and who to turn over to the ClanStars for induction."

"Understood, Commander," A'Alhakoth said.

She rose, nodding. A'Alhakoth had not expected to win such an argument with a woman like Kathra Omezi, but she still had wanted to make her case. She was sworn to obey, but Kathra had listened, acknowledged, and made her decision final.

Now A'Alhakoth could choose to leave the Mbaysey, or execute Kathra's orders. Not that there was any doubt on the topic, but that was exactly what comitatus meant.

"Thank you," A'Alhakoth said.

"You'll do fine," Kathra assured her. "Or I would have assigned the task to someone else. Never forget that."

A'Alhakoth nodded again and left Kathra's office, heading to her quarters for homework she needed to read.

The Commander knew her better than anyone, having been in her mind. She might have thought Daniel would know, but he had apparently not pried into any of her secrets that she wanted to hide from the man. He had probably not understood that working hard not to use the power of a god made him even more interesting than he normally would have been.

But the Commander believed in her.

A'Alhakoth supposed that meant she should, as well. She had an enormous task ahead of her.

THIRTY-THREE

Hadi Rostami studied the scan results that his bridge officers had built up. *SeptStar* had long since left the edges of even the maps of Free Worlds space that the naupati had purchased from the locals at Tavle Jocia, the vessel heading towards the galactic core itself.

The Ishtan had set the course initially. Kathra Omezi had left the Free Worlds from Thrabo, but Hadi did not need to follow her exact course, especially as it had zig-zigged several times, according to his scouts.

They had already crossed a number of systems to get here, none of them inhabited by any culture with even industrial technology, which made any of the species around here just iron age barbarians he could ignore. That might change when the Sept decided it needed forward bases in a future decade, but that would be well after the Free Worlds were no longer.

Hopefully, he or someone else would have destroyed the Mbaysey before then.

But the map on his personal screen did not bring him joy. Hadi took a deep breath and held it to center himself.

They had waited here long enough to build such a scan because the Ishtan had directed him to.

Daniel Lémieux had vanished from their sight, which meant that he was in jump, traveling away from the place *SeptStar* had been heading before. The chef would need to emerge somewhere so that they could track him again. Better to simply wait and then begin a new track.

Hadi decided that he needed an update. Visiting the Ishtan was no more objectionable than dealing with any other alien, but he always emerged feeling like he needed a shower. Except that there was no way to wash the trace of their thoughts from his mind.

At least, he supposed, Amirin Pasdar had been able to send an officer that would treat the Ishtan like valuable, sentient allies. Some of the men Hadi knew would have considered them little better than tracking dogs.

That would have been a mistake. Possibly a terminal one, but certainly Pasdar's alien allies would have likely moved on, rather than providing their assistance to the Sept.

He rose and exited his day office for the quarters of the Ishtan.

Guards were unnecessary at their hatch. No sailor would willingly enter such a place except him, and they had ways to enforce that with their mental powers if they chose. At the same time, they were content to let their bodies rest in this space, while sending their minds somehow out thousands of light-years to find that creature whom they hunted.

He entered, stifling a sneeze at the strange musk in the air. It was always present, but perhaps a bit more prevalent today. Hadi wondered if it represented frustration on their part.

Four furry snake bodies stirred as he took his chair, the focus now of twelve eyes.

"Why are these worlds not more advanced?" he asked the

room without introduction. "Those that are populated. It was my understanding that civilized, interstellar cultures have been in this area of space for many thousands of years."

Urid-Varg, they replied in a simple harmony tinged with rage and regret. *These were K'bari worlds, when the K'bari were still a trade federation. Until the Destroyer built an empire on their necks. After a time, they resisted, with the aid of others, and a terrible civil war broke out. Urid-Varg was driven away, but his followers still revered him as a god. They did not accept his demotion to mere creature. The wars were terminal in many places.*

"So the Anndaing and others helped the K'bari destroy themselves?" Hadi asked.

Such local history had never really mattered before now, and only really mattered because he was a scholar and a bureaucrat focused on building the longest logistics chain in human history.

The Anndaing mostly watched, they replied. *And sold weapons and ships to their allies, as they do. The K'bari did it to themselves.*

"And the K'bari are the natives we might find on these worlds?" he pressed.

Descendants of that people, if they survived the fall. Most would not have, and we have never bothered to ask if others did, as these worlds are not capable of even space flight so they represented no threat to the Ishtan or the rise of another Urid-Varg.

Hadi leaned back and considered this odd bit of trivia. Earth history was filled with epochs of colonization, where a more advanced culture displaced one at a lower level of technological development, either by conquest or extermination.

Would the Sept see these worlds as already-tilled fields to take over?

They would, the Ishtan harmony replied. *You are an edge case in even considering the ethics and morality of the situation, rather than just seeing an opening to exploit. The Sept are most likely to establish a variety of what your mind calls forward operating bases on these K'bari worlds, in their own expansion pulse. Whether they conquer the Free Worlds space first or second is beyond our ability to determine.*

Hadi wondered if he would go down in Sept histories then as an explorer, when viewed by future generations, when he was really just an assassin.

But that was not anything he needed to worry about. They would lead him to the chef, which would let him kill Kathra Omezi as well.

Then the Seven Clans would determine what to do with the information he brought back to Rhages.

So we expect, but that will be after our departure.

Hadi nodded and rose. He had the answers he needed. The chef would be destroyed. The Ishtan would either join the man in death, or retire to a monastic lifestyle somewhere. Hadi would return home.

And the Sept would be able to get serious about conquering the galaxy.

THIRTY-FOUR

Boneyard.

Joane nearly giggled out loud at the word itself, as this Anndaing Cargo-2 emerged from jump and settled down a safe distance from a planet, alone in the darkness and maybe the galaxy. She saw the scanner ping the neighborhood and show reflections of nothing at all on the screen in front of Raja, seated just in front of her on the shark's bridge.

Joane rather liked the trademaster in charge of *Windrunner*. Daniel had bribed the woman's crew with good food, but she and Raja had nerded entirely out over ship design and the little engineering details until even Raja's other crew were rolling their eyes.

But Raja's engineer, a big Anndaing male named Bipahl, was severely lacking in the area of dreaming about hot-rodding space ships. He just wanted to keep *Windrunner* sailing and fix the ship when things broke. Raja was the one who went beyond.

Similarly, Tragee, the male Pilot, and Kayna, the female Loadmaster, were quiet kinds of sharks. A Cargo-2 didn't have a lot of space to haul megaloads of stuff, so Raja had worked hard to turn her ship into something of a flying observatory for the occasional scientist and ambassadors and trademasters visiting newly-contacted worlds. Whatever modules you needed plugged in.

Having a pristine-feeling ship helped.

Raja looked up and Joane could see the gleam in the eye pointed towards her. She wondered what look Daniel was getting, standing on the other side, closer to the pilot.

"What's the scale on the scanner?" Joane asked, leaning forward and grinning at her new partner in crime.

"Scaled out carefully to show anything that might be a risk to us," Raja replied. "Otherwise, you've got nothing but random rocks floating in space here."

"And nobody around that might be a problem?" Daniel spoke up.

Joane leaned back enough to catch his eye. He would be searching in his own way, but she doubted that he would see anything like an automated killer robot that way.

He saw minds.

"Nobody is even aware of this planet, Daniel," Raja said. "I didn't know until we watched the clip from Wyll Koobitz, and I'm pretty tight with the Merchants Bank people. This is one of those military secrets that I have to take to my grave kind of thing. But it also means I'm something of a made shark now, so thank you for getting me here."

"Wyll wouldn't have done it if he didn't trust you, Raja," Joane reminded her. "Believe me. The comitatus is all about that sort of thing."

"I'm really looking forward to meeting this Commander of yours, one of these days, just from what you two have told me," Raja smiled and flexed her hammer forward. She turned to the pilot now. "Tragee, take us closer and start listening for challenges. Just because there aren't supposed to be any doesn't mean we don't stay alert."

"Are you expecting someone?" Daniel asked sharply. "I thought that Wyll stated we were headed to a secret system that nobody ever visited. You can't put a major base or anything here, or word will eventually get out."

"You might have missed the part that the Bank itself monitors this system," Raja turned her hammer at him. Joane watched the bridge lights dim a shade as the engines came up. "Trademasters who come here without authorization get their credentials revoked. That includes my whole crew, so none of us would ever be able to fly on an Anndaing vessel as crew again. Nobody is going to risk that, but you still have to worry about smugglers who might make a run in here to see what they could steal."

"I see," Daniel said, but it was obvious to Joane that he didn't.

"Most of these ships are not flyable, Daniel," Joane said. "The effort required to rectify that is significant, so it would be obvious if someone had tried. That's one of the reasons that many were landed on a planetary surface, that and the Ovanii built ships that way, unlike the more fragile vessels the Mbaysey have, or the larger Anndaing haulers."

"Are the bigger ones still around?" he asked, possibly still a little confused.

"No," Raja said. "Those are stored at one of five major naval bases the Anndaing maintain. If they ever need to call up the Armada again, those monsters form the fighting wing, but they are too big for your needs, since they are at least half the size of those Septagons you described."

"Oh," Daniel said as his eyes got a little big.

Joane wondered if he'd snuck into someone's mind at some point and looked at their memories, but had never been able to ask. Not that it mattered that much.

Ovanii Battlemasters weren't what Kathra needed, anyway.

Daniel had been given an ancient, printed book, rather than an electronic one, and had translated enough for her to look at. An Ovanii Assailant would be a terrible vessel to find, sufficiently large to take on several Sept Patrols and smash them by itself. Or crush *SeekerStar* and *The Haunt* with ease. The notes were ambiguous as to whether any here could be repaired, but the smaller vessels, translated as Duelers, were in generally good shape, if you spent the time and money to bring everything back on line.

One or three of those would make lovely pirate vessels to slip back into Sept space and blow things up. Not that Joane got excited at that prospect.

Perish the thought. She was just a nerdy, petite nobody out to explore the options of maybe finding or buying a ship Kathra could use for trade.

You'll believe that, won't you?

"So now what?" Daniel asked, possibly completely lost at this point, as one might expect a chef to be.

He was in the wrong context, after all. Joane could fix that.

"So now we go visit the morning market and see what fish the boats have brought into port, and what vegetables the farmers want to sell us," Joane said.

Okay, so maybe she'd been paying closer attention to the conversations with Ndidi than everyone else, but that was their problem now, wasn't it?

"Ah," Daniel's eyes finally uncrossed and he turned to her. "And Kathra and Erin will be in a position to plan lunch and dinner. Thank you."

Joane smiled. They made a pretty good team, even if she was going to need a couple of other women with her on the next mission like this. Maybe Areen for Daniel and Nkechi or Obi for her to fool around with.

Gods below forbid she got so horny she considered letting a man touch her, even someone like Daniel.

Raja was calling up a map of the new world, this forbidden place called Tnesu, as the ship started sailing into the planetary atmosphere. The ancients had picked this place because it was mostly stone, with very little water, so not all that pleasant a planet to even visit, let alone live on.

One massive continent nearly straddled the southern hemisphere, with several ranges of mountains that served to dry the air out nicely and deflect storms. Throw in some grasslands to capture the dust and dirt blowing, and there was an area down there with just minimal annual precipitation for low grasses to grow, but nothing bigger.

Ships, whole fleets, had been soft-landed here after they had surrendered to the Anndaing fleets, and then shut down for long-term storage. Like centuries at this point. But the Ovanii had built rugged and durable things.

They had just misunderstood that those polite merchants they had thought they could push around were willing to go junkyard dog on them eventually. One badass Assailant cruiser wasn't going to win if the other guy suddenly showed up with several hundred armed freighters and a willingness to absorb terrible casualties so they could get close enough to knife you.

Nobody had been willing to show Joane any sorts of battle reports from the engagements themselves, but everyone agreed that Ovanii warships were extremely capable things. And that the Ovanii had still gotten their asses kicked so hard that they functionally ceased to exist as a culture today.

Sure, there were probably a bunch of farmers somewhere now, with really good legends. And a homeworld or home sector out there that had unleashed them on an unsuspecting galaxy in the first place, but the Anndaing were still the undisputed masters of this range of space.

Joane didn't need to know any more than that.

Raja seemed to be reading her mind at this point.

"They really going to let you walk away with one of those ships?" she asked, slightly in awe.

"I have no idea," Joane replied. "That's a negotiation between Kathra and Wyll. We don't even know where we are, so we can't tell anyone anything, other than what we find and if we rate it interesting enough to bring some of the other women on a future trip. But it would be nice to be on the ass-kicking end of things for once, instead of forever being chased off by the Sept when they show up. Pirates we could handle, but Sept always came in packs, like dogs or sharks, and we were never strong enough to fight them directly. And a Septagon might even be too much for a Battlemaster to handle."

"That's even more frightening," Tragee offered, showing that he had been paying attention, even as he made adjustments to take them into the atmosphere.

"*Oui*," Joane agreed. "But hopefully we have convinced the right people to help us, and in doing so help themselves."

The other three generally agreed at that point. They were all just pawns in something larger, and knew it.

But Joane could see a much more interesting future for herself and the Mbaysey coming.

THIRTY-FIVE

CRENCE WAS on the bridge when *Koni Swift* came out of that last jump, the one that put them out on the very edge of the planetary system known to the humans as Tavle Jocia, although they still had at least one and maybe two jumps left, depending on how tight he wanted Jine to run the first one.

It was a massively busy system from the number of signals he could see on his boards. That was to be expected, from what Omezi had told him. Two major trade corridors crossed here, one running from Sept Imperial space to a border outside anything on an Anndaing chart, and the other running almost perpendicular to *Koni Swift*'s course getting here.

Nobody really knew about the Anndaing sectors, but those were a long ways away, even in a fast ship. Across a wide swath of darkness.

At least all the traffic around here looked civilian. Not that he was sure what human militaries would look like, but everyone here was transmitting an identity beacon on the frequency *SeekerStar* had used and talking in the clear.

Crence had even configured a second beacon for *Koni Swift* that read like they were just another ship sidling into port.

"Thoughts?" he asked the bridge.

"Nobody caught us getting here," Dane replied. "Doesn't mean they aren't trying."

Translation: let's do this thing and stop screwing around.

But Dane was too polite to say that out loud.

Most of the time.

"Jine, gimme a jump a little high and close enough we can talk to the station without too long of a delay," Crence ordered. "But make it look professional. I want everyone else coming along to be graded on the fin we cut today."

"Coming up," Jine replied, pressing buttons.

The second jump was a short one. Almost a blink you could miss if you weren't paying attention. Then they were above the north pole of Tavle Jocia, as the planet organized its orbital traffic.

Things were thin up here, by design.

"Tavle Jocia Flight Control, this is Anndaing merchant vessel *Koni Swift*," Crence said into the radio, attaching his current coordinates in a file format and numbering system that humans could understand, silly creatures being stuck with only ten toes to count on. "Request lane approach and docking assignment."

He had also included the relevant bits they would need in order to figure out where and how to dock a ship like this. Crence still hadn't had time to rip out a full airlock and replace it with something closer to Free Worlds standards.

Maybe if there was a derelict around here he could buy parts from for salvage? Weirder things had happened, and he was happy to haul home bits and pieces of human technology that Wyll and his people could tear apart.

They'd also pay well above market value, since it qualified

as intelligence gathering on this first trip, and they'd want to know as much as they could.

"*Koni Swift*, this is Flight Control," a female human voice replied several seconds later than she should have. Sounded female. Closer to Kathra Omezi's or Joane's from the conversation recordings he had been watching morning, noon, and night. "We have no records of Anndaing vessels calling here before."

She left it dangling like that. Crence wasn't surprised. Bureaucrats liked things easy and predictable. A whole new alien species and trade competitor arriving was probably triggering all sorts of alarms in various places. Hopefully friendly ones.

He glanced over at *SeekerStar*'s birthplace, that massive ships foundry that the human Isaev used to make new ships, wondering how he might get an invite to a tour. Scans from in-system weren't likely to be viewed hostilely, at least not today. That would probably change later.

"Flight Control, we're new in this sector, but have traded with humans in the past," Crence said. Technically, it was true, which was the best kind of truth. Plural. Kathra Omezi AND Daniel Lémieux. "We're prepared to handle your atmosphere, won't add anything dangerous, and all have our medical records updated. Plus we have cargo those humans suggested might go over well here."

Yeah, parse that.

He smiled to himself.

"Dane, scan the Isaev platform hard, but make sure you scan everyone else just as hard, and only do it once," Crence ordered.

Koni Swift was a simple Cargo-6 design, with space for three rows of cargo pods to be slipped out of their silos sideways down each flank, plus the massive cargo bays central and aft. Good scanners, but nothing equipped for espionage, or anything like that. More guns than most Anndaing ships, but also usually farthest from home.

And pirates rarely ask politely.

"*Koni Swift*, assignments and operating procedures have been transmitted," the female finally said. "Operations staff will be there to greet you on arrival."

She left it at that, not that Crence was surprised. Whole new alien species has just shown up and wants to trade? Everyone will want to get in on the action.

Hell, he'd probably get rich just from what he would normally score in margins, even over this distance.

And the Guild would pay top credit for anything else he learned.

Especially if there might be a war going on somewhere close.

THIRTY-SIX

Daniel found he was the odd woman out, but that was nothing new. On *SeekerStar* and *WinterStar*, he'd been the only male, most of the time. Here, he was the landshark, totally at a loss as to what all these ships he was seeing meant, at least in engineering terms.

They represented power. That much was obvious.

That the Anndaing had even admitted that these ships still existed meant that he and Kathra had gotten through to someone important with the possible risk that the Sept presented.

It helped that those *salauds* on Rhages were such incredible sexists, specists, and whatever other *–ists* you wanted to discuss. They would tend to make enemies anywhere they went, firmly convinced that they were the supreme power in the galaxy.

Having been the most powerful being in many different sectors across the lifetime of his memories, Daniel could have told them better, but they hadn't asked.

And then they'd shot him and his ship in the back with an Axial Megacannon more than once.

Thing like that tended to leave people like him less than polite on future encounters.

So he wandered along in the wake of Joane, Raja, and Bipahl. The air was thin and dry, and he had a small equipment belt around his waist with two canteens, just like the others did. Both even had a pinch of salt thrown in for the humans and some citric acid from the spice rack to make it a little tastier.

Daniel glanced up at the sky, but found it an unsettling gray-brown that had nothing to do with pollution. It just represented the dust that a planet-sized continent generated. At least the volcanism was at a minimum, from what Raja had said.

He was surrounded as he walked by massive fortresses designed for war. Hundreds of them, stretching every direction. Castles in steel and enamel paint.

Except that these were really dragons, asleep in their caves until the day they needed to range out and unleash their terrible destruction again.

Joane and Raja were looking for one in particular, comparing numbers on nearby hulls with the documentation that Wyll Koobitz had sent along with them.

Ovanii warships reminded Daniel of trilobites from ancient Earth. Teardrops with the tail blunted off and relatively flat. Maybe disks that had been stretched in only one direction.

The bows were wide and smoothly round, but he could see the armor plating, overlapping outward like scales. Gun turrets could be deployed up or down from the decks to engage, while not risking the edge armor itself.

There were a lot of such pimples on these hulls, from what he had seen flying overhead as they landed.

The narrow ends contained engines on the sides, with a weapon emplacement at the center of the flat end, designed to specifically engage someone coming up from behind. Scorpion tails? No…. Skunks.

And they were huge. *SeekerStar* was nearly sixteen hundred meters long, but that was the length of the core cylinder needed to let the wheel spin smoothly. It still looked like a dragonfly holding a wedding ring in flight.

These were rounded scones resting on massive legs. The biggest ones were not as long as *SeekerStar*, but as wide as the ring and simply solid, conveying the strength of a mountain.

"We're here," Raja announced, stopping in front of one of the monsters.

It looked like a castle wall to Daniel. Twelve or fifteen meters tall on a dozen legs, with a space below high enough to drive a truck under, extending in both directions as far as the eye could see. Gray in places, but it had also been painted by someone to show off panels in almost every color imaginable, little squares and hexagons like cute freckles on the outer hull.

He followed them underneath the ship, musing about the poetry these gruff warriors had created, so at odds with their public image as terrible marauders plaguing the spacelanes.

Raja led them to a landing leg, where she compared a keyboard to an image on her pad and began typing. A ramp lowered from the ceiling and Daniel heard hatches slide open above for them.

So, still powered after all this time? Or was this the showpiece that the Anndaing used for demonstrating either the vessels or the technology?

Joane and the two sharks ascended into the vessel, so he joined them.

Inside, Daniel was reminded that the Ovanii were generally a little over two meters tall, plus or minus. More than half a head taller than humans, relatively. Kathra's height, but even wider. Built like forceball players, too, although that thought brought back a terrible memory, Angel departing from *Pain du Soir* on that last night, the thing that was finally too much, when he decided to sell the restaurant to Lucrèce for the cash the man had in his wallet.

How far we've come in just four years.

Daniel had never been back to his former restaurant. Had only stayed on Genarde itself for long enough to book passage off-planet the next morning. Rather quickly, he had wandered his way to the edge of the Sept empire and gotten himself hired by Kathra as her personal chef.

And then the adventures had truly begun.

The interior of this warship was as colorful as the exterior. Or maybe he'd just spent too much time with the poverty of the Mbaysey. Maybe folks with too much money decorated the interiors of their ships with pretty swaths of random color in geometric designs, including the floors and ceilings as well.

The others had the same impression, from the murmurs and commentary, but even *Windrunner* tended to be monochromatic in a soft green Daniel might have called turquoise.

Daniel could see that changing, as Raja touched walls almost reverently as they walked. He suspected she might be slobbering with the anticipation of hiring a new interior decorator when she got home.

Four decks thick, from the numbering system in place here. Each deck was about three and a half meters of space, with armored tops and bottoms protecting you.

"Do we need something this huge?" Daniel asked the others.

"This is just a Dueler, Daniel," Joane turned to him with a smile. "The Assailants are several times as big. But most of this was used to haul people and supplies. Like the Mbaysey, the Ovanii were nomadic, carrying their entire tribe with them. So this is more like a ClanStar as a warship."

"Oh," seemed to be about all he could manage in response. That made sense, but multiplied by the thousands of ships in the various squadrons, they must have numbered in the millions or tens of millions as a raiding force.

No wonder they had been a threat. He had been imagining them too small.

The group ended up on the bridge. Daniel supposed you would call it a bridge. That was what other cultures did.

He liked to think in terms of kitchens, instead. Feeding people instead of destroying them. Maybe he needed to design more interesting warships, one of these days?

"Gravity?" he asked, contemplating that this ship was flat, where humans walked on the inner side of *SeekerStar's* rings, or swam in space when you were down in the core.

"Almost as good as the systems we use today," Bipahl replied, moving to a station and sitting, but pointedly not touching anything.

The ship should be powered mostly off and then locked, and nobody was sure what the limits of behavior might be. Where would the Merchants Bank folks decide that enough was enough?

"So you just power things up and take off, like in a Spectre?" Daniel asked the women.

"Effectively, yes," Joane said. "And sneak up on some Sept base, hiding in the darkness to support forward invasion forces. Steal what we need. Blow up the rest. Slip away. The Ovanii were masters of that sort of thing, from what you've shown me."

"Well, yes," he agreed, still a little confused about the whole thing.

Daniel looked around and wondered if Kathra would add something like this as a new warship and move here, or keep *SeekerStar*. The Ovanii hadn't done individual fightercraft, unlike the Mbaysey, so there were no landing bays sufficiently large to handle anything beyond two SkyCamels or one of those standard transports the Anndaing flew.

They spent about ten minutes on the bridge, just in pure wonder, before moving on. Engineering was just as impressive, taking up the entirety of the two middle decks for about the middle third of the width and aft quarter of the ship. Personal quarters followed the ring hallways that wrapped around inside the armor, with that same teardrop shape before running straight and slowly converging.

What must it have been to be Ovanii in those days? Daniel had memories of folks who had known them, but no Ovanii directly in his mind.

He suspected that they would have recognized Kathra Omezi as one of their own, though, just from the little things about this ship and how they had built it. Even the colors, although Kathra had not gone that far. That brought him solace as he trudged in the wake of the other three, making sure they saw and touched everything on this supposed *Dueler* vessel.

He had lost the Star Turtle, and all other starships were really just *things* after that, rather than living creatures. He would not get emotionally engaged by just a ship. Only the people, like Kathra or Erin or Joane.

Joane seemed impressed, though. That was enough for Daniel.

He had a debt he owed a Septagon named *Vorgash*.

THIRTY-SEVEN

Kathra had all the women in their Spectres today, despite not expecting to launch them. She was down in *SeekerStar*'s command area in zero gravity herself, seated next to Ife and strapped in for maneuvering.

Nobody knew what was coming next, but they had arrived.

Ogrorspoxu. Central world of the Anndaing culture. Home of the Merchants Guild and the Merchants Bank.

SeekerStar came out of jump at the location that Morgan Wilzae, Trademaster In Residence at Kanus, had told her was the optimum, since she was going to be arriving as an unknown vessel.

There were ships coming and going constantly in this system, and rules to follow. If you were truly alien, they shuffled you off to a particular orbit until the authorities could figure out what to do with you.

Ogrorspoxu was a complicated experiment in orbital dance, just watching all the beacons identifying ships and vectors. Thankfully, Kathra had been speaking almost exclusively in Anndaing for weeks now, so she was comfortable without her two experts handy.

She would have other experts soon.

"This is Mbaysey vessel *SeekerStar*," she announced on the control frequencies. "Looking for an orbital assignment from which we can send shuttles to your station with documentation."

Again, straight out of their book. Hopefully, they would even recognize her name, since she didn't see *Koni Swift* anywhere on the lists of ships nearby.

Daniel, Joane, and Crence Miray might be anywhere by now, but they had come here first. She would track them down from here.

"Mbaysey *SeekerStar*, you are cleared for the orbital path attached, with standard deviations and spacing for speed," a male Anndaing voice replied after a few minutes. There was a file attached for Ife.

Surely, it hadn't taken them that long to get organized, so Kathra wondered who had been alerted to her presence before anybody replied.

"I've got this, Kathra," Ife said as she opened the file and read the contents. "We're almost in the correct location now and just a little maneuvering will get everything in place."

Kathra smiled at the woman. That was Ife's polite way of telling her Commander to get off her deck and go do something useful.

She rose and swam aft. As she was riding the lift down, Ife came over the comm.

"Kathra, I have a message from someone named Wyll Koobitz, asking for a personal audience," Ife said, her voice conveying some level of concern.

And personal audience sounded wrong. Made Kathra sound like some alien princess come to Ogrorspoxu, rather than a simple merchant tracking down a pair of wayward crew.

What had Daniel done to impress these people? Or piss them off?

"Any other details?" Kathra asked.

"Not currently, should I reply asking?" Ife continued.

"Yes," Kathra decided. "I'll head to my office. Let *The Haunt* know that they'll be in their seats a little longer. We may have to fly over there impressively or something."

Ife laughed and cut the line. Kathra rode down to the main deck and headed to her office instead of her ship.

"They're ready to talk," Ife said when Kathra opened the line to the bridge from her desk. "Audio and video capable. No scrambling."

"Understood," Kathra sat up and took a deep breath. "Put them through."

She rarely used the video channels, because it was cheaper and easier to just communicate by text most of the time. If she needed to talk to someone to their face, she could have them in her office, or fly to their ClanStar.

But this was the start of a new era.

Anndaing. Male. Older. Looked smaller than Crence Miray, but he had mentioned that he was tall and broad for one of his kind, so perhaps this Wyll Koobitz was just average.

Except the face didn't look remotely average. There weren't many Anndaing on Kanus, but the ones who were there tended to be exceptional in their chosen field of endeavor, whether it was trade, manufacturing, or service.

This shark put them all to shame.

"Commander, it is a pleasure to finally meet you," he said with a warm smile that flexed his hammer slightly forward. "My name is Wyll Koobitz and I am a representative of

Merchants Bank. Daniel and Joane have both told me much about you, as has Crence Miray and the crew of *Koni Swift*."

She nodded and smiled back at the man. At least she knew better what she was dealing with. Her people had come this far and chatted with this man.

That had to be a good sign. And Merchants Bank was the money in this sector, so he was politely telling her he spoke for the government, without ever being rude about it.

"Thank you, sir," she replied. "I have been looking forward to Ogrorspoxu, but the delays at Kanus were greater than I had anticipated."

Simple. Evasive. Clear without any clarity.

"May I invite you to join me for dinner in a few hours aboard the station?" he asked. "I have a chef brimming over with excitement to try out some of his new recipes."

"I look forward to it, Koobitz," she said, wondering what his game was. Recipes suggested that Daniel had been here long enough to teach someone new things, but wasn't present currently. "How large should I plan for?"

"I was thinking something compact," he said. "Myself and a co-worker. You and perhaps Erin, if she can be spared with you off-vessel. Or A'Alhakoth."

Okay, so this shark had spoken with Daniel under most friendly circumstances, or Crence had supplied more information than Kathra had been expecting of a simple merchant.

Assuming Crence Miray was a simple merchant, and not a spy of some sort, considering who she was speaking with now. And they had not uncovered Daniel's secret, or they would have likely already been trying to destroy *SeekerStar*, afraid of another Urid-Varg.

But he hadn't mentioned Daniel or Joane. Kathra considered asking, but this was an open line, available for anyone with the right sensor facing to listen to, if they were of a mind.

Dinner would be the sort of privacy where she could ask.

"I will bring someone," Kathra said. "A'Alhakoth remained at Kanus as my Ambassador, along with the rest of the Tribal Squadron."

"Excellent," he said, his eyes flicking off screen for a moment in that weird way they did at the ends of the hammers. "Say four hours, twenty minutes from now?"

"I am looking forward to it, sir," Kathra said.

She cut the line and keyed Ife.

"I heard," the woman said. "Stand everyone down?"

"Yes," Kathra decided. "Comitatus meeting in the dining hall in thirty minutes. You join us, Ife."

Kathra caught the woman's slight intake of breath, almost a gasp.

"I will be there," Ife replied, a little flustered.

Ifedimma Ogu always handled sensors and communications, while Obioma Nneka was the primary pilot and Ngozi Obi usually was in charge of the various gun turrets, at least so far as being in command when they had to be fired.

Ife had, in many ways, become Kathra's other second in command on the ship, like Erin, but never had been elevated to the comitatus. Might never, for other reasons, but if Kathra would have to become a mother soon, everything and everyone else would have to change along with her.

That would include bringing Ife and others into planning and command, especially if this was going to be larger than just the twenty-four women and one male of the comitatus.

Kathra made her way to the dining hall, in case Ndidi missed the message. The young woman was busy teaching Ebube some new recipe when Kathra looked into the kitchen itself. With Daniel not around, Ndidi was the primary chef, although she also was generally in charge with him here.

Like Ife, Ndidi would never fly Spectres. Possibly not command warships, although the brains and skill to command a kitchen would probably transfer over nicely. And Ndidi had as much killer instinct as Daniel did.

Time to recruit new chefs, and use the kitchen as a training ground for military command?

Kathra laughed to herself as Ndidi approached with a cupcake in hand, frosted in blue and with sprinkles of something on the top.

Kathra raised an eyebrow at the woman.

"Cupcakes can be prepared ahead of time, contain a jolt of energy, especially as the chocolate has some coffee mixed in, and I wasn't sure who I would be cooking for or when," Ndidi said simply. "Eat."

Kathra sat and peeled the delightful treat. Daniel didn't understand the obsession with chocolate, but he understood females well enough to include chocolate desserts. Ndidi was female. Her default was the chocolate that Zalman ClanStar produced, with other things thrown in for spice.

"Sit," Kathra told Ndidi as the woman started back into her kitchen. "You can cook later. The rest will want showers first."

Ndidi complied, eyes perhaps a little wider than normal behind those glasses that had kept this brilliant child out of a cockpit, when such poverty was the norm. If they could trade well here, without the Sept chasing them off every so often, how much wealth could they accumulate? Enough to fix the eyes of children and elders? Disease was uncommon, but genetics was what the tribe brought with it from Tazo, supplemented by the males allowed to contribute.

Should she recruit males to command positions in her coming fleets? It was a novel, painful question. Mbaysey was female. Sept was defiantly male. Even the Free Worlds tended that way.

Her own revolutions notwithstanding, could she afford to exclude a competent male, just because of his gender?

Ndidi had snagged a second cupcake and was nibbling at it as Kathra watched her.

"How good is Ebube as a chef?" Kathra asked between bites, her voice quiet enough out here that the other woman would not hear as she worked on something in the kitchen that involved banging pans occasionally.

"Competent," Ndidi replied. "Better than Ugonna on her best day, but perhaps not an artist at her craft. She can follow Daniel's and my recipes sufficient not to poison anyone."

Kathra noted that Ndidi didn't ask why. Just supplied the information her Commander needed, on the assumption that there was more going on. There was, but it was pleasant to see that level of emotional maturity in someone so young.

"You will need to recruit and train others to cook, both here and in the general crew kitchen," Kathra decided. "As well as intensify your language studies until you are fully, conversationally fluent in Anndaing."

"Getting there now," Ndidi nodded. "Perhaps a little better than the comitatus, at least at present."

"At present," Kathra agreed.

Ndidi had been there when Kathra met the clan leaders. And she was smart enough to see the shape of the future.

Change was coming. Major change.

Erin entered the dining hall with a cluster of the comitatus. Ndidi exploded off her bench and moved quickly into the kitchen, returning with a platter of cupcakes.

"Coffee is brewing and will be ready shortly," Ndidi announced to the women.

That explained Ebube's noises. Ndidi was always trying

to be a step ahead of Daniel, who was working to outthink Kathra and the others. Military-grade planning.

Yes, Ndidi would be a key part of the future. Along with so many others.

It was time to explain it all to the comitatus. They knew it instinctively, but they had perhaps never seen the shape that the future would take.

Kathra could see the river begin to delta before her.

THIRTY-EIGHT

CRENCE HAD SPENT enough time around Daniel and Joane to appreciate how stressed these new humans were at Tavle Jocia. And he had seen pictures of terran sharks that bore a remarkable resemblance to Anndaing, with their own version of the hammer that was a sensor unit detecting electrical signals.

Supposedly not as terrifying as the ancient megalodon or their smaller descendants the great whites from their home, but he knew he was still triggering some level of subconscious fear and dread with the folks on the Tavle Jocia station.

Not that he was enjoying himself or anything. That wouldn't be tactful now, would it?

At least his smile seemed to calm them. It was just the hammer flexing forward and back that caused pupils to unconsciously dilate at these various meetings.

One bureaucrat had given way to a second. A third. An eighth, if his count was accurate without checking his notes or counting on his toes.

Pretty sure he would either run out of people, or be

talking to the human in charge of the station itself before too many more such meetings.

This one was female. Named Beryl Cho. Human females had a different shape than males. Or Anndaing. Curvier, with the addition of breasts on the front that would slow a swimmer down, except that humans were land creatures through and through.

Older, from what Daniel and Joane had said, with wrinkles around the eyes and mouth, plus long hair with gold at the tips, gray in the middle, and white at the roots.

Not immense age, but not a pup, either.

He had been shown into her office, in a nicer wing of the station, from the decorations and furniture that was uncomfortable to someone with a fin to sit in.

Crence had been smart enough to bring his own tea bags. Also Daniel's fault.

"Ambassador," she began, but Crence had to interrupt her, lest she work up a good charge on a wrong path.

"Merely a trademaster, Madam Cho," Crence said. "I do not come with ambassadorial credentials from the Anndaing Merchants Guild. Merely their official greetings and a request to perhaps transport a trade representative from the Free Worlds to my sectors, so they can establish better protocols and ambassadorial-level interactions."

He smiled. It was a load of tuna poop, but nobody here could gainsay him. And even fish shit was useful, in the right circumstances.

"Trademaster, then," she said, cocking her head to the right as she did.

He wondered if that was like flexing only one hammer forward. He'd never tried it, but there was no reason it wouldn't work. Maybe later.

"So you have, as you no doubt realized, caused a bit of

consternation with your arrival," Beryl Cho continued as Crence watched her.

He grinned.

"And you have spent enough time around humans to have learned Spacer and handled the technical aspects of arrival and docking correctly," she said. "Who was it you ran into? Have the Se'uh'pal made it as far as your worlds?"

Crence felt his grin expand mightily.

"We've known the Se'uh'pal for many centuries, Madam Cho," he said. "They have made extensive trade ventures into our space. It was the humans that convinced us to visit you specifically."

"Humans?" she asked, obviously surprised.

But then, nobody had asked the right questions before now.

Hardly Crence's fault.

"Indeed, yes." Crence decided to perhaps have a little fun with her. The whole story would come out eventually, as he wasn't trying to keep it a secret. "We encountered the vessel *SeekerStar* and the Mbaysey Tribal Squadron in deep space while on an exploration voyage ourselves. They accompanied us to our capital world, traded some, and provided the sailing directions to visit you."

"Where is your system?" she pressed, like a proper trademaster should.

"As I understand your notations, a little clockwise around the wheel of the galaxy," Crence replied. "And well in towards the core itself."

"That's K'bari space," she said, confused. And referring to the barbarian lands that barely traded with anybody anymore.

"The K'bari are no more," Crence said simply, with a hint of a shrug from both shoulders and hammer.

"Did you destroy them?"

"They destroyed themselves long before us, Madam," Crence replied, without telling the humans anything about Urid-Varg if they didn't already know those tales. "We knew them in a previous millennia, when they were great traders across a wide section of the quadrant. And I come from well beyond K'bari space."

"Beyond?" she echoed.

"For the longest time, we thought K'bari space as primitive and largely uninhabited as you do," Crence smiled. "It was Commander Omezi that proved us wrong, although I'm given to understand that humans are relative newcomers to these worlds."

"We are," Cho replied. "Most of our trade is either with the Sept on human hulls, or with individual worlds, carried out largely by Se'uh'pal or Ch'sh'xx vessels, with a few others also engaged."

"So we were given to understand," Crence said. "I for one look forward to breaking the monopoly of the se'uh'pal."

"As long as you don't bring your wars into our space," she said with a bit of an edge to her voice.

"Our wars?" It was Crence's turn to be confused.

"*SeekerStar*," Cho said. "And the other vessel."

"Other vessel?" Crence asked.

"The one *Vorgash* had built at Isaev's shipyard," she continued with a nod over his shoulder. "*SeptStar*, I think they called it. We don't want anything to do with Omezi's war with the Sept."

"I can assure you I feel the same way, madam," Crence said.

Inwardly, he could feel the gaff hook his gills, even though his kind had evolved past such primitivity in the distant past.

He was stuck here when he had a piece of intelligence that people back home would probably kill for. Literally.

But he had to find out what in the four hells a *SeptStar* might be, because if the Sept was capable of sending warships into Anndaing space today, even just to hunt what they saw as a renegade, then the threat to the Merchants Guild had just gone through the roof.

"Just so we understand each other," Trade Ambassador Beryl Cho smiled at him now, looking remarkably like one of his own kind with her own shark smile.

"Oh, we do, Madam," Crence assured her. "We do."

THIRTY-NINE

"So now what?" Daniel asked as *Windrunner* seemed to hover about five thousand meters in the air above the *Boneyard*.

Tragee, Raja, and Joane all looked at him with different emotions. Boredom, more or less, from the pilot. Awe from the trademaster. Greed warring with *Triumph* on Joane's face.

Windrunner seemed to almost be a puppy straining at a leash, from the way the ship seemed to skim across the winds up here, but Daniel had seen Tragee flying it for long enough to understand that he knew what he was doing. Rather well, actually.

"Now we head home," Raja said after a moment. "Unless you have some other place in your instructions that I need to take you."

"*Non*," Daniel shook his head. "All Koobitz gave me was this place and the instructions for you."

"Should there be more, Daniel?" Joane asked.

"I do not know," he shrugged. "My original goal had been to learn more about the Ovanii as a people, so that I could better understand that odd mix of culture that drove them forever into deep space, rather than living on planets. Perhaps I was unconsciously trying to compare them to the Mbaysey in that."

"Have you found it?" Tragee, of all people, asked. "That thing that would make sense of them? To us, they were just terrible raiders who might appear in your skies, strip your world like locusts, and then move on."

"There was that," Daniel said. "But the Mbaysey did not set out to become Vikings. I could see that being an outcome in another few generations, however. Originally they just wanted to escape Tazo and the Sept."

"Do you think that the Ovanii had their own Tazo?" Joane asked. "Their own vile overlords to flee from?"

"Again, I do not know," he said. "Perhaps when we return to Ogrorspoxu I can find the right book in the right library and answer that question. But if so, it is not that uncommon a thing. Consider the ancient tales of Moses and the Egyptians. Would the natives of the Levant have seen the onrushing Jews as an Ovanii horde?"

Raja wanted to say something now. It was in her eyes and the way her hammer moved. Daniel turned to her and smiled encouragingly.

"Do you have Ovanii memories?" she asked skittishly. Possibly expecting a lightning bolt for her effrontery, but she only knew the pieces of the truth he had been willing to share with her or Wyll Koobitz.

He started to speak, but stopped.

Did he? How many of those ancient ghosts might have simply refused to communicate with him?

The K'bari were a gregarious people. Or had been, once upon a time. The Z'lud more logical and taciturn, but they also had possessed surprisingly complex philosophical systems, at least before the monster reduced everything into stark balances of good and evil.

Maybe he needed to write some Z'lud philosophies sometime. And love poetry.

But he was seeking the Ovanii. Memories of their peoples, or at least of their passage down the twelve thousand years of his former lives.

Daniel closed his eyes and made sure he had a firm grip on the back of Tragee's seat, just in case.

He dove inward. It was usually like swimming in a cocktail party when he did this, surrounded by hundreds and perhaps thousands of beings of all colors and species. The only thing that unified them was their former existence as erect bipeds, but Daniel already knew that Urid-Varg's original form had been humanoid.

How hard would it have been to exist instead as a Vida, or a Bhaorajj, to say nothing of the Atter?

The conversational hum quieted as he descended into their midst. Frequently, he found himself on one side of a glass wall, with all the rest opposite, but today they surrounded him, and it felt friendly.

"Do we know the Ovanii?" he asked simply.

He had done that before and gotten no answer, but now he had walked on one of that race's decks. Experienced their spaces and their dreams.

The Z'lud to his left all shook their heads in unison. Daniel was always surprised to see them hornless, but these were not the Upynth, even as they resembled both Upynth and Terran zebras, although their hides had more subtle stripes and more colors than either of the others.

These were Urid-Varg's second empire, after he wiped out all of his own kind and then began his long wander as other species began to rise to technology. The oldest of these ghosts had died perhaps nine thousand years ago.

A few Roahrt also shrugged. They had provided the Destroyer a few bodies, but he had not stayed around long enough to build himself a new empire. Perhaps outliving two before that already had jaded him for a time. Certainly, he had not tried again until the K'bari.

And look where that had gotten him.

Daniel turned slowly in place, practically gobsmacked that all of his ghosts seemed to be present today, even the ancients who were the Mnapyre themselves, Urid-Varg's people. Normally they were far more aloof and distant, refusing to even make eye contact with him.

What had changed today?

A K'bari stepped out of the crowd and approached.

Arsène. The one who had taught Daniel the K'bari language so that he could translate the book by Idir, the scholar.

He was taller than Daniel by a few centimeters, with pale green eyes, and yellowish-tan fur that covered his body in a fine pelt. The man had three eyes across the face, with the nose below that stretched into a snout halfway between feline and canine for size.

Petite horns that swept back from his forehead and then outward always reminded Daniel of an ox.

Daniel bowed. Arsène returned it.

"What has changed?" he asked the ghost, gesturing to the crowd around them, almost humming with warmth and excitement today. Arsène had always been one of the friendliest.

"You have always understood evil, Daniel Lémieux," Arsène replied simply. "Given the power of Urid-Varg, you have time and again refrained from exercising it."

"*Oui*," Daniel said. "The Left Hand of Evil."

Arsène nodded.

"All expected you to succumb anyway," the ghost said. "Such is the nature of the power you hold, terrible as it is."

It was Daniel's turn to nod. He had never met any male

that he would have trusted with this power, and only by subverting himself to the women around him had Daniel been able to control it. Areen. A'Alhakoth. Erin. Ndidi.

Kathra.

"And now?" Daniel asked, breathless as he realized that all of his ghosts had joined him on a precipice now. He could see eternity at the bottom of the cliff, waiting to swallow them up forever.

Would that be a bad outcome, given the power at his command?

"It would," Arsène answered, surprising Daniel all the more.

"How?" he gasped.

"Because you have changed, Daniel," the ghost said. "Previously, you understood evil and resisted it. Now, you have chosen to actively fight it."

He started to deny those words, but they died on his tongue.

The Sept Empire.

It was Urid-Varg, without the Destroyer himself seated at the center of that web.

Arsène nodded.

"They will continue to expand, and do so by force, as none can resist them," Arsène said. "Or rather, like always, those who can resist will wait too long and be unable to stop the thing later, when they might have succeeded today."

"The Sept Empire must be destroyed," Daniel said aloud. For the first time, he really meant it.

The crowd responded in their own ways, about half nodding and half shrugging.

"Perhaps broken is a better term," Arsène said. "No culture deserves to be annihilated, if people still support it, but their power to impose on the weaker must be ended. The K'bari are no more as a stellar civilization. We are unsure if the Z'lud even exist today as a species. The Mnapyre are known to be gone, as Urid-Varg chased the last of them down and personally killed her, to prevent another from rising to challenge him later."

"Are there Ovanii here?" Daniel spread his arms wide at the group, but nobody answered.

Nobody answered.

There were only those records that the Anndaing had preserved, and even then they were generally lost behind a forgotten language after so much time.

Daniel wondered if he was the last person alive who could read Ovanii love letters without resorting to a computer to haphazardly guess at translations and miss the idioms that made their art so poignant.

So painful.

Because there were no Ovanii left in the galaxy but him.

He opened his eyes and found himself on the bridge of *Windrunner* again. Three others stared intently at him, mouths agape and eyes huge.

He found that he was crying, but that was acceptable. It just meant that he would need to find some Anndaing scholars and revive the language. Translate the dramas and poetry first, so that others could learn the words and build some positive memories of those ancient marauders, lost so long ago that they were nearly forgotten, save for the terrible tools of war they had perfected once.

"Are you okay?" Joane asked quietly.

"There are no more Ovanii," Daniel replied quietly. "I asked all my ghosts. Every single one of them was there. That was the first time that had ever happened."

"And the tears?" she continued.

"We are going to go break the Sept," he said bluntly. "In that, we were united."

Joane had been inside his head enough to understand the

power of that statement. She paled under that dark skin, almost turning umber and gray. The others knew less, but perhaps that drove a greater fear.

"And now?" Raja asked tentatively.

"Ogrorspoxu," he said simply. "We need to see a shark about buying a warship."

ISHTAN

FORTY

Hadi felt the Ishtan calling him. It was a polite thing, almost like a knock at the door, except that it was in his mind. He acknowledged the pulse of energy and contemplated his office. Some paperwork that needed reviewing, mostly reports from various department heads about current statuses of things and future needs, but the sorts of details that an aspbad had to focus on daily.

Nothing that could not wait, and no meetings in the next few hours.

He rose and exited his office, heading around the curve to the door that separated the Sept Empire from the Ishtan homeworld, at least in his mind.

Entering, he found the four as usual, reclined on their couches and waiting for him. Hadi took his accustomed chair and studied them.

They had an excitement about them today. He could not put his finger on any one detail, but they moved with greater energy, perhaps. The three eyes seemed to glow as they focused on him.

Daniel Lémieux has arrived, they sang in harmony in his mind. *He is at his destination. Kathra Omezi has joined him.*

Hadi paused, slightly offset by those words.

"Was she not before?" he asked, perhaps a bit more sharply than he had planned to.

Correct, Hadi Rostami. They have orbited different stars ere now, but have reunited.

Hadi waited a moment before exploding. He needed these allies to complete his mission. Without them, he might visit a million stars and never catch another hint of Kathra Omezi and her so-called tribe. Such was the depths of the galaxy in which she might hide, once she passed beyond the Free Worlds.

"I understood that we sought to destroy them both," Hadi said carefully.

He is far more dangerous, they announced. *Without the scion of Urid-Varg, the woman is just a simple human that does not represent a threat to the galaxy.*

Hadi caught a glimpse into the mind of their combined entity as they spoke. An ideogram, for lack of a better term to describe it, showing the chef superimposed over a mad god intent on wreaking destruction on the entirety of the galaxy. Kathra Omezi was just a footnote, comparatively.

"She is part of the deal," he reminded them carefully. "Her destruction is why the naupati was willing to put this ship at your disposal."

And so she shall die, they replied. *But the chef must be utterly crushed. With him gone, we might provide you with the tools to seek her yourself, Hadi Rostami.*

He caught a second ideogram now. Himself, with a second image superimposed.

They could alter him to give him that sensitivity? Would he still be human at that point?

It would not be coded into your genetic structure, Hadi

Rostami, they supplied the answer. *After seven of your years, it would fade completely as your cellular existence overwrites itself.*

"But for those seven years?" he started to ask, petering out of words.

You would be more than human, they confirmed. *Not enough to be a threat to galactic order, though.*

Hadi quailed at the image of galactic order as they envisioned it.

In their minds' eyes, the Sept empire was a grain of sand washed up temporarily on a beach. Poised briefly, as it were, before the tide swept it out again.

And so it is, Hadi Rostami, they agreed. *Nothing more. All of Urid-Varg's empires were longer-lasting and more powerful. The Sept will remain a thing for perhaps another few hundred years before it splinters.*

"How can you know that?" he gasped.

You contain that knowledge yourself. Only a few of your so-called human empires lasted more than a few generations. Other houses will rise and challenge the beings that make up the Sept. Byzantium would have absorbed them. Chin as well. The Sept cannot.

The Sept cannot.

Hadi felt his own doom inscribed with those words.

The Sept cannot.

Nothing he did would matter in the grand scheme of things. Even in the smaller scheme of his generation.

SeptStar could destroy the Mbaysey without any survivors and it would not change one thing about the future of the Sept Empire itself. Hadi could be turned into a demigod, and nothing would save the Sept itself from falling.

Thus you do not present a risk, were we to do this thing.

"How long have you planned it?" he asked, breathless with the immense implications.

Was this was nihilism tasted like, this coppery hue at the back of his throat? Or was it fear?

It has been an option since we encountered Amirin Pasdar, they answered. *Such was his personal ambition that he might have wrestled the Sept away from its current lords, but you convinced him to regain his humanity instead.*

Hadi swallowed past a tongue suddenly too big.

Could Amirin have truly conquered the Sept itself, given whatever mental powers the Ishtan might have blessed or cursed him with?

The probability lies beyond the fourth standard deviation, the voices spoke in his mind. *Nothing measurable would have changed, save that the Sept itself would have fractured for a generation. Perhaps he could have built something better in its place, but that is a low-probability outcome, given human nature as we have seen it.*

Broken the Sept Empire? Brought it down in pieces?

Affirmative, Hadi Rostami.

"What will he do now, without those powers?"

He will attempt the same, but the probabilities of success are lower, they answered. *Your success in ending the existence of the Mbaysey will increase his chances by perhaps as much as seven percent, but your failure would not materially damage his standing enough to prevent his attempt.*

Hadi let the enormity of the thing wash over him. This might be the opposite of nihilism, whatever an expert might call it. He had wondered if pursuing Kathra Omezi bore any value.

It both did and did not, in ways that his mind raced furiously to calculate.

Amirin was going to attempt to make himself emperor. Somehow. Hadi could see that. It had quietly been present in their relationship as long as he had known the man.

Ambition. Not married to an understanding of power far beyond what humans were capable of.

Hadi Rostami could have powers no human had ever been granted, save for a chef from Genarde. He could assist Amirin, or thwart him.

Correct, they observed. *Stopping Amirin Pasdar from succeeding extends the current span of the Sept Empire to perhaps three hundred years before the cultural probabilities render estimation random. Assisting him guarantees their immediate fall, with the opportunity to create something else that might last longer.*

Or it might also fail within your lifetime.

How much did he wish to replace the Sept with some other dream? Hadi was unsure. But he was a scholar and a bureaucrat, not a fire-breathing warrior intent on scribing his name into the face of a mountain for all to read.

And on that pedestal such words appeared:
My name is Ozymandias, king of kings:
Look on my works, ye Mighty, and know despair!
Nothing besides the stumps of two legs remained.

The words of the unknown, ancient poet were there in his head now, a memorial to futility.

But he also had the opportunity to destroy Kathra Omezi, somehow. To fulfill that dream that had driven not only Amirin, but also himself.

If the Mbaysey were successful in fleeing Sept law, others would be emboldened. If they instead saw that no depth of light-years might protect them from Sept justice, they would remain behind, unwilling, perhaps, to risk their culture and existence.

Certainly, the Mbaysey would be erased from history, except as an example. A warning to future generations of either the Sept, or the thing that he would help Amirin Pasdar create.

Hadi found peace within himself. The chef would need to be destroyed, but his allies would be ready to depart at that moment. He would need them to transform him, somehow, into the thing that could continue the quest to destroy the Mbaysey afterwards.

It cannot be undone, Hadi Rostami, they reminded him.

Truth, but he would have seven years to use such power to change the galaxy. Longer if a scientist could figure out how it was done and replicate it.

They cannot. We will assure that no successor to Urid-Varg ever rises, even as we assist you now.

He nodded, withholding judgment until he emerged from whatever chrysalis was about to engulf him.

He felt the four minds focus on him now, probing deeper than they ever had.

Hadi screamed in mind-ending agony.

FORTY-ONE

Kathra was reminded today of Morgan, the Trademaster In Residence at Kanus, but only as a scale against which to compare, with Crence Miray at the other end.

Physically, Wyll Koobitz was an unimpressive Anndaing. He lacked that physical presence that Crence had and Morgan did not, but possessed something else instead. A charisma, perhaps, that calm determination that would make him stand out in any crowd of sharks, even bigger ones.

His skin wasn't as dark as Crence's, but his eyes were brighter, seated across the table in a dark green jacket and lighter green shirt. The shark on his left, Obaj Gendrah, had a similar look and fashion, even a similarity about his person. They might look like brothers, but Wyll was the elder, and Obaj was obviously the younger.

Kathra had brought Stina Carte, Spectre Sixteen, with her today. All of the comitatus was one, but Stina was the only *Anglo* currently serving, a brunette with straight hair and skin so golden it was almost painful to look at.

The green eyes probably made her appear like only a

related alien species, if you had only known the Africans from Tazo ere now. Certainly, she was not that different from A'Alhakoth, save in height and round pupils.

It was a quiet statement for Wyll.

See how many species, how many cultures might rally to my flag?

She was sure he'd read reports of her arrival and activities at Kanus before she came here.

Kathra sipped her tea and enjoyed a scone that Daniel might have made, if he was stuck in an alien marketplace at dawn and was expecting hungry comitatus women to descend on him soon.

But it was also tasty. Daniel had taught someone how to mix these ingredients and make the result palatable to both human and Anndaing.

Small talk had been general and vague, following Anndaing cultural mores that sought to chat for politeness's sake before getting down to the serious business.

They almost reminded her of the Sept in that, except for the parts that she actually liked.

Koobitz put his mug of tea down and studied her now. The tea was also a human thing. Kathra found it bland and a little bitter, but Wyll Koobitz had explained that Joane had drank it thus and proclaimed it acceptable.

Kathra could see teasing that woman later about how Anndaing culture was going to adjust to one woman's odd indulgences.

"It is my hope that Daniel and Joane will return soon," the shark said simply. "Flight times are always iffy, and I don't know how long they planned to be at their destination, but they could have been back as early as yesterday."

"Where are they, Ambassador?" Kathra asked bluntly.

She had no proof that they hadn't been killed at some point, despite the tea and scones.

Koobitz turned deadly serious. She'd been around plenty of Anndaing over the last few weeks to understand the change that came into his eyes and the set of his hammer.

He turned to Gendrah and fixed that shark with a terrible glare.

Kathra hadn't pried too much, but she had the impression that the younger cousin reported to a different member of the Board of Directors from Koobitz, making him something of a friendly spy, perhaps sent here to make sure that Koobitz stayed within bounds.

Gendrah nodded, whatever message passed between the two in that look.

"We have sent Daniel and Joane to a secret naval repository, Commander," he said quietly.

"Why?"

"Daniel was inquiring about the Ovanii," Koobitz continued, perhaps a shade uncomfortable. "Their history as wanderers, much like the Mbaysey. Their culture. Their memory, if you will."

"Yes," she agreed. "He found a book at Thrabo and translated it, placing it roughly in this sector of space, but thousands of years ago, if he did the math correctly."

"He did, although how such a thing got to the Free Worlds is probably an epic tale unto itself," Koobitz nodded. "My best guess, based on what Daniel told us, is that an Ovanii ship escaped at the end and ended up closer to your sectors eventually."

"Escaped?" Kathra perked up and stared at this diplomat with shark teeth.

"The Ovanii threatened the entire Anndaing in their time," he replied succinctly. "Thousands of warships traveling in roving packs. Raiders. Marauders. Vikings, to use the term Daniel had for them. It was sufficient threat for the Merchants Guild to summon our fleets together."

"Was it now?" Kathra asked, tilting her head a little to study his body language. She didn't have Daniel's tools, nor his experience with so many members of the species as he would have had flying here, but she was the Commander of the Mbaysey.

She had other experience.

"The *Call to Armada* resulted in a fleet sufficient to break the Ovanii as a people, Kathra Omezi," he said flatly, possibly threatening her and the Tribal Squadron, but doing so in a polite-enough manner. "When they surrendered, as an alternative to being annihilated as a species, we took all of their ships and stored them against future need."

"What happened to the Ovanii afterwards?" Kathra asked.

"We set them down on worlds well outside of our current colonies, dropped them to the early metals age, and watched them like terrible angels from above for a few centuries," he replied, eyes bulging a little to focus on her.

That much body language she understood. Stina was an afterthought, as was Gendrah. This was just the two of them.

"And after a few centuries?" Kathra asked.

"They reverted into true barbarism, as we had expected," Koobitz answered. "On most of their worlds the population simply died out as they fought each other rather than outsiders. On others, they forgot everything except legends of coming from the sky. They had forgotten us, so we left them in peace."

"Are they still there, or have they died out now?" Kathra leaned forward and placed both elbows on the table.

Koobitz smiled genuinely now. It had an edge of embarrassment and perhaps pain to it.

"We decided to send a ship to find out, when Daniel arrived," he said. "That vessel is not scheduled to return for another seventeen days at this point. That's how far away we settled the Ovanii when we decided to accept their parole."

"Why did you not scatter them onto your own worlds and absorb them?" Kathra turned and stared at Gendrah now, including him in something that might be classified as a crime against an entire species, depending on how one approached the ethics.

"The ancient records are unclear," Gendrah spoke up now. "We think that they rejected such an option as an affront to their warrior culture, and chose a different path instead."

"Barbaric continuity instead of passive absorption into the superior culture?" Kathra focused some of her ire on the two sharks. "Has Daniel told you about Tazo?"

Koobitz actually licked his lips before speaking, which was a mannerism she hadn't seen in one of the Anndaing before now.

How close to some Anndaing cultural nightmare were the Mbaysey, then? How much did the Tribal Squadron bring back unpleasant memories of the very Ovanii Daniel had stumbled across and wanted to research?

"Joane actually was the one who spoke of Tazo, Commander," Koobitz said quietly after a moment. "She gave us an abbreviated history of the Mbaysey, including the ClanStars and the escape that culminated in Daniel joining you originally, plus a highly-sanitized explanation of what has happened since you encountered the being known as Urid-Varg."

"Did Daniel tell you that I killed that *salaud* myself?"

"Yes." Koobitz was wary now. "But not until after it had modified Daniel in ways he has not explained, except that he speaks and reads many dead languages that humans should have never encountered."

"Urid-Varg is destroyed," Kathra announced flatly. "Daniel is incapable of becoming him."

"How can you be sure?" Gendrah asked now, some delicate emotion under his tones that she could not identify. Fear perhaps? Or wonder? "What has he done that gives you the confidence that another Destroyer can never rise in his place?"

"Submitted himself, body and soul, to the comitatus," Kathra said. "To me."

She could not give them the truth, lest some fool of a shark decide to try for the gem of which they were hopefully still ignorant. That just might trigger the exact, violent confrontation that they seemed to fear lay just under these polite words.

She had wondered why Koobitz required a second before now. The sharks had enough of the truth to be nervous, but not enough to be reassured.

"All of my women watch him like hawks, gentlemen," Kathra continued, gesturing to Stina. "Any deviation on his part will result in his death. He knows that. Accepts it. That truth has actually kept him sane, after what Urid-Varg did to him, as Daniel Lémieux is no longer truly human, as you or I understand such a thing."

"Tell me about the Sept," Koobitz suddenly spoke up, pivoting the conversation. "Why should we fear them? What will they do when they discover the Anndaing?"

"The Axial Megacannon on the bow of a Septagon can destroy cities on the surface of a planet from low orbit," Kathra said. "I have seen the results when someone angered the Sept enough to be made an example of. That is one of the reasons Yagazie decided to remove the Mbaysey from the reservation on Tazo when she won our freedom from Sept slavery."

Kathra paused to take a breath, before what erupted from her mouth turned to acidic fire.

"I could have brought Erin with me, but chose Stina. Erin has a barcode tattooed on her right cheek, done in solidarity with her grandmother," she continued, tapping her cheek to show the place. "Ezinne had that mark because she was *property*. Not a person. A *thing* that a Sept nobleman *owned*."

Both sharks recoiled a little now from the ferocity of her words. The anger in her voice. The fire no doubt sparking in her eyes.

"We knew that our freedom was a temporary thing," Kathra said. "A piece of paper from a court that would only last until the powerful ones who lost *property* found a way to overturn it. Or subvert it. We fled them. They pursued. Even beyond their own borders. The Sept eventually invaded Free Worlds space with a Septagon, trying to destroy me as an example to any other people who wanted to be free. They will come here eventually. You are not even humanoid enough to rate under their laws, Anndaing merchants. Merely intelligent animals, much like the Vida or Atter. The Se'uh'pal will continue to serve them as alien traders, because the Se'uh'pal are apolitical creatures, only interested in profit and loss. Their language does not include a word for *morality*. They use Spacer when they have to discuss such an alien concept."

Kathra leaned back now, aware that she had probably looked like she was about to come across the table at those two. Unintentionally, but body language across species was always a complicated thing to understand. Especially as heated as she had gotten.

"So if they came, you would fight them?" Koobitz asked, his voice as subdued as his hammers now.

"One of the reasons we wanted to visit Kanus first,

instead of proceeding to Ogrorspoxu, was to determine its feasibility as a base from which the squadron might explore, while generally being safe from piracy and other problems, gentlemen," Kathra answered. "That would free *SeekerStar* up to perhaps range into Free Worlds space and beyond, looking for the bases we already know that the Sept must have built, to have delivered a Septagon to Tavle Jocia."

"What would you do to such bases?" Gendrah leaned forward now, his elbows on the table in a manner almost identical to what she had done.

"Destroy them," Kathra said simply. "Without such things, the Sept are greatly curtailed, because of the logistics necessary to feed four hundred thousand crew."

"Four hundred thousand?" Gendrah gasped.

"Three hundred on the Septagon itself," Kathra nodded. "Another hundred thousand on the Patrols they bring, plus the ships that would be necessary just to haul food around. And that is only one Septagon squadron. They have many."

Koobitz started to say something, but Kathra heard her name being spoken.

She cocked her head and waved the shark to silence as she focused her mind on that sound.

Except it wasn't a sound. Nobody in here had said her name. It was a mental touch, much like Daniel did, but this wasn't Daniel.

It was alien. The colors were wrong. The flavors were off. Even the air tasted differently.

Kathra came back to herself and turned back to Wyll Koobitz. She pulled out a comm and pressed the signal to contact *SeekerStar*.

Koobitz had leaned back, in a body language she could only classify as *concerned*.

"Whatever defensive systems you have aboard this

station, I suggest you activate them right now," she said simply.

Gendrah had a look of confusion, but Koobitz nodded. He reached into a pocket inside his jacket and pulled out a device remarkably similar to the one in her hand. Physics was physics, and Anndaing hands were similar enough to human ones for an engineer designing a tool.

"Commander?" Ife was on the line, sounding breathless, like she had run from the washroom to take this call.

"Sound the alert," Kathra ordered the woman. "Prepare for combat immediately. Ife, you will take command of *SeekerStar* until I can return. Do not allow Erin to launch *The Haunt* unless you yourself think it appropriate, but do not spend time trying to get me to answer questions, because I will know less than you do and I am not sure how quickly I can rejoin you."

"Understood," Ife said. In the background, Kathra could hear the alert sirens begin to sound. "What has happened?"

"The Ishtan have found us," Kathra said. "Assume the Sept are with them."

She cut the line and focused on Ambassador Koobitz. He had turned sallow, but was regaining his color as she watched.

"When this emergency is done, I will have questions," he said simply.

"You may not like the answers," Kathra replied.

"I am aware of that, Commander," he said. "But if your enemies have come this far to attack you, they may have just become my enemies as well."

They nodded at each other, the promise of a future reckoning put off for now.

"Now, can we help you get back to your ship?" he continued.

"No," Kathra decided, rising and prompting the other

three to join her. "The battlefield will be too dangerous for me shortly, as I came in a SkyCamel and not a Spectre. Plus, I make a promise to a dangerous, old woman, back at Kanus."

"What was that promise, Commander?" Gendrah asked, confused.

"To outlive all of you."

FORTY-TWO

Daniel still wasn't sure how he felt about everything he had learned at the boneyard, but he at least had more answers than before. If the questions had also multiplied madly, at least that was a predictable thing.

None of the problems would be his to solve. Kathra would be in charge, as was appropriate. He was just her chef.

They hadn't exactly taken their time returning to Ogrorspoxu, but Tragee had perhaps plotted his various jumps with less precision, zig-zagging as he did, just so nobody seeing them suddenly appear might be able to guess their origins.

The Merchants Bank was deadly serious about keeping the secrecy of that world tightly contained.

The had hit the farthest navigable edges of Ogrorspoxu's system with the previous jump. Stayed there long enough for Daniel to fix everyone one last meal as a group, before whatever was going to happen when he returned to meet Wyll.

Much would have changed, probably on both sides of the equation.

Seeing that golden-red star faint in the distance out the bridge window now just reinforced all that.

Before, all of this had been merely an academic exercise. Locate another long-lost species, like the K'bari, and learn their story. He had mused with several of the women of the comitatus about whether a star-traveling people could ever actually go extinct. Several of them were educated enough, sharp enough to have strong opinions on the topic, as one would expect from a tribe of warriors intent on doing the same thing.

Nobody knew, but the consensus was that you could thin yourselves out too far to maintain viability. *SeekerStar* and all the other vessels kept sperm banks as repositories for exactly that reason. More than sixty-three hundred women, but only fifteen hundred men, plus donations acquired over time at various stops.

Still, plenty to keep the tribe intact for a time. Even a single ClanStar, if it got separated from the others, could maintain the tribe for generations with careful planning.

Raja was studying him as Tragee prepared the last jump. Joane had found a seat off to one side, but he was too keyed up to sit.

"So now what?" she asked.

And that was the crux of it.

"That depends on your boss," Daniel said. "And his bosses."

"You think they will deal?" she asked.

"He would not have allowed us to even know that such a place existed, if they weren't close to a deal in their own hammers," Daniel said. "The question is what they will want from us in exchange, and whether Kathra will be willing to pay that price."

Raja nodded. They were all operating above their pay grade right now. Playing with the gods, as it were, except that

Daniel already contained a mad god within him. Only Joane knew that truth.

"You folks ready?" Tragee asked, tilted his head to bring a withering right eye upon them.

Daniel almost expected him to roll that eye, but Tragee was like that. All he wanted to do was fly. Politics was for folks with too much time on their hands and not enough stars.

"Jump," Raja said simply. "We'll be home soon and the adventure will be over, Tragee."

"Thank the goddess," he said as he triggered the drives.

They rode in a frozen tableau for a few minutes as they dropped down close enough to Ogrorspoxu to come under terminal flight controls. You had to have a comm lag under five seconds to talk meaningfully, anyway.

Windrunner dropped back into space and settled down to begin maneuvering.

"Hey, that's odd," Tragee said absently.

Something about his tone had Daniel's head completely around and Joane up out of her seat before the echo died.

"What?" Daniel demanded harshly.

A finger went out and touched the screen between the two seats.

"*SeekerStar*, if I'm reading this correctly," he said, turning his hammer to look up at Daniel. "Yours?"

Daniel looked at the list of ships close to the station.

Sure enough, *SeekerStar*. They were still too far away to see anything but a dot of light if they looked in the right direction, though.

"Can we hail them?" Joane asked.

"I'll handle it, Tragee," Raja said. "You talk to the station."

Windrunner jarred. It was like an earthquake running through the plates of the ship, plus a sound like someone had dropped a stack of ceramic plates on the floor. Daniel had to grip the back of the pilot's seat to avoid being thrown to the deck.

"What?" he managed.

"Oh, shit, we're taking fire from somewhere!" Raja cried. She flipped a switch and her screen changed. "Someone's got a targeting lock of some kind on us, but it's nothing like I've ever seen before."

"Show me," Joane commanded, her voice suddenly deep and angry. She glanced at Daniel, but he was more than willing to let her handle things.

Raja flipped more switches as the vessel rocked a second and third time.

Ranging fire, growing more accurately, although Daniel had no idea how he knew such a thing.

One of his ghosts, he supposed.

"*SeptStar*?" Raja asked, blankly. "What does that mean?"

On the screen, Daniel could see a smaller, sleeker version of *SeekerStar*, charging out of the darkness. It had the same cylindrical shape, with a smaller ring around the outside and a thicker torso. Guns at both ends. Turrets around the rim. Those were the ones hammering the hull of *Windrunner*.

Daniel knew what would happen when the bow cannons finally found them.

"Evasive maneuvering!" Joane yelled sharply. "NOW! All engines open. Pitch, roll, and yaw, Tragee, if you want to live. Do we have guns?"

"What?" Raja seemed lost.

Daniel staggered to a nearby seat and planted himself. There was little he could do, but if he was strapped in, it was possible to step outside the vessel and see what was happening from an alien perspective.

"DO YOU HAVE GUNS?!?" Joane snarled.

"Yes," Raja replied meekly.

"Take command of the guns and return fire," Joane ordered. "What is the most armored section of this vessel?"

"The bridge," Tragee answered, hands dancing across keys as Raja seemed paralyzed.

"Order Bipahl and Kayna up here then," Joane took charge. "Better they be safe with us if the ship gets broken in two."

Daniel finished strapping the harness around his body and took a deep breath.

Time to fight them on terms they understood.

FORTY-THREE

Hadi still had a hard time seeing only the physical world, as he now had some bizarre extra sense that was not bounded by the walls and steel of *SeptStar* around him. Perhaps only his imagination saved him.

Fortunately, he was a bureaucrat, and not an artist. That would keep him closer to sane.

SeptStar had slipped quietly into this system, cutting across the arc of a chord while chasing the chef across the galaxy, when it became obvious he was returning here to meet Kathra Omezi.

She was here. Hadi could see her, in ways that were not immediately obvious even to himself.

Hadi somehow knew that she was aboard that massive station in close orbit, even as her vessel lurked nearby. Close, but well away from where today's action would be.

The chef was closer. And the Ishtan had led him to the man. He was their target anyway.

Somehow, they were in his mind now, even though he was on the bridge of *SeptStar* in zero gravity, rather than out on the ring where his office was, or their quarters. Four of them, wrapped around him like furry, pink tentacles.

They had placed a destination in his mind. Hadi had relayed it to the pilot seated nearby. *SeptStar* had jumped to those coordinates from the edge of the darkness, almost in perfect synchronicity with his target.

Had they been more accurate, he could have landed exactly behind them, in the perfect kill zone for the bow guns.

A Septagon was designed to kill things that way. Hadi had commanded one of the great ones. As it was, he was atop the little ship almost as soon as they arrived.

"Open fire as you bear," Hadi ordered his gun commander as they locked onto the vessel.

The thing was alien. Barely a third of the size of one of his Patrol vessels from the old squadron, yet it was flat, as though it had gravity field inducers under the decks.

Were the generators so small that the ship was at one third gravity at all times? Or had the aliens developed something better? More efficient? Smaller?

The Ishtan had not crossed this sector of space in their deathless quest for Urid-Varg, so they had no explanation for the people he could see, or the thousands of vessels plying this system around him.

On *SeptStar's* rim, three of the guns began to hammer at the vessel bearing Lémieux. The range was long but not impossible for them. The Ram Cannons on the bow would require the ship to come about if he wanted to hit them, though.

That was next.

"Pilot, ride the gyros hard," Hadi said loudly. "Bring us about to engage and chase."

"Aye, sir," the man responded without looking up.

Hadi had originally picked this crew for Amirin to

command, selecting the best he had from all his officers and men on *Vorgash*. All men he trusted. They would give their all for him today.

"All hands, stand by for maneuvers," the pilot announced on the intercom.

If you weren't strapped down by now, you had no business in this navy, so any injuries you sustained would just be proof of that.

If he was really upset, Hadi could always order such a fool put into a lifepod and fired into an alien system as the ultimate punishment. He had no doubts that the locals would either capture such a worthless specimen or eat them.

Either way, it would no longer be his problem.

SeptStar rattled heavily.

"Enemy vessel is returning fire," the gunner said. "Weapons better than particle cannons, from the scan. Not as powerful as the Ram Cannon."

Good enough. Particle cannons could damage the ship, but not badly, unless he just sat there for an hour and let them. Ram Cannons on the station would be too far away to even hit *SeptStar*, so he would be safe. Only a vessel maneuvering to close with him now would be someone to worry about.

SeptStar's ring continued to turn, bringing new turrets to bear and allowing the old ones time to cool and recharge. He could sustain a killing fire all day without risking weapons being damaged from overuse.

Downrange, his target finally began to move, pivoting like a worm on a hook trying to escape a fish. It wouldn't do him much good as *SeptStar* had the wind on him, poised above and behind the tinier vessel. Anything the chef did now would just be telegraphed to *SeptStar*'s gunners and pilot, allowing Hadi to respond just as quickly.

His only chance lay in flight, and the possibility that he

might be able to outrun *SeptStar*'s valence drives enough to get away.

Every second he remained in this system was just one more closer to his own destruction.

Better, even in flight he could not escape, no matter how hard he tried, as Hadi and the Ishtan guiding him could find him, every single time he thought to stop and catch his breath.

I have you now.

A heavier impact jarred the entire hull. The little popguns on the alien had been astonishingly accurate, but weren't heavy enough to damage *SeptStar*'s armor.

This was the thump of something larger.

"Who's firing on us?" he demanded, looking around.

"Contact," the scanner officer called out without looking up from his screen. "I have *SeekerStar* on an intercept course. Repeat, *SeekerStar* intercepting."

"Have they launched?" Hadi asked hungrily.

SeptStar had been specifically designed to crush Omezi's squadron of one-woman craft in battle, using an entire array of lighter turrets on the rim and main hull. None were large enough to even threaten the cook, but a significant portion of Omezi's power relied on those antique Spectres. Kill those and he went a long ways toward killing her power.

"Negative on secondary launch, sir," came the answer. "Only the warship."

Damn her anyway.

Hadi had assumed that it would take Omezi time to return to her warship before it could engage. *SeptStar* was smaller and a little lighter. He could run her down as well as the chef, or outrun her through jump, but if he did that now, he would lose the surprise he had on the chef, and the ability for a quick kill.

SeekerStar had not waited for Omezi to return, but moved immediately to fight him.

"Engage *SeekerStar* with the aft battery only," he ordered. "Keep the rim turrets forward. Fire the bow Ram Cannons as soon as they have arc."

"Yes, sir," the various voices rang back in harmony.

His trap had just been reversed, but he had time to kill the chef yet before he and *SeptStar* fled. He could always return for Omezi later, even if the Ishtan decided that they were done with Lémieux destroyed.

They had indeed modified him into something more than human, though perhaps less than a god.

But he would visit his terrible wrath upon everyone before he was done.

FORTY-FOUR

IFEDIMMA OGU HAD SEEN MUCH in her forty years. She still had memories of Tazo as a girl, before Yagazie had finally gotten them all into space. And Ife had served Kathra faithfully since the day an assassin's bullet promoted the youngster to command, far earlier than she had ever expected.

Ife was not comitatus. She understood the line drawn between the women who were sworn as Kathra's personal troops and the rest of them that merely served. That Ife was generally Kathra's second in command among the ship's crew just placed her first behind all the comitatus.

At least until today.

Kathra had warned the comitatus that change was coming. And done it with Ife in their dining hall with them. None of the women had acted surprised, and many had welcomed her warmly, even as she was more than a decade older than any of the rest of them.

But the Sept had arrived.

Ife's primary job was sensors and communications. She

saw the ship drop out of jump, just one of many that were registered in her subconscious.

Until a second ship came out behind it firing.

This one was larger, almost like a more compact version of *SeekerStar* or *WinterStar*, built along those same lines anyway, so that it was alien among all the local craft.

Kathra had already called and told her to rouse the ship, following some unknown instinct that warned her.

Obioma was flying them into battle. Ngozi was programming the guns. Adanne was aft, mothering her engines like chicks. Ife had already warned everyone that she would be pushing them all as far as they could go.

Possibly breaking them.

Anything to protect Kathra. And Daniel, too, if that was him on the smaller vessel, that little Cargo-2 currently being bombarded by the intruder.

"Ife, I have the range," Ngozi called from above her, all of the seats having been ripped out and installed on the rim, instead of being awkwardly placed on a level.

Ife took one last look at the scan of the ship. The beacon identified it as *SeptStar*, in case she had any doubts.

As if she would go after pirates with any less ferocity.

Isaev must have built that ship for them. It had identical lines to *SeekerStar* in so many ways, only smaller. That would make it faster on the valence drives fleeing or chasing. And she could see three times as many point defense batteries as *SeekerStar* had.

Someone was laying a trap for The Haunt, *you filthy* salauds.

"Erin, this is Ife," she called into the squadron circuit.

"We're ready to launch," Erin replied with an angry growl.

All Spectre lights already showed green. How many women had been just sitting in the watchroom, waiting for the alarm to go off? Of course, Kathra was away, so the comitatus was prepared to go rescue her at a moment's notice.

"Stand down on launch, Erin," Ife decided, not even taking a moment to revel that she could give that order today. "The target is an escort with plenty of guns to annihilate you if you close."

Ife heard the brief angry squawk that emerged before Erin jammed her teeth together.

Ife was in command today.

May the Goddess have mercy on all their souls.

"Ife?" Ngozi repeated, as if she had missed it the first time.

"Stand by, Ngozi," she said.

In her mind, Ife could see the dots turn into vector lines. If *SeptStar* was built like *SeekerStar*, he had a gun turret located dead center between the four engine wells. The ship had the wrong facing to engage, but that would change if this turned into a running chase.

"Obioma, bring us up and flare the bow to the left," Ife ordered. "Keep us just enough on line to hit him with the Ram Cannons."

Obioma actually turned and looked at her like she had lost her mind, but Ife smiled.

Command. She suddenly had a better understanding of how Kathra had to deal with all the headstrong women of the comitatus, at the same time she routinely butted heads with the clan leaders.

"Rear cannons on *SeptStar*," Ife said, instead of snapping at the woman.

A light came on in Obioma's eyes.

"*Salaud*," she muttered under her breath and began stabbing buttons.

"Ngozi, adjust your firing arcs," Ife said.

These women trained for this religiously, but none of the Mbaysey Tribal Squadron had ever been in a pitched battle, other than *WinterStar's* death at the hands of *Vorgash*.

Still, they reacted quickly and smoothly. Ife leaned back and studied the vectors again.

SeptStar would be chasing Daniel, but if *SeekerStar* moved off his stern, he either had to turn to engage the bigger ship's guns, or allow Ngozi to pound on *SeptStar* without response.

Which enemy do you wish to fight, because you cannot get us both, connard?

Ife felt the great ship shift as the gyros took hold. Out on the rim, everyone would be aboard a small ship as a massive wake passed under the keel.

Ife remembered harbors and wakes from her youth.

"Fire, Ngozi," Ife ordered.

She had the stern. *SeptStar* was off their line and also turning on his gyros to line up on Daniel, moving his rear Ram Cannons even farther out of the way to shoot back.

Ife had no idea how long it might take an Anndaing merchant to recharge everything for a second jump away from trouble. She just needed to distract this *salaud* long enough to protect Daniel, and maybe teach this Sept *connard* not to act like a pirate in someone else's front yard.

At least the little Cargo-2 was firing back with everything he had, but those were just particle cannons. Little, like a slap, rather than a fist or an elbow to the face.

That was Ife's job.

"Firing," Ngozi stabbed a button on her screen.

The beam was a strobe of light emerging from just below them and fluorescing across solar wind in an instant.

On her scanners, Ife watched the impact spall chunks and plasma off the rim of *SeptStar*.

Good, Ngozi had understood who their enemy was. Or

at least what. The important equipment would be down in the central hull, if this ship had also been made in Isaev's yard. Armored and protected by bulkheads and depth.

Cannons were out on the rim, but that wasn't why you fired into the ring. Damage there caused the ring to jam, throwing off everything else. *WinterStar* had actually shed pieces when the ring didn't survive under the abuse from *Vorgash*, according to the stories Ife had heard.

In either case, a little damage out there could cause the entire vessel trouble.

Ife had been flying ships of this design for decades. She understood the weak points probably better than anyone in the solar system right now, which was why Kathra had put her here.

And then placed her in command.

"Up your rate of fire," Ife ordered. "Burn out the guns if you have to. We are on home turf for repairs and they are not. Worst case, we flee to Kanus for repairs. Punish them, Ngozi. We only have to fight once and not for long."

The woman stared at her with the whites of her eyes visible, but that was understandable. This ship was as much her baby as it was Ife's.

"It is a tool, Ngozi," Ife continued. "Use it like a hammer. We can buy another hammer tomorrow, but we have to win and do it right now."

Ngozi nodded and pressed several other buttons.

On her board, Ife saw all the rim turrets open up. They could not do much at this range, but anything might be the straw to break this camel's back.

It was good.

Now she just had to protect Daniel.

And kill this Sept *connard*.

FORTY-FIVE

Daniel left his body behind and extended his mind outwards. Losing the Star Turtle had cost him power and range, but not so much that he could not do this.

Windrunner had begun to move, but it was a freighter, not a Spectre. They were moving on a vector, and Tragee had to flip the ship around and open the engines to move them to a different line.

If they survived, killing all that motion would take a while, but they had to survive first. That was Raja's job. And Joane's.

Daniel stretched out to *SeptStar*.

It felt like *SeekerStar*, when he was out flying with Kathra. That weird mix of minds split evenly between the hub and rim. He presumed the name meant it had been made by Isaev, as that *salaud* was all about money.

Daniel could see *Vorgash* returning to Tavle Jocia and camping while they did the same thing that Kathra had done. And they could afford to build something like that.

He assumed the Ishtan had led them here. There was no other way that ship, those people, could have found him.

Iruoma had killed two of them, leaving only four.

Even in his reduced state, he could hold four of their minds at bay.

Except there weren't four. Or rather, there were. Four Ishtan. And *something.*

What?

They presented as a single entity, but Daniel could see the swirls of a human mind in there, like a cake he had baked with chocolate and white wrapped around themselves.

No. The human part was at the center, and four Ishtan minds were protecting it.

Him.

The range was far too great to do anything but watch, but Daniel could also taunt them. Perhaps he might even distract them while the others escaped.

Plus, in the distance, he could see the warm home nest of *SeekerStar* suddenly appear.

Kathra had come.

Good.

Except he didn't smell her presence. Erin and the others, yes. But the brightest mind he saw was Ife.

How joyous!

She looked like Erin or Kathra from here, focused down with a diamond intensity like the finest chefs achieved when they pulled the masterpiece from the oven.

Daniel did not try to send her even a warm feeling. He turned all his rage on the imperials.

Four Ishtan minds, wrapped around a human like arms. What did that mean? None of the other humans on that ship even registered to Daniel, except as a background flavor. A hint of nutmeg mixed with salt, like an amateur looking for exotic in the kitchen.

The human noticed him now. It was like a sleeper suddenly stopped snoring and the eyes opened.

Daniel thought a rude gesture in his direction, watched it impact.

You will die now, the imperial said.

He had a name, even. Hadi Rostami. It didn't mean anything to Daniel, except that the four Ishtan were one, without any name other than Ishtan. They had long since lost any individual identity, if they ever had one. His memories of their world did not suggest such a thing.

You wish to try me, silly human? Daniel pulsed back at the man. *Can you even make a soufflé?*

It didn't make any sense. It didn't have to. That was one of the ritual insults chefs exchanged when they were feeling feisty, followed by a bake-off to determine who had the better *fu*.

Such wars were often as tense as chop socky movie climax battles, before they ended.

This fool was just a sailor.

You will join Urid-Varg in death, Rostami snarled across the gap.

I already have, human, Daniel snarled back, just trying to make the man twitch. *Do you think death with protect you from me?*

Gods, this was silly. Around them, the world was a firefight between three spaceships, racing madly away from Ogrorspoxu and exchanging fire.

He lies, the four Ishtan broke in like a Greek chorus now.

The rest of your race calls you from the grave, Ishtan, Daniel turned his rage on them, mocking them as only a French chef could. *Can you not hear them? It would be better for everyone if you killed yourselves and stopped trying to control the galaxy. Your evil is greater than anything I have ever done.*

That blow seemed to strike a soft spot, but he doubted they even knew what a soufflé was in the first place, let alone how they might craft one to win in a kitchen.

He watched them turn inwards for a moment, as if ignoring Rostami to consult one another so that they could determine whether Daniel Lémieux really was full of shit, rather than an oracle proclaiming the future.

Somedays, it was hard to tell those sorts of things apart.

Around him, he felt *Windrunner* rattle as the smaller guns continued to hammer the hull. He felt the surge as Tragee got the engines fully on-line and the ship began to accelerate, but this was a freighter, not a warship. He had no doubts that *SeptStar* could run them down eventually.

Rostami's mind started getting closer and Daniel understood that Tragee had pulled a fast one. Instead of racing away, he had spun the ship almost end for end and was accelerating the other way. Or rather, killing all forward momentum as hard and fast as the engines could, and forcing *SeptStar* to either pick a single jousting pass to kill them, or do the same.

With Ife and *SeekerStar* coming for them.

Daniel didn't understand naval warfare, but he didn't have to. Raja and Joane were quietly chattering back and forth with ideas as his body listened.

For all her nerdiness, Joane was still comitatus, a mighty warrior with a pistol on her hip. A woman absolutely fearless.

You failed, Rostami, Daniel mocked the man with his sharpest tone, hoping it wasn't about to be proven a lie as the closing range let *SeptStar* kill them and flee Ife.

The man fixed harsh, angry eyes at Daniel across the space. That was at least as good a description as anything. Rostami wasn't human anymore. The Ishtan had done something to him. Not as great or powerful as the gem, but more than anybody else in Daniel's amazing memory.

And then Rostami screamed in an agony so intense that Daniel collapsed back into his body.

FORTY-SIX

DAMN THEM, what were they doing?

Hadi hadn't detected any communications linking the two vessels he was engaging, but both had reacted in perfect synchronicity, with *SeptStar* trapped between them. The alien freighter had gone into turnover, not pointed directly at *SeptStar*, but slowing so abruptly that he would overshoot them unless he either got close enough to ram them, or tried the same maneuver with *SeptStar*.

That would be suicide with *SeekerStar* coming up his stern. He would come to a dead rest exactly in front of Omezi's flagship, where the Ram Cannons might cut him in two.

Worse, *SeekerStar* had moved to a flank in such a way that he could either bring his bow guns to bear on the alien, or his stern guns onto *SeekerStar*. Not both.

Damn you, Omezi. You should not be this good.

He howled in his mind, where his crew could not hear. Nobody could, but the aliens.

Another alien presence continued to mock him, but Hadi had given up speaking to the chef. He understood the man better now. Saw how Urid-Varg must have changed him in order to do the things he did.

It would not help Hadi kill him, because the chef had far more power at his command, but Hadi could chase him and Omezi now.

And he owed that *Rabic* fool much pain.

You failed, Rostami, Daniel Lémieux said across the space separating them.

Hadi just snarled wordlessly back at the man. Around him, *SeptStar* continued to rattle as *SeekerStar* began to score hits commensurate with the alien gunner.

At least the freighter was starting to come apart under the pounding. Pieces of hull and armor were beginning to flake off under the impact of his own particle cannons.

Soon enough, he could flee the scene, having killed one of his foes and leaving the second for another day.

SeptStar jolted so hard that Hadi was thrown against his restraints. There would be exquisite bruising tomorrow.

He started to speak and someone drove a white-hot dagger directly into his mind.

Hadi could only scream mindlessly as someone died.

FORTY-SEVEN

"Cut *SeptStar* off," Ife ordered Obioma as Daniel's courier came around hard and started pushing her engines.

She could see what that pilot was doing. Better, *SeptStar* had two choices now. He could try for the same maneuver in a much more fragile ship, with her bearing down fast and all her guns ready to hammer him, or he could declare failure and just accelerate, allowing Daniel and *SeekerStar* both to escape.

"Ram Cannons ranging now," Ngozi called. "Locked and firing."

That first hit jarred *SeptStar* far worse than any of the others. Ngozi had finally developed the feel for firing in motion. Ife could see the need to practice under more realistic combat situations in the future, especially if the Sept had just gone from an occasional pain in the ass to stalking them in the high grass for an ambush.

Panthers in trees on a dark night.

Ife snarled back at that *connard* in charge over there.

"Whoa, something just broke," Obioma said, staring at

her screen as she tried to out-guess the other pilot. "*SeptStar* seems like she's drifting rather than maneuvering."

"Hit them again, Ngozi," Ife yelled. "Everything you have, pour it into them now. That same spot on the rim, if you can. The central hull if you cannot. We must have found a soft corner."

Ife watched the two women react and plot. Daniel's ship also seemed to understand, as all three of the little popguns on it opened up at the same time, rather than pulsing sequentially as they had.

What was there on the rim of *SeptStar* that would cause such a problem? Surely, they hadn't put their bridge in such a place. If they had mirrored the design that closely elsewhere, the bridge was above and behind the main guns forward, where they could spot while flying, but keep the Ram Cannons central.

That section of *SeekerStar* was generally quarters for flight crew. *SeptStar* hadn't launched anything in this battle, but he also didn't look like a carrier. *SeekerStar*'s primary striking power was in the twenty-plus Spectres Kathra could send after a pirate ship.

"Keep pounding," Ife said absently.

She had only been planning on chasing the ship off so that Daniel could escape, but if she had just hurt him, Ngozi needed to get a knife into the gap again and again.

Could they actually score a kill today?

The Mbaysey owed a mighty debt for *WinterStar*, even though nobody had been killed when the ship died. Kathra had still lost her first flagship, and the first casualty of what would turn into a greater war based on today.

SeptStar was their answer to get back at Kathra. Ife could see where it would be a problem for *SeekerStar* and *The Haunt*. Many small guns to kill Spectres. Lighter vessel, so it could outrun them through valence space, which was how the Mbaysey had always managed to escape Patrols and that Septagon in the past.

Something had gone wrong over there, though.

"Okay, they've fixed it, whatever it was," Obioma said. "Ship's under control again."

"Hit their rear turrets, Ngozi," Ife said. "Misses might damage the engines."

"On it," the woman growled. There was almost a note of triumph in her voice.

Like maybe it was possible to take on a Sept warship and not just survive, but *win*?

The Mbaysey had never once won. They had only endured, time and again fleeing deeper and deeper into darkness to escape.

Even Kanus and Ogrorspoxu hadn't been far enough to escape those *salauds*. Or this *connard*.

"Is he coming about?" Ife asked, not trusting her own screens now, since she was too busy being in command.

She would need to talk to Kathra about making some changes up here soon. If Ife was going to act as an aspbad, she would need someone else on the sensors.

What was the galaxy coming to?

"Negative on maneuvering," Obioma said. "I'm smelling fear. He's starting to accelerate, but we have a small advantage in speed right now. Should we give chase?"

Ife studied the situation like a naupati, rather than a sensors officer.

Saw the vectors align in her mind.

Acceleration. Inertia. Maneuverability. Armor.

"Drive him, Obioma," she decided. "Push him, but let him out-accelerate us. If he is fleeing, he's going for a jump and wants us to stop hurting him. Don't give him the chance to pull a reverse as we get going too fast. Ngozi, just pound on him until he is gone. Obioma, don't get too close, and stay off his flank as much as you can."

More shots hammered the ship. Ram Cannons were terrible beams, designed to engage much larger ships. Accuracy wasn't all that great, but the impact was awesome when they did.

SeptStar fired back, but his heart didn't appear to be in it.

Something in the crew quarters on *SeptStar* had caused the whole ship to black out for perhaps ten seconds. She wasn't sure what idiocy had put something important in such a fragile location, but that was the difference in Daniel being dead and escaping.

"He's gone," Obioma announced, but only after Ngozi had scored two more hits on the central hull. One engine might be permanently off-line until they got repairs at someplace like Tavle Jocia.

Except that Ife knew in her soul that they would limp all the way to Sept space instead. No aspbad would want a potential enemy like the Free Worlds to see how badly *SeptStar* had been spanked in its first battle.

Especially not if the Sept were going to go after the Free Worlds soon, like everyone assumed.

"Stand down from combat and vent the engines forward until we can slow enough to turn without torqueing anything important," Ife ordered.

SeekerStar couldn't stop in less than a half-day at this speed but they could kill some momentum and let the rest of the system catch up with them, turning much more carefully than attempting the ancient maneuver known as a bootlegger on a ship this big.

"Repair teams, start your work," Ife said over the intercom.

They hadn't taken many hits from counter-fire, but a few. Plus she could tell by the way the ship sounded that things had broken. Nothing important. Perhaps as much maintenance as two months of normal sailing in an hour.

Still, they had won.

Ife had won. Taken *SeekerStar* into battle against a ship that her sensors showed was at least a peer, and defeated it.

A comm line blinked. The alien signaling.

"Thank you, Ife," Daniel's voice said, with Joane echoing her.

Nothing more, but somehow Daniel had known Kathra wasn't aboard.

But it was Daniel. He was like that.

And the Sept would be back for them. Ife had no doubts about that.

But you lost badly, connard. *Do you have the courage to try again?*

FORTY-EIGHT

Hᴀᴅɪ ʟᴏᴏᴋᴇᴅ ᴀʀᴏᴜɴᴅ ʜɪꜱ ʙʀɪᴅɢᴇ, studied the pale faces trying to absorb what had just happened.

At least he had managed to get away, although he had no idea how.

And now he knew what it felt like to be inside another mind when it died.

The Ishtan were no more. Extinct. Whatever gods they worshiped have mercy on their souls.

"Damage report," he croaked as the ship limped across valence space on only three generators.

Someone sent him a readout showing all the red and yellow spots where *SeekerStar* and the alien freighter had damaged the ship.

Only one really mattered. The Ram Cannon shot that had passed through the crew space where four deathless Ishtan had waited, their minds wound up with his own as they screamed their death agonies directly into his soul.

Hadi had the faintest memory of having echoed that scream outward, tearing at the minds of his bridge crew, but he would go to his grave blaming the alien snakes instead.

Nobody in the galaxy except Daniel Lémieux knew the truth now. That Hadi Rostami was no longer human. That he had been altered by those alien creatures before they died, then absorbed some of that agony into himself as their bodies were torn apart and vented into the cold tomb of space.

"Course, sir?" the pilot croaked back, looking like a man who had just woken in a jail cell after a three day bender.

Hadi considered his options. There was a forward resupply base that would be the first step. After that things got complicated.

"Zabol," he ordered. "But prepare for a long sail back to Ardabil after that, rather than a Free Worlds port."

"Understood, sir," the man's voice was slowly regaining strength.

What must it have been like to have Hadi Rostami scream directly into your mind as he thought he was dying?

How many of these men would be broken as a result? Or come to fear that their commander was somehow no longer human?

How many would he have to kill to protect this new secret, at least until he could have a long and dangerous conversation with Amirin Pasdar about the future of the Sept Empire?

FORTY-NINE

Kathra waited on fidgety feet as the two ships both landed in the same bay below her and the outer hatches locked, allowing atmosphere to flood in. Through the window, the Cargo-2 bearing Daniel and Joane looked worse for the wear, having been nearly broken in two under the horrible fusillade of fire. Next to it, the SkyCamel looked almost quaint.

It was a tight fit, but not that bad, as both pilots appeared to be experts. Kathra would need to meet this Tragee fellow, if he was as good as Erin in such a confined space.

"Commander, they'll be a few minutes," Wyll Koobitz said, approaching from her side. "We should move to the conference room and prepare."

She studied the shark closely.

Wyll Koobitz was far more than he had first appeared, and even then he had given off hints of being a major figure.

Since the battle had ended, Kathra had seen a whole other side, as he started giving orders that were obeyed without question or hesitation.

What are you, Wyll Koobitz? What is your position?

But she nodded and followed him into a larger room than the one where they had met before. Caterers were in the process of laying out a spread representing almost every color under the rainbow.

She found a comfortable chair and allowed someone to bring her a glass of a sweet juice in a shade of green. One of them Daniel had approved. Or Joane.

Wyll joined her, as did Obaj Gendrah again sitting beyond him. Other Anndaing as well, but it was obvious that the rest were merely aides and couriers.

Kathra wondered at what point she would meet actual members of the Merchants Bank Board, the men and women who controlled Anndaing space. Ruled was too strong a term, from what she had learned, but they controlled the money, and with it the power in these sectors.

Erin arrived at the head of the line, with Ife and Ndidi along as Kathra had ordered, the rest of the comitatus remaining behind to protect the ship against *SeptStar* suddenly returning, even though her ship was now safely under the big guns of the station.

The Sept commander might be desperate. A'Alhakoth had attempted to ram *Vorgash*, after all.

Daniel and Joane followed closely behind, in the company of two other Anndaing Kathra did not recognize. She rose to greet everyone, liberal with hugs, even for the surprised sharks.

It had been a close thing. Daniel might have survived, and maybe been able to bring Joane with him, but it would have also revealed far more than Kathra was prepared to at this time.

"Weren't there four crew on the Cargo-2?" Kathra asked as she was introduced to Raja Zoodrah, Trademaster of *Windrunner*.

"There are," Raja replied, stepping back to look up at her. "But Bipahl insisted on supervising the repair crews and my loadmaster Kayna is overseeing the removal of the two cargo pods so repairs can begin."

"I see," Kathra replied. "I would still like to meet them at some point, so I can thank them as I thank you and Tragee for getting Joane and Daniel home safe."

"That was Joane, Commander," Raja said. "I've never been under fire before. We would have gotten destroyed if she hadn't given me expert advice on how to evade *SeptStar*."

Kathra looked over at Joane and saw the quiet pride in that woman's eyes. Even more so than Daniel's but his eyes promised a story when it was just the two of them.

Rather than talk, the larger group attacked the food, with Daniel and Joane explaining all the plates and trays and vegetables to everyone equally between them.

Eventually, they settled at long tables that reminded Kathra of the trestles in her dining hall aboard *SeekerStar*. She had Erin on one side and had dragged Ife to sit on her other, with Daniel and Ndidi outside that and Joane across, next to Wyll Koobitz.

They ate. It was a complicated mélange of tastes, but everything was alien to her tastes, however amazing it was. Daniel declared it a success, which seemed to be the thing that the Anndaing were looking for.

Servers brought wine, coffee, and tea as they ate, making small talk that very pointedly ignored all the critical discussions that were needed. Like where Joane and Daniel had been, and what they had seen.

Wyll clapped his hands—fins—together and looked around. The servers and aides cleared the room like a bomb threat had been announced, pulling the door shut tight behind them and leaving only the four Anndaing and five humans in the room.

Kathra studied his face.

"How did the Sept find you here, Commander?" he asked her simply, as if they were alone and the rest of the group elsewhere.

Kathra felt the surge of anger pass through Erin's thigh, touching hers under the table. Kam, Iruoma, and Nkechi would react the same way were they here,. They had all met the Ishtan personally at Tavle Jocia.

"It was not the Sept," Daniel spoke up, causing all the sharks to look that way.

The humans knew the truth.

"Who, then, Daniel?" Koobitz asked.

"They were called the Ishtan," he said.

Kathra felt her own surge of emotion course through her stomach.

"Were?" she asked, in harmony with Koobitz and Gendrah.

Daniel turned to her and she saw the truth in his eyes.

"Urid-Varg destroyed most of their species eleven thousand years ago," Daniel continued, turning back to the Anndaing. "The six survivors had mental powers of some sort, but were weaker than the Destroyer, so they waited patiently, quietly stalked him as well as they could ever since, perhaps helping some of the revolutions that inevitably brought down his various empires. I never did get the truth from them."

"You've met them," Koobitz accused.

"*Oui*," Daniel nodded, and then nodded towards Erin. "They kidnapped me, Erin, and several others at Tavle Jocia. In our escape, we killed two of them. Iruoma did. The other four got away, and obviously joined up with the naupati of *Vorgash* after we had fled."

"And followed you here," Koobitz declared.

"I felt them when we arrived, Wyll," Daniel answered as Kathra watched the two of them.

"I did as well," Kathra said.

Daniel's head came around sharply.

"They called my name and I sounded the alert that got *SeekerStar* in motion," Kathra continued.

Daniel nodded at some previously unguessed clue.

"You said were," Gendrah spoke up now. "They are no more?"

"I am surprised the entire station did not hear their death scream, Obaj," Daniel spoke to the other merchant. "It struck me like a migraine, but I was also fighting with them when Ife killed the *salauds*."

"Ife?" Kathra turned to catch the woman blush, even as dark as her skin was.

"Ngozi, actually," the woman said. "We hit them at long range with a Ram Cannon shot on the rim of *SeptStar*. The whole ship seemed to shut down for as long as ten seconds afterwards."

"*Oui*," Daniel agreed. "Their dying screams stunned the entire vessel as those deathless creatures were annihilated."

"What do you mean you were fighting with them, Daniel?" Wyll Koobitz asked. "You mean Raja and *Windrunner*, correct?"

"No," Daniel said.

He turned to Kathra now and with his eyes and face alone asked for permission to extend the conspiracy to four new players, including three male Anndaing.

Females could not use the power. Could they convince the sharks that it was a human thing, as a form of insurance? What lies would Daniel need to spin?

Still, she nodded. He was as comitatus as the other women seated here, including Ife. That blade cut both ways, because he obviously believed strongly in what he was asking, and Kathra did not have all the details.

Daniel reached down now and pulled his outer shirt up and over his head, tossing it onto the table, and then removing the piece of thick cloth he kept over the gem.

It glowed with an inner fire as it was revealed.

The sharks all shrank back with cries of surprise that quieted quickly to a dangerous silence. Kathra knew she could escape the room, the station, and the system if they needed to, but at a cost of these as potential allies.

Daniel would not do this recklessly.

"I was fighting with them mentally at that moment," he said simply. "Distracting them from what Ife and the others were doing. What Joane and Raja were doing. I heard them die."

There was a long pause.

Gendrah had paled. Raja and Tragee had shrunk in on themselves in interesting ways that must have a story behind them.

Wyll studied Daniel like a predator spying a stupid tuna swimming along.

"What is that thing, Daniel?" he finally asked. "And how did you come to possess it?"

"It is the mind gem of the biggest, most ancient of the Ishtan to have ever lived," Daniel said. "Urid-Varg killed it and then tried to wipe out the rest of the species so they could not stop him in the future. The six escaped the anti-matter bombs dropped on the surface of their world and swore to follow him forever. They did, only because Kathra destroyed the thing after I killed his body."

"You claim not to be Urid-Varg," Wyll said accusingly.

None of the sharks made a motion. The humans, Kathra included, were poised at the edge of violence, however unnecessary it would be here.

"I am not," Daniel said. "I can never be that powerful, because the gem amplifies native powers, and the Mnapyre were far in advance of humans or Anndaing on that front. Plus, Urid-Varg had inscribed himself into a second gem that contained his mind and memories. This gem contains all the people he rode before me. Those are the ghosts I inherited. The K'bari language and the Ovanii. There are many others."

"You are Urid-Varg, then," Gendrah accused.

"No," Daniel said, holding out a hand to the two closest men. "If you take join hands, I will show you the truth that Kathra and the entire comitatus already know."

Gendrah paled nearly to a great white, but Wyll took Daniel's hand. After a moment, Obaj did as well.

Kathra watched the two men fall into Daniel's mind.

"I wondered," Raja said absently.

"If you ask him now, he will show you as well," Kathra said. "All of my women bind with him thus regularly. We know his mind better than he does, so that we also know his soul."

They waited.

It felt like forever, and hours might pass inside there, but only moments on the surface.

Wyll and Obaj regained themselves with starts of surprise.

Wyll turned to her now and focused both eyes on her like a hunter.

"I understand the Sept now," he said with awe in his voice. "And the Mbaysey."

"Then you understand everything that needs knowing, Wyll Koobitz," she replied.

"And I was correct," he turned to Obaj Gendrah and got a hollow, almost fearful nod out of the other Anndaing merchant. "I sent Daniel to a place on a hunch I could not explain, and I know that he did not influence that decision, because I saw the truth of it in his own mind."

He trailed off and took a moment to catch his breath.

"The Sept are coming," he said a moment later. "We knew that from an intellectual standpoint. The battle today just proved that they could range this far. And they will return, because Hadi Rostami is another one like Daniel, but without the gem. He will be able to find you anywhere in the galaxy once he returns in strength."

"*Oui*," Daniel said quietly. "But your solution will work on both counts, Wyll."

"Oh?" Kathra asked, looking at both men, and everyone else.

"I sent Daniel to a secret military base to look at a vessel that once belonged to the Ovanii, Kathra Omezi," Wyll said. "I had planned to determine if it would be a wise choice on the part of the Anndaing Merchants Guild and the Merchants Bank, were we to discuss leasing you such a vessel, so that you could go fight the Sept in their space, rather than allowing them to intrude on ours."

"And?" Kathra asked.

"And I think it would be the wisest choice I ever made to engage you as a pirate, Commander," Wyll said. "To send you after those *salauds* and let you damage them as badly as your vengeance demands. Or whoever you send in your place, as you did promise to outlive us all."

"Daniel?" Kathra looked one way, and then the other. "Joane?"

"They were a mighty people, Kathra," Joane spoke up. "Ancient warriors unafraid to sail into the darkness and explore the galaxy. Terrible marauders, as well, but they built glorious, beautiful machines that would let us do vengeful things in turn to the Sept. I vote in favor."

"I see," Kathra said as a placeholder. "Daniel?"

"*Oui*," he said.

He held out a hand and she took it, becoming him for a long moment to experience everything he had seen and done since he left her side at Kanus.

Kathra opened her eyes and blinked back tears at the pain and rage that Hadi Rostami had broadcast at the galaxy as the Ishtan died. But she also agreed with Joane. Such a vessel would allow the Mbaysey to take Yagazie's war to the Sept Empire and make it personal.

"Yes," she said to Wyll. "We will negotiate, but those are mere details."

The shark nodded, still a little in shock from the things he had learned.

"And," Kathra continued, "we will call that ship *SwiftStar*."

READ MORE!

Be sure to read all five books in the Star Tribes series.

WinterStar
SeekerStar
SeptStar
SwiftStar
MorningStar

Available from your favorite retailers!

ABOUT THE AUTHOR

Blaze Ward writes science fiction in the Alexandria Station universe (Jessica Keller, The Science Officer, The Story Road, etc.) as well as several other science fiction universes, such as Star Dragon, the Dominion, and more. He also writes odd bits of high fantasy with swords and orcs. In addition, he is the Editor and Publisher of *Boundary Shock Quarterly Magazine*. You can find out more at his website www.blazeward.com, as well as Facebook, Goodreads, and other places.

Blaze's works are available as ebooks, paper, and audio, and can be found at a variety of online vendors. His newsletter comes out regularly, and you can also follow his blog on his website. He really enjoys interacting with fans, and looks forward to any and all questions—even ones about his books!

Never miss a release!
If you'd like to be notified of new releases, sign up for my newsletter.

I will never spam you or use your email for nefarious purposes. You can also unsubscribe at any time.

http://www.blazeward.com/newsletter/

Connect with Blaze!

Web: www.blazeward.com
Boundary Shock Quarterly (BSQ):
https://www.boundaryshockquarterly.com/

ABOUT KNOTTED ROAD PRESS

Knotted Road Press fiction specializes in dynamic writing set in mysterious, exotic locations.

Knotted Road Press non-fiction publishes autobiographies, business books, cookbooks, and how-to books with unique voices.

Knotted Road Press creates DRM-free ebooks as well as high-quality print books for readers around the world.

With authors in a variety of genres including literary, poetry, mystery, fantasy, and science fiction, Knotted Road Press has something for everyone.

Knotted Road Press
www.KnottedRoadPress.com